the sky is not blue

MAD BEAR BOOKS

*This is a work of fiction.
Any similarity to actual events or persons is purely coincidental.*

© Sandie Zand 2013

All rights reserved.
The moral right of the author has been asserted.

Published by **Mad Bear Books**
www.madbearbooks.com

ISBN Nº 978-3-943829-06-8

Cover image: Jessica Dent, self-portrait

Thanks to:

Kim Curran, Brian Talgo, Jane Alexander, Liz Tipping & Viv C for thoughtful criticism, Paul Shepley for boat advice, Malcolm Erskine for unwavering admiration, various vineyards for creative sustenance, my family for believing it possible… and Freddie, for making it so.

*For the little girl with mousy hair
who lives inside us all…*

*Let there be, for a time, no driving aim;
No mission, no goal, no fury'd intent.
Notice the hours—how they lengthen and breathe:
Like dust in the sunset, thy soul is content.*

eight beats

THE RADIO was still beside the bread bin in the kitchen. Same radio. Same bread bin. Same old kitchen. I turned it on, rotated the dial to find a decent station, and it crackled in reluctant search for the unfamiliar. I need music. It fills the gaps. There's a song for every eventuality, lyrics compressing entire concepts into a handful of words, squishing whole stories into five minutes. The song makes everything manageable. But the years with Zak and the band had proved how brevity brings triteness. To encapsulate something well in so few words requires a great deal of cutting out, a lot of summing up. Reams of thought must be crushed into one brief line, mountainous feelings dismissed in eight beats.

The song in my head when I opened the front door had been *In My Life* by the Beatles. I didn't bother chasing the thought. It was just some subconscious awareness of being back here after all this time. A more appropriate Beatles' number would be *I'm A Loser*, but I'm not chasing that thought either. That wasn't why I came back. This isn't the trip down Memory Lane. I've always resisted reminiscence, the ache for the forgotten, that irrational pull, I'm not the sentimental type. I don't travel backwards.

But here I am, for the first time in thirty four years. The solicitor said I should go through my mother's papers, looking for policies, share certificates, any useful stuff not documented in the will. It seemed worth a punt. At this stage anything was worth a punt. Speculate to accumulate. Anyway, Mervyn wanted me at his retirement party and had paid for the flight. He'd tracked me down again, his voice crackling over the wire, wrapping around me like an old blanket.

"Chrissy… sweetheart, I'm sorry, bad news, your mother's died."

"How did you find me?"

"Did you hear what I just said?"

"Yeah. Sorry. I'm a bit out of it."

He'd caught me at a bad time. I was in Portugal, high in the hills and nearing the end of my tolerance with that particular crowd, that particular location, that particular distraction. There was a party, we were all stoned. I was watching my lover flirt with a newcomer. She was an artist, young – all brown muscle and edges – casual, relaxed, detached from effort as only beautiful people with their lives ahead of them can be. For my lover, she was a challenge with promise. I'd long since ceased to be a riddle worth solving. Mervyn's news about my mother was so far removed from any thought I had at that time as to glide over my senses unhindered, not pausing long enough to resonate.

"What did you say, Merv?"

"I said your mother's dead."

Alice looked ancient. Easily into her late eighties, maybe older. Clothes that had once touched curves hung pathetically over sharp shoulders, dragging her towards the ground in future readiness. She stood on the doorstep for a minute or so before I could place her. Alice. Neighbour, childhood aunt of sorts, and my mother's closest friend. She handed over a rigid cardboard box, lighter than her shaky hands suggested, and waited to be invited in.

"What's this?"

An opaque mist clouded the old girl's eyes. Marine blue viewed through a mid-day haze. She paused, lips moving in tiny, silent quivers, echoing the question, holding it still long enough to work a reply.

"It's your mother, Christine."

So this was life's end. Plaintive evidence of existence – a container filled with dust, modestly hidden in a blank cardboard box – an inability of those left behind to let go. To think any semblance of humanity survived in a handful of dross required unfeasible belief. It wasn't a person, it was a problem. I'd expected to leave with the promise of a couple of hundred thousand for the house, a few insurance policies perhaps, the meagre contents of a savings account, not a box of dirt.

"What am I supposed to do with it?"

"I don't know, dear. Take her home, scatter her somewhere nice – it's up to you."

I knew someone once who had an old dog. A hideous thing, covered in lumps and bare patches of weeping skin. It had lost most of its teeth and she had to soak bread in milk and egg to feed it. It died and everyone except its owner was relieved. We could all see the benefit, for us and it, of the Big Sleep. There were about eight of us sharing the house at the time and three of the guys were instructed to dig into the night so it could be buried. Appropriately, its owner, Judy, had said. She wept. Someone else read a poem. And one bloke who'd always proclaimed himself an atheist, performed the actual ceremony, complete with a tree-hugging-pseudo-religious impromptu speech that left me thinking he'd lied all along. People are strange when it comes to death. It was Alice's superstition, not mine, but I took the box, said I had jet lag – what does she know, she's probably never been more than twenty miles from this pit – and got rid of her.

More than anything, I was stunned by how old she was. The Alice I remember was curvy and bouncy, quite pretty in a barmaid kind of way, and usually had toffees in a pocket in her apron.

I liked her when I was little.

They're near the old lifeboat house. Pat has the vodka and she's not sharing anymore. She swings the bottle towards her mouth, misjudging speed and direction. Marion's trailing. She just can't keep pace. But Chrissy has never felt so alive – she's sharp, edgy, and can walk all night if she has to – she's not even cold. She's alive. Vibrant. Pat shouts "on there, you and me, winner calls the shots, right?"

I phoned Mervyn, waited for him to finish talking to someone in the office. I didn't recognise the name – there was hardly anyone there from my time – but the gist of the conversation was familiar. They were going to print. I shouldn't have called.

Whilst I waited, half-listening to half a conversation, I paced the rooms. Looking, but not touching – part-visitor, part-curator – struck by both strangeness and familiarity, noting the location of objects long forgotten. The whole place was like a sealed vat of old, damp air. It had been shut tight for weeks, maybe months, I don't know how she lived. I opened windows, let in the fragrance of the sea, but it didn't remove the stench. It was ingrained. Surfaces imbued with the steam of domestic effort. Simple menus learned with raw marital enthusiasm, perfected over decades, served and consumed in apathetic routine. There were fifty years of repeated repertoire in those walls. My mother had persisted in using a pressure cooker long after the rest of the population moved on, its low-level hiss and steam on the windows dominating long Sunday afternoons. No wonder the wallpaper looked depressed.

She could spend all day in that kitchen. I'd be in the other room, at the dining table – slowly, carefully, pencilling in my school notebooks – and he'd be standing behind, rigid. Anger waiting for release. I hadn't looked in the cupboard but I knew the pressure cooker would still be there.

Pat's at the top, straddled across the ridge tiles, hair blowing. She looks elated. "Come on then, bitch, if you're brave enough." Unless Chrissy does this, there'll never be an end to it. One of them has to fall. One of them has to finally get the last word.

Mervyn's voice brought me back.

"Sorry babe, shit's hitting the fan. You're there then." He sounded tired. He used to thrive on deadlines, now they were killing him.

"Yeah, thought I'd just check in."

"Everything okay?"

"Fine, yeah, it's fine. You?"

"Will be, by weekend. Oh, hang on..."

He called to someone, the conversation muffled as he covered the mouthpiece. I went upstairs. The air there was more medicinal –

menthol chest rub and floral disinfectant. Apparently she'd been nursing a cold when she fell. Flies feasted on an open bottle of cough syrup and sticky spoon on the bedside cabinet, and there was the same suffocating dust, the same violent need to open windows wide. Not much had changed – painfully tidy, God-awful bedding and matching curtains, dark-veneered furniture – but there was something else. Something faint, unknown. Perhaps it was slow rot, her loose flesh as it evaporated on dry bones. Perhaps the smell of loneliness, fear. I came downstairs again anyway. I had a feeling, were I to open my own bedroom door, I'd find it exactly as I left it: unmade bed, copy of *Jackie* tossed on the floor, *Ziggy Stardust* spinning at 33 revs, reduced to the sad click-click of needle on plastic. Though it was equally possible my father had removed and burned the lot.

"Where the hell have you been until this hour?"
"It's only ten o'clock."
He draws himself up. Rigid. Still.
"Answer the question. Where have you been?"
"Marion's."
He slams a hand against the banister. The girl hears her mother upstairs – a familiar creak on the floor – she's on the landing. Listening. A safe distance.
"You left the Madderns' at twenty-one hundred hours."

"I was walking home."

"An hour? Do you think I'm a fool, girl? The distance between the Madderns' and here is one point six miles. Even at the walking pace of a dullard you'd be hard-pressed to take more than fifteen minutes. You will account for the missing hour."

"I was just walking around."

He stands silent. He believes in pauses.

"Go to your room, Christine. Punishment duty for a week. There are rules. You know them and will abide by them, or God help me you'll learn the hard way."

I could imagine his seething when I'd gone. Absent without leave. A little worry perhaps, on my mother's part at least. They'd have heard by then what had happened. People would have been searching. A neighbour might have mentioned seeing me at the station with a large rucksack, or Spencer might have called, looking for his camera and money, though this was unlikely. Slowly my parents would have pieced together random conversations, the events at the harbour, the missing clothes, and concluded the obvious answer: *she's flown the coop.* There'd have been calm resignation, relief even. She would have tidied my room, he would have gone to his shed to paint more relics, burn his gaze into his own mistakes for a change. Their lives would have been still again.

"Sorry angel." Mervyn. Back again. "I'm a man down."

"Look, I can..."

"Danny broke his leg last night. Drunken bastard fell off the bloody kerb. They're like headless chickens here today. Got to go, babe, I'll call you later."

So, I don't travel backwards, though some contemplation of the past is inevitable. I've kept in touch with Mervyn all these years, after all. I've visited the UK often enough, but never here. Stepping onto the station platform and slipping through time to a vaguely familiar strangeness – a sense of possibly having been here before – had been a little disturbing. Though I knew it could be viewed with detachment. I could focus on the contrast between what had changed and what had not, and leave the personal alone. It was just a bit unsettling rather than traumatic, a little odd. It was only for a few days. Tourists, there seemed to be more of them and I can't understand why they still come. Flights are cheap these days – flights to warmer, more interesting lands. What do they hope to find in a place like this?

"I like it when the other children come, Alice."
"Do you, Christine? Why's that then?"
"Because it means it's summer!"

"Ah-ha, I see. And what do you like about summer?"

"Summer is best because you don't have to go to work and we can go to the beach and all the holiday children are here."

"Well then, why don't you go and make friends with some of them? Look, over there, those two little girls are making a sandcastle. Why don't you go and ask if they want any help? Go on, Christine, I'll just be here."

"No. They won't want to play with me."
"Why ever not?"
"They just won't."
"Oh, you are a funny little thing."

The station was tiny, provincial, and yet impersonal. It could be anywhere, there's a sameness to these things when you've travelled a lot. The town itself, the businesses – at a glance nothing seemed out of place, although I was sure in the past three decades many would have changed hands at least once. But it looked as I think it always did: buckets, spades, ice cream, fishing nets, the usual junk you find in a seaside resort. A shop selling surf gear had caught my eye – surfing has gone upmarket, the window display was über-modern – but apart from that it all appeared much the same. Holidaymakers everywhere. And the art galleries, of course. The jewels in the tourist board's crown. Whether there were more or less, I didn't know. Less art, more outlets probably. I didn't meander. I wasn't on holiday. *My tears are falling like rain from the sky, is it for her or myself that I cry?* Trite, but I couldn't get the song out of my head. It was my own fault, I shouldn't have dredged it up.

I've never met Regret either. I don't look backwards, don't look forwards. I am now. What's gone is lost, what's to come is irrelevant until it arrives. The present is all we have. I suppose it's a hangover from my time here.

I had things to do and ran the list over in my mind. Change the linen on my mother's bed, clear out the medicine bottle and kill the flies, throw the shabby dressing gown into the bin and strip the room of unfinished detritus: historical fiction, bookmarked at chapter three, the wooden hairbrush with its eerie embedded strands of white, a plastic medication dispenser for the senile, segmented into days of the week. Monday, Tuesday and Wednesday's slots were empty. I could get rid of those things, scrape the room back to its bare minimum like a cheap hotel. It'd be comfortable enough for a short stay.

Or I could open that tightly closed door to my old bedroom.

It was only a room. Slim chance it'd be completely empty – she wouldn't have let him do that – and, equally, my stuff wouldn't be there. The step back in time would be no greater than in the rest of this dump, the cupboards, the scrap boxes, now scattered over the sitting room floor – the walk down Memory Lane had happened. It was a space. They were only things. Behind that door might already be the cheap hotel room – a bed, curtains, Spartan calm. If not, if by some incompetence on her part there were only floorboards and bare walls, so be it. And if, for some incomprehensible reason, the copy of *Jackie* was still on the floor, the covers were still hurled to the foot of the bed and *Ziggy Stardust* was still spinning on the turntable, what could it possibly do? Things. They were only things.

When she can move again, Chrissy says thank you to Jack and the landlady and the other helpers because tomorrow this will be all round town and her parents need to salvage something. She says she needs the toilet – "it's fine, honestly, I'm okay by myself" – walks steadily down the dingy corridor keeping her back straight, her pace even. But she doesn't stop at the entrance marked ladies. She walks through a side door which leads into the delivery yard, goes to Spencer's place because she knows he isn't there, breaks a window, opens the door, lets herself in, takes one of his cameras from the flat – it's his favourite – and empties the cashbox he keeps under the counter in the studio. Then she goes home, packs a few things, and just makes the last train.

The warmth outside seemed unable to penetrate the walls of the house. Christ it was a dump. I phoned Mervyn back. There seemed little point staying. I'd found nothing of any importance, no policies, no savings accounts – only junk, the scraps of meaningless lives. There was probably an early evening train. I could be at his place by nine.

"Tonight?" he said. "But you only just got there."

"There's nothing here, it's pointless."

"And the house? What you going to do? Lock up and leave? Thought you were skint?"

"I can sort it from there."

He didn't speak. I could hear the mania in the background – voices, telephones, life. Here, nothing beyond the crackly radio in the kitchen, some kids shrieking in a neighbouring garden.

"You can't. I'm not around, got things on." He sighed. "Come on, Chrissy, what's a night or two? Just sort things out, stick to the plan. Look, I've got to go. Deal with it, eh? We'll talk tomorrow."

He hung up, disconnecting me from the buzz of the city, leaving me alone with the past. I went back upstairs and stood before my old bedroom door. Touched it. Pushed without any real force. It was jammed, as it had always been. My father believed fervently in *good working order* – a legacy of his military days – and it could only be that he'd wanted it this way. Control. Like the squeaky gate he refused to oil at the bottom of the path. He needed to hear people coming. Friend or foe. In my case, the noise gave him time to hide in the shadows of the hallway, *where the hell have you been till this hour?* He was a man damaged by his own expectations. That and those missing war years. John Albert Barker believed if a person kept a straight back, a closed mouth and a guarded countenance, his dignity would be assured. Dignity was important. My mother and I knew that. I don't ever remember him laughing. The silent legacy of his war was a wound too raw for a child's eyes, a festering sore no tending could ever heal, no medal could ever assuage, constantly irritated and reopened by the slideshow of bloody snapshots behind his eyes.

And the failings of his new crew.

Me, my mother, our shoddiness, our lack of attention to detail.

He and Zak had more in common than either would have believed possible had they known each other. John Albert Barker, unlike some of his original crew, had survived the war. Zak Zook, unlike some of his crew, had survived rock and roll and its gross excess. And they were failures for it. Coming out alive was pointless when all you'd been was gone. Success was *there*, in the middle of the noise, not on the edges in the banal calm. Had John Albert died in battle, his name would be publicly etched in stone, respected and remembered. But I had a feeling there was another blank cardboard box somewhere in this house. Equally, had I not switched flights in 1982 and arrived early at the hotel, had I not looked past the two naked tarts to take note of scattered pills, the empty Jack Daniel's bottle, the deep sleep of my husband – had I not *attended to the detail* – Zak's name would also be etched forever, his passing regretted, the ruin of potential acknowledged.

And I was sure, had either man known in the heat of things what actually lay beyond that noise, they'd have willingly swapped survival for eternal glory.

touch

TWO MAIN beliefs sustained Marion Styles and without them she would be someone else. Firstly, there was good in every person and situation – even the worst of atrocities brought out the positive qualities of *somebody*. To say God was vengeful was a common, but awful, misunderstanding. Sending tsunamis and earthquakes to remind mankind how to *feel* was not an easy call – these things hurt our Lord much more than they hurt us. Secondly, she passionately felt it the duty of the young to care for the old. That her life had provided ample opportunity to nurture both these beliefs was a blessing for which she was more than happy to thank God – both privately at home and publicly here, in church, once a week.

"Amen."

The rumble of voices punctuated the prayers with a full stop. Pews rattled as those able to kneel pushed themselves back into a seated position. Marion no longer took to her knees to pray, her bulk these days likely to wedge between the seat and the back of the neighbouring pew, but did at least lean forward uncomfortably – in solidarity with the more nimble, if nothing else. Pete called her Rubenesque. She considered herself fat, but worried more about the vanity of such thoughts than the weight itself and so her size had, over the past thirty years, slowly moved in only the one direction.

Church was one of four places in town at this time of year where locals outnumbered the holidaymakers, the others being the doctors' surgery, job centre and various care homes for the elderly. Marion and Pete were aware of the irony of such distinct contrast – sun, sand and excess versus poverty, sickness and death – and as they'd long reaped the benefits of the healthier group, felt it only right to dedicate a portion of their free time to the other.

This portion had grown exponentially over the years. Sunday was now the only day they had together, alone, as a couple, with no social responsibilities beyond morning church attendance. Sundays were a guilty treat. Sundays were their marital salvation. There had been a time when these precious afternoons were spent in bed, naked bodies fused in sunlight though open curtains, tenderness reconnecting two as one at the end of the working week, reinforcing love for the start of the next. But Marion was far too self-conscious for daylight sex now. These days they were more likely to take a walk on the beach, read the papers over tea in the garden or, in the colder months, light a fire and sit in silent togetherness. They'd once joked about being like an old couple and its echo had lingered, an uncomfortable truth.

The last hymn was one of her favourites – the line *there's no discouragement shall make him once relent* bringing, as usual, tears to her eyes and a lift to her spirit. A physical lift, growing taller as her chest swelled, neck stretched upwards, her diaphragm pressing air outwards, raising her voice so she could share the joy. It had the same effect on the rest of the congregation; she always sensed the rising passion during this song. It was a good choice for the end of today's service – three fewer old dears at Trewartha Nursing Home, a shortage of funds at the Hambly Daycare Centre and dear old Alf Foxall critical after his recent road accident. Faith needed a little help at times.

They reach the lifeboat house. Pat stops, as though this was always the destination, leans against the wall, dangerous, reckless. Chrissy says "are you going to share that bottle, or what?" Marion gives her a look. Pat stops smiling. She says "want it, bitch?" and throws the bottle over the wall. She points to the roof of the lifeboat house, which is just about level with the top of the wall, and she's swaying a bit. Marion looks nervous. The sweat makes Chrissy shiver. Pat shouts "on there, you and me, winner calls the shots, right?"

Marion noticed Alice Tippett exiting the church, nervously approaching the worn steps down to the path, startled by the contrast of sunlight to the internal gloom. She nudged Pete and pointed.

"Give her a hand, she's all wobbly, bless her."

Marion had watched them all age, as they had watched her too. For many of the old dears there was nothing now to do but succumb to deterioration and death. For herself, there was still a chance to savour life even as time moved ever onwards. She'd watched Pete decline as well. He wasn't healthy – too big, too unfit, too stressed – and reminded her in so many ways of her father at the same age, unexpectedly close to the end of his life. Dying prematurely, her father had never reaped the benefits of decades of hard work and community kindness. Marion wanted more for herself and Pete, something to give real meaning to their shared effort over these past twenty five years. She didn't want to find herself a widow too soon, as her mother had done, with no more than regret for company.

"Morning, Alice." She touched her lips to the old girl's cold cheek. A shaky hand, stronger than it looked, gripped her forearm briefly.

"Marion. What a lovely dress. How are you, dear?"

They walked slowly to the exit gates, Alice retaining her clutch on Pete's arm, though perhaps more for its comfort than support.

Marion smiled and offered hers too. There's an almost instinctive tendency to stop touching the elderly and it's a loss they feel. She'd been told this on more than one occasion over the years.

"Have you seen Christine?" Alice said.

"Christine?"

Marion closed a hand over Alice's arm. The chill of the old woman's flesh seeped into her own. Chrissy. Surely not.

"Barker, dear, you remember? She's here to sort Elizabeth's affairs."

"I didn't know."

After more than thirty years a person ought to have forgotten a hurt, but it stung as if it were still raw. Chrissy, and today of all days. Ironic.

"She'll get in touch, I'm sure," Alice said as they walked up the hill towards her road.

"Who are we talking about?" Pete said. He glanced at his wife, a fragment of a frown creasing his brow. "I take it someone you don't want to see?"

Marion shook her head. "It's nothing. Not important."

Pete tried to catch her eye but she focused ahead. Nearly there. Just the corner to turn. Chrissy. Less than the length of a football pitch away.

"She looks well, dear." Alice said, patting Marion's arm. "Though you'd not recognise her. Goodness, no. Very glamorous. Travels a lot too. She's a photographer, you know. Had pictures in all sorts of magazines. I suppose all that glamour is part and parcel of being a rock star's wife."

"Ex-wife." Marion said. "Their divorce was all over the papers."

"Who are we talking about?" Pete said.

"Just someone I knew as a kid."

They reached Alice's gate and she invited them in for a cup of tea. Marion stared over the low hedge at the Barker's dull green door and let the question hang. Pete touched her arm.

"You okay?"

She shrugged him off, apologised to Alice and declined the invitation. "It's dad's birthday. We're taking flowers to the crem'."

Local churchyards were full and, with the exception of one or two ancient families whose plots were secured in advance of both birth and death, had seen no internments for decades. The dead were burned eight miles out of town, their existence marked by rows of identical white stones in orderly array against a sloping green background. The drive was a distraction. Marion sat in the passenger seat cradling a flower arrangement. There were only four recurring reasons to leave town: regular visits to their parents' resting places, the weekly trip to the wholesalers, a monthly shop at the supermarket five miles east, and for pleasure trips, holidays, as and when they had time and urge.

So, Chrissy had travelled.

Or had she just kept running?

Pete turned the radio down and glanced briefly at Marion, profile rigid and shadowed by the bright sunlight beyond her window. They drove in silence for another mile. She reached forwards and turned the volume back up. He tapped the steering wheel with fat, blunt fingers, breathed in the suffocating air, checked the fuel gauge, checked his wife.

Marion inhaled deeply, sickening herself with the heavy scent of the bouquet. The church had been filled with flowers for her father's funeral. An aroma of freshly cooked fish and chips would have been more appropriate; it was almost all he'd ever known.

"Are you going to tell me?"

"What's to tell?" Her eyes pricked, a heaviness pressing her down, a desire to ask him to just drive and keep on driving, until it grew dark and they ran out of fuel and she broke properly. But how many miles would that take? She'd already travelled thirty years on half-empty.

"Who is she?"

"The bitch who caused dad's heart attack. I don't want to talk about her."

Marion seldom swore. She heard the bitterness in her own voice, matched its sharpness with the set of her mouth. Pete gripped the steering wheel, stared ahead and they drove the remainder in silence.

So Chrissy had travelled. Escaping duty, responsibility. Doing things her way, as she always had. How free she must have been. Marion, too, sometimes felt like running away, though she knew she had nowhere to run. She and Pete were not impulsive people, they were steady and reliable. Those were the words people would use to describe them if asked. Steady and reliable. Good words. Decent attributes. She looked out over the crematorium's neat expanse. A groundsman on a quad bike moved slowly across the horizon, the chug of his vehicle taking the edge off the silence. A seemingly endless stretch of dead. Yet only thirty years' worth.

"What do you think they'll do when they run out of space?" she said.

Pete's upper body emerged from the car's boot, one hand clutching a grubby bag containing a small gardening fork and trowel.

"I don't know," he said, squinting against the glare. His face was red and sweaty. "I expect they just buy another field and extend."

"And when there are no more fields?"

He closed the boot lid.

"Not our problem," he said with a dry laugh. "We'll be long gone by then."

the backward glance

MERVYN WANTS me to go to France. Not the *forever into the sunset* trip – though Christ knows I've been laughing that one off long enough – but next week, for a few days. Go to France and sort out the decorators because he's too busy in his last working moments. As though it matters. As though at this late stage in the day he can prove the bastards wrong. If he hadn't screwed up with Mrs Levy the Fourth, she'd have been out there keeping an eye on the decorators. Then again, if he hadn't screwed up with Mrs Levy the Fourth, he'd have got his promotion and would have nothing to prove. I mentioned this.

"Plus it seems pretty stupid to build yet another house for the benefit of future ex-wives and their leeching lawyers," I said.

He hung up.

I'll go to France if he's paying, but he can sweat a few hours first. I owe him, I do realise that. But he's like a big dopey dog, any encouragement is too much. He slavers with expectation only to be hurt when nothing else materialises and time has shown me it's best to keep him down, so the occasional passing pat on the head is appreciated for what it is.

He turns from passive pet to ferocious carnivore when with his pack at the magazine. I do miss that glorious tacky life – the banter, working hard, playing late – though I wouldn't go back. There, he doesn't ask nicely or wait on the off-chance and had I known when I met him how high he'd rise, I might not have bothered pursuing the dream. Might just have settled on a slightly overweight, chain-smoking ticket to security. Hindsight is a wonderful thing.

Mervyn saw the weakness in Zak long before I did. He'd introduced us. By the time he regretted it, I was in too deep. *Grab your camera, Blondie, I need you to cover the Plutonium gig, Jake's gone AWOL, I'm not waiting any longer for the idiot. Pictures, interview, couple of backstage shots… you know the score, you'll be fine. Okay? This is your moment, babe, it's what you've been waiting for, don't let me down.* We were all passionate about music, we wouldn't have survived at the magazine if we weren't, and we hung around with bands, it's what we did. They and other journalists were the only men I met and I was never going to date a scribe when there was a musician in the offing. Zak was a star, Plutonium a success, it was the dream. It was everything I'd known it would be. Nobody knew then we were witnessing the start of the decline. Zak was amazing. And stronger men were rejected back then purely on the basis of their ranking. Drummers, for example. Nobody screams or throws their knickers at the drummer, it's a fact. Lead singers have an automatic advantage – it makes a person overlook the defects. Add this to the wave's crest, that absolute peak of success, and it's impossible to see weakness, all you see is strength. When someone can shut a hundred thousand people up just by raising an arm, and make them scream again just by singing one note – that's power, that's control, and anything they can't do, or won't do, or maybe never intended to do, is absolutely invisible.

But you'd think anybody riding that wave would concentrate, so they don't fall. You'd think only a fool would screw things up when they've achieved so much. It's only later, when you're in way too deep, that you discover you picked that fool.

"Jesus, what's he been taking? He's on in ten minutes. Ten freaking minutes! Christ, Chrissy, can't you control him?"

"You're his manager, you sort him out. He's at work – not my problem."

"Just get him some coffee... water... anything."

He's slapping Zak's face.

Chrissy sits back, dangles her legs over the arm of the chair, the new soft leather of her boots outclassing its weary fabric, pitted with cigarette burns and sticky with old beer spills. She laughs. Tips back her head, hair dropping over the other arm and grazing the dirty floor.

"*Ask one of the lackeys,*" *she says.* "*I'm not on the payroll. I'm sick of doing your job for you. He's a loser – I know that, you know that – which of us is going to dump him first? You know what?*" *She gets up from the chair, heads towards the door,* "*I'll tell you who. Me. I'm out of here, had enough, I'm done. You can tell him that when he comes down.*"

Zak's wafting his manager's hand away apathetically, groaning, drooling, unseeing.

"*Yeah? Well good idea, it's you makes him miserable anyway. Prize bitch. Why couldn't you just be like the other chicks? Everything's such a goddamn issue with you.*"

I'm travelling backwards again. Not advisable. But it's what happens when you let the mind wander. When you've made the mistake of opening the door and inviting someone in just to fill the gap between one failed phone call and the next. When you're standing in a forgotten history, waiting for some silly old woman to stop staring at the walls and remember why she's called round. Alice obviously had something to say, but it was taking time. She hesitated, blinking those cloudy, surprised eyes and talking in that laboured way – taking forever to contribute nothing. A vagueness, a forgetfulness you wanted to slap. *Just get on with it.* Eventually she reached the point. My mother enjoyed the cliff walks; it would be a good place to scatter the ashes; maybe we could go together.

Christ.

So I told her I wanted to put them in the garden.

"Oh." That absent stare again, just missing by a fraction – there but not there. "She really wasn't very keen on the garden, dear. She had a man who came, after your father died, you know. She never really spent any time... the shed, you see. She hated it. You know, with your father and... the war damaged so many. So many lives were spoiled..."

She retreated into memories of six decades past. It was doubtful, but possible, things were less muddled in her head. That getting it out was the problem. She plucked something invisible off her cardigan, showed no signs of heading for the door and after a couple of beats, I gave in, put the kettle on, made two cups of tea and passed her a piece of kitchen paper.

"Sorry, dear, I'm a nuisance, I know."

I didn't want to encourage her. I just felt I should do *something*. I don't delude myself with an image of benevolence. I don't crave the warm glow of extending kindness to others. On the rare occasions I do make the magnanimous gesture and feel that warm glow, I understand the motivation – habitually kind people are painfully needy. Alice probably did think it a kindness, but to me it was panic – back against the wall. There was no warm glow sitting watching her snuffle, just a desire to get her out of the house and my life. She'd like to talk about my mother. She'd like to wander down that memory lane at the sort of pace someone of her dotage just doesn't have time for. She'd like, no doubt, to impress upon me the life my poor mother led – with him – as though I can't work that out for myself. As though there's any point even contemplating it now, after all these years, and with both of them dead and burned. As though I'm not full enough already.

Alice told me my mother liked sewing. It wasn't something she did when I was a child. But apparently, at some point between my leaving and his suicide, my father stabilised, took his medication properly, and my mother had time to sew.

"She was altering a dress for me," Alice said.

"Oh."

"Upstairs. Your old room, dear. I wonder if we could...?"

So we went to my bedroom and I opened the door with a hefty shove, saw what had been done with the space – left almost as it was. Almost, but not quite. That which said *Chrissy* had gone, that which said *Christine* was still there. A more paranoid person might have assumed it was deliberate. A calculated creation by someone who knew that one day I'd have to come back, even if only briefly and reluctantly, even if only after they'd gone.

There was a sewing desk now, beneath the window which looked out over the grey rooftops towards a tiny triangle of blue in the distance. A sea view of sorts. The bed was dressed in the same candlewick bedspread, my alarm clock still ticking beside it. Anyone who didn't know better would think it was a guest room, but my old teddy was propped up against the hump of the pillow, waiting. The record player was there. The albums had gone of course, and the posters. Obviously. They were up and down as a matter of rote; my father removing them, me replacing them. He had no valid excuse to take them away and, whatever else he might have been, he was a stickler for his own rules of fairness. He couldn't sneer or hit over an inoffensive poster carefully stuck to a melamine cupboard. He could do no more than sneak in when I was out, planning his mission with well-trained thoroughness, and quietly remove them. He knew I wouldn't ask for them back.

A half-way house – my room and yet not – and its memories screeched in the silence. Alice stood near the desk, stroked a hand over the sewing machine. She cried again, quietly. I opened the wardrobe. I don't know why, I didn't expect to see anything, it was just an automatic movement, an echo, a routine more familiar than I could have imagined. But it was full. My old clothes. The ones I had to discard because my rucksack was only so big; the ones I'd long forgotten. I closed the door, opened it again. I couldn't help it. I needed to see it all – clean, pressed and neatly ordered. No dust. No musty smell. I wondered what sort of person would do this.

"Christine? Are you all right?"

The girl with the mousy hair sits on her bed, silent. She listens, hears the slight creak of a loose floorboard as her mother shifts position on the landing.

"Christine? He says you can come out now."

The girl stays silent. Another creak – louder this time – as her mother removes her weight from the loose board, taps nervously on the bedroom door.

"Can I come in?"

The girl says nothing.

In punishing her mother she does not affect her father, but still she says nothing. Somebody has to feel it. She can't bear all of this alone.

Her mother's face appears around the door.

"Come on, love. Come down and eat your dinner."

"No. I don't want to."

Her mother moves to the bed. She sits beside her daughter on the candlewick and touches her back gently, tentatively. The girl stiffens. The mother removes her hand.

"Why does he hate me?" the girl says.

"Oh, love, he doesn't. He just likes us to follow his rules. He needs order, Christine. It makes him feel safe."

"What about us? When do we get to feel safe?"

Okay, so I do sometimes look backwards. It's hard not to. Things can't be forgotten. A little something lingers; a tiny fact, a remembered smell, the defiant ghost of an emotion seeking substance, needing to become whole again. Unless you have a massive bang to the head, or the sort of mental trauma to leave a person mute and shaking in the corner of some shrink's office, there's no way to obliterate the past. Even then, there's a residue. What has been will always influence what follows. In trying to forget, but failing, the facts become warped rather than destroyed. There's a danger they just become damaged. The more you try to alter the past, the more you'll succeed. Only not in the way you'd intended – by replacing, rewriting or forgetting – but by turning an unwanted clarity into an impossible-to-shift muddle.

But still there. In essence.

Once you've lost the grip on that original undesired truth, once it's been twisted and distorted into something just as painful but now intangible, you really are screwed. You can either move forward in the fog and never understand why life hurts so much, or you can start to think about the whole damn truth again, in reverse, until the muddle fades and you're back where you first started – although by now, half your life has gone and you're not sure you can be arsed to plod through the rest.

A rock or a hard place.

"I've got it, dear." Alice held up a carrier bag. A thick one, from the sort of quality shop my mother could never afford. "She'd finished. It was ready. Bless her."

She wiped her nose with the kitchen paper, turned to the window. We should have gone, slammed the door shut on the room, but I was transfixed. Held tight in that marginally altered space, almost drowning in the soupy mix of truth and lie. I touched the clothes. Stroked the arm of a long-forgotten cheesecloth shirt, its stiff ridges of cream and blue juddering under my nails, grasped a wide trouser leg, spotted the matching jacket with tacky faux leather patches on the elbows. A birthday present. And from nowhere, Pat's voice, *oh you lucky bitch, I want it, I want it.*

I hadn't managed to forget them, of course, Pat and Marion. I hadn't managed to make them part of that foggy muddle, those worthless years, none of it special enough to keep. Though I had intended to come and go without contact. But Alice seemed calm again – her generation didn't weep for long – and there was still the danger of that other conversation, so I asked after them. Stupid. The minute the question left my mouth I regretted it. Because until *I* could remember – until *I* could weave my way backwards and find the truth – these things were best left in their dark closet, untouched. But I'd asked. As I waited for her to thumb through the dusty index of her memory, I could only try to second-guess the answer.

In the best case scenario, Pat would have finished art school, forgiven me, and headed west in search of more and more. Marion would have got her grades, gone to university, met some dorky guy with a zillion prospects, raised at least four super-clever kids and would now be settled in commuter-belt paradise, probably not a million miles from here, hosting charity fundraisers. They'd have seen me in the papers all those years ago with Zak, and Marion would have laughed out loud and said *oh my God she did it, she actually went and married a rock star* and Pat would have been impressed and angry and excited and jealous. They'd have wondered *does she ever think about us?* They'd have liked to think *yes*, but they'd have known I didn't.

a repetitive chorus

IF I HAD TO describe my childhood in one word, it would be *quiet.* The house, my parents, myself – all quiet. This is hindsight, of course. Quietness was normality to my young self. School must, in fact, have been a noisy shock. But, in any case, my head had never been silent. I played mutely with toys, all the chatter contained within. I was content. Silence only became the enemy later and then there was a simple train ride to endless noise. Losing myself to the incalzando rhythm of the city had been a salvation of sorts.

But people invent their own histories, one way or another. Selectively editing the past to impress or amuse or garner pity. It's the way we tell stories. Everything should be taken with a pinch of salt. Even when thousands retell the same tale there's the question of perception – kings and queens, their greatness, their goodness – and a wilful removal of the mundane. All those regal documents to sign. All that silent play. My mother had kept a history, a record of what had been, but it wasn't accurate. Pictures of Christmas and birthdays, school uniforms and plays, as though my whole little life had been busy, as though I'd had nothing but state functions with which to pass my time. There were no candid shots of my father in disapproving flow, no visual record of hours spent rewriting homework – *sloppy Christine, do it again* – no reels of film to depict those long days poking at the soil or talking to my dolls. My childhood was clearly one of important events and broad smiles – brief captured moments, no more than five minutes real time – the rest all but gone, the foggy hangover of a bad night's sleep.

Perhaps I should stick together my own collage. My own series of events pressed tight against each other for maximum affect. But I don't dwell on it – my pain wasn't special. I never starved or had to walk outside in winter without any shoes. I was never molested by a drunken uncle. I didn't even have an uncle. Neither did I have to share a bed with a crowd of bony siblings, rise at dawn to light the stove and cook breakfast, nurse sick parents, climb up chimneys and down mines, or beg for money in the rain. I had a comfortable upbringing. I have no claim to misery. There is no mass normality anyway, though this too is hindsight.

It was another glorious day, hot and bright. The sun has a knack of suggesting promise. Heightened colours bring hope, as though we might dodge the darkness forever. Holidaying families washed over the warmed landscape, nestling in gaps bathed in sun. They clustered where the colours were brightest, choosing to ignore pavement cafés on the shadier parts of the street, to avoid viewing points in the shadows of the harbour wall. They gravitated, instead, to the areas of most promise – vying in uncomfortable closeness, driven by that unquantifiable sense of optimism.

A family ate a late continental breakfast at a nearby table. Father, mother, two young daughters. Well-dressed, neatly groomed, healthy and affectionate. Holidaymakers. The elder daughter helped the younger one cut open a croissant and spread it with jam. The father poured tea for his wife and she thanked him politely, with a genuine smile. Such manners are often lost in familiarity.

"So, what shall we do today?" the father said, glancing at each child in turn. The elder girl shrugged. He pulled a silly face and she laughed.

"Beach, beach!" The younger child wriggled on her seat, flakes of croissant dropping onto the table as her hand bobbed up and down.

"Yes, yes," the father said, laughing, "the beach is an absolute must, but what *else* shall we do?"

"I'd like to look round some of the galleries, darling," the mother said. She stroked the younger child's hair, smiled indulgently and wiped stray crumbs from the child's face. "After we've been to the beach, of course."

"Okay." The father beamed around at his family. "Everyone in agreement? Beach this morning, galleries this afternoon and then *I* thought – because *I* have a vote too – we should have dinner at that nice-looking fish restaurant over there. Agreed?"

The town was filled with these utopian families in summer. Thirty years on, despite my own more glamorous travels, my freedom, the distance between me and the little girl I'd once been, it still cramped my stomach to watch them. I turned back to my coffee. Heard the scraping of chairs as they stood, gathered their things and went to the beach. A gull circled, its eye drawn to the crumbs on the floor.

They're near the old lifeboat house. Pat has the vodka and she's not sharing anymore. She swings the bottle towards her mouth, misjudging speed and direction, her arm numbed by drink, anger and cold. Now her cheek is doubly wet. She's ahead of them, walking backwards so she can see their faces – "I hate you" – then turning, staggering on, up a narrow road that leads nowhere. They follow because they knew this would come. It has to be seen through. Even though it's freezing and she's hogging the booze.

Marion's trailing. She just can't keep pace. But Chrissy has never felt so alive – she's sharp, edgy, and can walk all night if she has to – she's not even cold. She's just alive. Vibrant. She's waiting for Pat to really start, and she doesn't give a damn because this has been coming forever. They reach the lifeboat house. Pat stops, as though this was always the destination, leans against the wall, dangerous, reckless. She's smiling, but it's twisted and ugly. It could go either way from here. There's a part of her that wants to be stopped.

Chrissy says "are you going to share that bottle, or what?" Marion gives her a look. Pat stops smiling. She says "want it, bitch?" and throws the bottle over the wall.

Pat's hands are free now, so she climbs. The wall isn't very high, but there's a hell of a drop the other side. She points to the roof of the lifeboat house, which is just about level with the top of the wall, and she's swaying a bit. Marion looks nervous. The sweat makes Chrissy shiver. Pat shouts "on there, you and me, winner calls the shots, right?" and jumps the four foot gap, over a lethal drop onto teeth of granite and the sea's raking thirst. She's clawing at the frost and scrambling up to the ridge. Marion looks at Chrissy. She's terrified, you can see it in her eyes. But it's not as if they haven't been on there before. In summer, to watch the sunset. Sober.

Pat's at the top, straddled across the ridge tiles, hair blowing. She looks elated. "Come on then, bitch, if you're brave enough". For Chrissy, it's no longer about Spencer. It's about every challenge levelled since she was six. "Can you stand on one leg? I can. I bet I can do it longer than you".

Can you sit on a cold roof?

Unless she does this there'll never be an end to it. One of them has to fall. One of them has to finally get the last word. It's perishing. The wind's getting up. The tide's coming in. Pat shouts again. Marion says "don't be stupid" as Chrissy climbs onto the wall, stands with arms wide to counterbalance the drink, the wind, the adrenalin.

I knew yesterday, when I spoke to Alice, the night on the lifeboat house was real. She didn't mention it, of course – far too polite to open anybody's old wounds – but just having asked about Pat, having spoken her name out loud, had disturbed a narcoleptic memory. This morning I woke to an echo of clarity – not tangible enough to touch, not sad enough to make me cry; just an overwhelming ache, a smallness. A pointlessness I'd long forgotten. But memory is unreliable. I reminded myself that and got up, drank coffee, sang along to the radio, but didn't quite manage to lose the ghosts hiding behind each door and curtain, the expectation that I'd find my father sitting silently in his chair, waiting for me to do or say something I'd forgotten to do or say, waiting for me to explain myself. So I walked to the harbour in the morning sunshine, immersed myself in the noise of tourists busy making entries for their own albums of broad smiles, listened to the chatter of their precocious kids, the flapping of flags and clanking of steel cables against metallic masts, the repetitive *caw, caw, caw* of feathered toddlers mid-tantrum.

But the echo didn't fade.

There's something else. Something I can't quite hold. And it's trying to persuade me to dredge over what I can, force clarity to come. Because people don't really forget. There's always the residue.

The girl with the mousy hair sits with her parents outside a café by the harbour. The chair's too high and her feet don't reach the floor. She clings to the side of the seat with small, sticky hands and swings her legs. Her body tilts back and forth in rhythm.

"Stop that," the father says, quietly so only she and her mother can hear. "Sit still."

Her mother catches her eye, gives a little smile, a subtle nod. The girl stops swinging her legs though she still keeps a tight grip on the chair's edge.

"Can we go now?" the father speaks in that low voice again. He hasn't touched his tea. It's probably gone cold now. The girl eyes up his uneaten scone but doesn't ask if she can have it.

"Just a few minutes, John," the mother says. "Dr Morrison said an hour, small outings, just an hour."

The girl watches a family walking past. The children, two boys, have buckets and spades. They're heading for the beach.

"Are we going to the beach, mummy?" the girl asks.

This is the first time they've all been out together. It's a Special Day.

"She's covered in food," the father says. "She's got it all over her clothes."

He too is holding the sides of his chair. He nods at the mess on the little girl's t-shirt but doesn't make any move to wipe it away.

"It's only a bit of jam," the mother says in a light voice. "I'll sponge it off when we get home."

The girl turns, sees the holiday family retreating – she can just about make them out in the crowd, heading towards the beach. The children swinging yellow and red plastic, the older boy with fishing net held high, the younger one holding onto his father's hand.

"Can I have a bucket and spade?" she asks her mother. "Can we go to the beach?"

She's never been to the beach. Even though it's here all the time. Six years old and never played on the sand. She's seen children on beaches in storybooks, with their buckets and spades, digging. The little girl likes digging. She digs the soil at home, though she doesn't have a spade – she uses a stick.

"Is it an hour?" the father says. "It must have been an hour now. I want to go."

"Yes," the mother says. "We can go home."

"Not to the beach?" the girl says. It was supposed to be a Special Day.

"Not today, Christine," her mother said. "Daddy needs to get home. But I can see if Alice would take you some time? That would be nice, wouldn't it?"

Places like this are menacing. There's something evil about ancient fishing ports. Narrow streets reaching out from the quayside like arthritic fingers, grasping at the hills, clutching the earth against the pull of the tide. Unloved boats held tight in the harbour's palm, rigging clanking to the pulse of the sea, slumped in beds of foul water and rancid mud, with no more than a daily wash of flotsam to ease the boredom – broken plastic buoys and crates, the dirty froth of engine oil. Towns like this are filthy, haunted places. But it's what the tourists pay to see. They think it an authentic echo of simpler times. *Such a beautiful place*, they say, *if only it weren't so busy.* They promise themselves they'll come in winter, when it's quieter. But they never do. If they did, they'd see a different dream. They'd see what I see. Streets still and barren, unwelcoming, their paradise raw and defenceless against the anger of a neglected sea. In the absence of sunshine and plastic windmills on sticks, they'd see life behind the postcard imagery, deprived of pretty views and holiday pastiche. People rotting in ugly structures from less cosmetic decades; utilitarian boxes far removed from the essence of culture; whole generations untouched by the artistic buzz in the streets below, dulled by grey concrete and hard slog. If they looked hard enough they'd see the reality of the whole world, condensed into one repetitive chorus – the beat of a stormy sea.

As any photographer can tell you, reality is a perception. The pleasure of the camera is its capacity for illusion. A desire to capture the truth ultimately only traps an insular lie, holds it for eternity – for endless interpretation – and the past becomes whatever the present desires. Just like every deliberate click of the eye. Every vision committed to memory, isolated from what came before, what followed after, caught from the angle of the beholder, held fast for future recall. And yet it's lost. From the moment it lets go of all that surrounds it, it is lost. The truth, if ever it existed at all, is gone and what remains is a new vision, from a new perspective, surrounded by other remembered events that were never even close at the time. So if I do think back, it's with a photographer's eye. I understand the fallacy.

An old fishing tug pulls into the harbour after a leisurely forty minutes round the bay, its haul a group of pensioners on a day trip from some miserable province. The captain wears traditional fisherman's garb, knitted in Malaysia by small fingers in dire conditions. It's what his customers want. He doubtless maintains a stock of fishing stories too, complete with accent and local jargon. Looking at today's crowd, he probably stuck to ornithology – they were all too close to death to relish stormy nights and boats that never made it home. Had he known at sixteen how rich the pickings would one day be, perhaps he would have tempered his work ethic, saved a little energy for these lonely, dusky years. He doubtless finds pleasure enough in loading and unloading the female cargo, taking their smooth hands in his sandpaper grasp, their buxom warmth into the fold of his arm, *lean against me, darlin'*.

But he'll wish he was ten years younger.

One of today's passengers, overblown and underdressed, leans into his embrace with a coy giggle and makes a meal of the low steps. She probably hasn't been touched by a man in years. Her sharp-eyed friend snaps *oh come on Doreen, he's got another six of us to see to*, and reluctantly she relinquishes her catch, rues the cool breeze where his arm had been. Eventually the moment will vanish from both of their pasts.

And if I had to describe my teenage years in one word, it would be *surreal*. At some point – I don't know exactly when – I was shunted off the main rails. Just fractionally. A few millimetres or so. Enough to feel the slip in dimension – the sense of being a little bit early, a little bit late – but not enough to obliterate the world travelling alongside, not enough to render me obviously derailed. Youth became an echo, as though it had already gone, or was only a half-conceived idea of something yet to come and now, with thirty four years of noise as a buffer, it's a gaudy blur ending in a strange city – everything too fast, at an oblique angle. Only logic can claim me as part of its colour, but it's where the *something else* lies.

Marion's back with her dad. He's a bit thinner than he once was but he's still too fat to climb so he runs into The Smuggler and brings out a few strong men. One is Jack Crozier who used to fish but now takes tourists round the bay. It's Jack who gets onto the roof. It's solid and almost dry. It doesn't dip and twist with the wind, doesn't keel over and make a man pray. It's a pleasure trip.

He's glancing from one girl to the other – he can't be in two places at one time – and shouting "ROPE GET ME ROPE I NEED ROPE" and somebody must already have it because it appears near his feet just seconds later.

Just as Pat takes off.

It lands in a loose coil, clunking against the slate and slithering halfway down the roof again. In the silence between flight and fall; the brief halting of wind, sea and the jangle of the harbour – in the silence of a communal held breath. But there's no splash. Chrissy looks at the sky.

Pat must have done it. She must have flown.

Between them, the men from the pub get Chrissy down. The landlady of The Smuggler brings a blanket, wraps her up and takes her inside. She sits across from Marion in front of the fire and thaws.

Marion is crying. Her dad says she has her A-levels to think about, she doesn't need this, and though she doesn't say anything, you can tell Marion agrees.

There are some broad smiles. A few clear snapshots of the time. Spencer. I remember Spencer with all my senses. Even now, I feel him, smell him, see his eyes, taste his mouth, hear his words. I knew that passion. It was real. There are times I can reach out a hand in the dark and swear I touch him. And Pat. So brutally close. A furious loyalty. A measure of all I was and all I was not. Every clear recollection I have from those days hangs on these two passions. To have once felt so fiercely for other human beings seems bizarre to me now. To have lost it, even more so. I just don't know whether the destruction came because such force was unsustainable, or whether it was incidental and the end had a more mundane source; some surplus boring details long forgotten. I know what the argument was about. But not where it came from, or where it took us.

"Again? You're always with him. He doesn't love you. Not like I do. He just wants someone to listen to him. On and on. It's not love – you're his one-person fan club."
"So? He still loves me."
"Really? How come he never says it?"

If I had to select only one photograph from my mind to illustrate those years – one brief captured moment, one small song – it would be the darkness of that last night, the wind, the spray, the screeching, the sheer bloody futility. The chasm chasing through me as those two passions crashed and burned. It would be a vast, black snapshot of nothingness. There's a part of me that says Pat did jump, it's the sort of crazy thing she'd have done, but then I think it must be false memory – that the story evolved – because it's not something I could have forgotten. So I wonder if she's alive. Whether I'd find her if I looked. I wonder whether I got all the memories wrong and for her I'd be no more than a passing acquaintance from a time long gone and, for Spencer, I'd be a vague remembered kiss, the recognition of an old fragrance, a dim awareness of the naked limbs of youth connecting like virgin jigsaw pieces. I wonder if any of it happened, whether I was ever there, whether I'm actually here now. Maybe I was the one who jumped. Maybe the past thirty years have been the biggest fallacy of all. Of all I think I remember there is nothing but this moment I can prove as truth and that itself is gone in seconds, into that same unreliable past, and I'm left to question *did I think that just then?*

I shouldn't have come back.

Marion is still here, on the other side of the harbour behind a steamy window and a long queue. According to Alice she runs the family fish and chip shop with her husband. So much for a university degree and high hopes. Given Alice's poor recall, Marion would be the easiest way to clear things up. She'd been there, below – a vague white face interrupted by thick rimmed glasses glowing in the floodlights of someone's jeep – staring up at the lifeboat house roof, at us, as Jack Crozier jumped the gap. But I don't know whether I can do it. I don't know whether she wants to remember.

Below me, the captain readied his boat for the next catch, worn ropes draped with seaweed straining as it tried to tug free from the harbour. That prison of impassive stone, tarnished from years of oily caresses; managed, maintained, but never safe from nature's grasp. Three hundred years of man's futile attempts to control the sea and it still charges over when angry enough. I had my camera. I wanted to zoom in on Marion but the window was impassable, so I focused on the pleasure craft instead, brought Jack Crozier's face closer. It was him. Still here. Trawling for tourists more years than he ever did for fish. Travelling, over a lifetime, miles over sea – but barely moving inland. Here always, just like his father, just like his grandfather. Incredible. I bet he still thinks himself a fisherman.

Marion too. Repeating her parents' lives despite the dreams. No executive husband, no commuter-belt paradise, no time for fundraising.

Just fish and chips. Scrubbing and serving and asking the same questions over and over. *Salt and vinegar?* Acting as human guide-book for people who live far more interesting lives. People who come and go and smile and talk about the weather. Knowing for them this is novelty, for them this is a break, for them this isn't somewhere they could be forever. We'd have nothing in common, once we'd finished discussing Pat.

one won't hurt

THE ONLY people I've spoken to in three days are Mervyn, Alice and the tedious Malcolm Fenchurch from Boyd & Fenchurch. I don't like silence, I don't like solitude. No particular reason, I just prefer company and noise. It didn't need analysing, just rectifying, so I bought another radio to save moving the existing one around. The new one is digital, not quite in sync with the analogue, and the déjà vu catches me every time I go upstairs.

I'd been through everything, it was the solicitor who was dragging his feet. There were no more policies, no hidden papers – everything he had was it, full stop – yet he was taking a lifetime to have one simple document typed up for signature.

"Do you know how long," I say, "it took to organise and execute a *Plutonium* shoot in the Rockies? That's Colorado. The States. America."

"I know you think..."

"Not just people – equipment: instruments, lights, rigging, generators, make-up, dressers... have you any idea?"

"It's not..."

"Forty eight hours."

Okay, I was exaggerating. It was forty eight hours after we'd landed and wasted half a day waiting for equipment trucks who'd taken a wrong turn at Utah and not realised until they hit Salt Lake City, and there'd been weeks of preparation before that. But still.

"Look, I'm sorry, I am, we're just really busy and short..."

"It's a bit of paper. How long can it take?"

There could be nothing keeping a second-rate solicitor so occupied he couldn't produce a simple document. Unless folk had been dying off in their dozens and he was up to the light-fittings in probate claims; or there was a mad rush on housing and everyone wanted to move in before summer's end – which couldn't be the case because the estate agent hadn't yet marched forth with a queue of potential buyers for my mother's house.

The whole town runs at an immeasurable pace.

He breathes little sighs. Moves papers. And I wait because I can sense him weakening.

I don't often play on the band thing, or Zak's name. I changed back to Barker about twenty years ago when the seventies became an embarrassing stain to be scrubbed away, the association with Zak a key that no longer fit any doors. Lately there'd been a revival, the era was now retro-cool. I may even change back. When I first spoke to Fenchurch it was the name he used and I'd sensed his excitement when I confirmed I was that Chrissy Zook – *how many could there be?* He said he was a fan of *Plutonium* which, having now met him, surprised me – he was at least a decade younger than me – maybe there was a chance of resurrection for Zak and the guys after all.

"I've got that album," he says now, "with the Rockies on the sleeve." He has a soothing voice, I'll give him that. Another sigh. "Okay, if I have to type it up myself it'll be ready tomorrow, close of play."

My mother read an article about the wedding in seventy five and found out where I worked. That I was alive. She obviously hung onto the details and phoned the magazine when my father died, nearly two decades later. It was the early nineties and I was long gone. Mervyn was still there, though only just. His father-in-law bought the magazine in ninety five and promoted him to group editor of a much larger playground. Those old offices were closed. Had my mother left that initial contact any later, nobody would have found me this time round. But Mervyn kept in touch with her after that first call. I'd no idea.

He found me then through Zak – who himself had only just tracked me down, to tell me he was sober, he wanted to try again. I told him no. Then it was Mervyn, calling out of the blue to tell me about my father, to try and persuade me to get in touch with my mother. I'd spent a decade moving on and suddenly everyone seemed to want me to travel backwards. We argued. Mervyn has strong views on family and they don't match mine at any point. Our edges are, shall we say, very irregular. It probably riled him to realise at that point how a twenty-year sporadic affair had revealed no more than flesh. But ten minutes of chatting to my mother and he thought he knew it all. I remember the conversation.

It was nineteen ninety one.

He said I was the most selfish bitch he'd ever known. And my instinctive thought was *well, you never knew Pat.*

It was the first time in eighteen years I'd had a clear thought about her. It was a revelation. Not like recalling some half-baked acquaintance from school – someone so forgettable that even when you do remember them the curiosity extends no further than *have they done better than me?* before you tune them out, forget them for another two decades – but like remembering you're alive. Something so obvious and fundamental you can't believe you forgot. I wondered where I'd been all that time to have completely erased myself. The world tilted. It was clear to me then, it had tilted before and I'd forgotten about that too.

I moved on again, found a new crowd – good

people, fun people – and another year passed before I remembered the night on the lifeboat house roof. Before I thought about the night Pat flew. It just came back to me. I'd tilted low enough to let it in. And I can't work out where the tilts start and end. It's like being hypnotised once and never being certain you've come out of it. I feel fine now, but I've felt fine before. There's no context, no way of knowing whether I right myself each time or whether every subsequent tipping takes me further down. All I know for sure is that I lost four years to that first phone call. So when Mervyn tracked me down again in ninety five to tell me his happy news, there wasn't much I could say to congratulate him. I just asked him to come over. I just needed him. He got a seat on a plane the next morning, broke his vows to Mrs Levy the Fourth, and my world readjusted at a pace of one day for each spoiled year.

As he seems to have the knack of righting me when I tip, it wasn't the best news that he didn't now need me to go to France, or that his retirement had been indefinitely postponed.

"So why the change of plan, Merv?"

"It's complicated, babe, just magazine stuff."

"Like what?"

"Just stuff. They need me to stay on a bit. Look, we'll talk later, got to go."

This place was pushing me. If he thought it

an appropriate moment to reconcile with his wife, he was wrong. At least Fenchurch had promised the goods. I could leave soon. But to where, I didn't know.

They sit in the wind and darkness. It feels like forever. Invisible spray hits the walls, arcs high, scatters and falls on them like dew. Pat doesn't look so confident now. She's stopped shouting. She's crumpling – she'd probably fall if her legs weren't frozen into place – and crying. She's really crying. Maybe she wants to let go but can't. Chrissy has never seen her like this – so empty of anger.

But Chrissy can't open her mouth. It's all she can do to bring one frozen hand to her face, wipe the wet from her lashes. If she could unclench her jaw, her teeth would begin to chatter, her whole being to shiver and shake, and she'd lose control. If that happened, if she lost that rigidity, the momentum of hate and fear and pain would be unstoppable. So she just watches Pat, and it hurts, but she can say or do nothing.

Various songs have appropriately summed up my life over the years. There isn't one constant. I have favourites, or should I say a few regulars seek me out from time to time. It's ironic, given my dislike of the backward glance, to appreciate words which emphasise the past. Words which hurt. But it'd be false to choose a reflection on the basis of what you wish reality had been – either a song fits or it doesn't. There's no bending the rules. And these persistent musical reminders can't be avoided, reopened wounds won't cure if they're left to fester, and maybe the mind knows this. Maybe it's a trading off – short-term pain for long-term survival. No matter how good a person is at staving off the inevitable, there comes a moment when a niggle morphs into a craving and it's impossible to refuse. Like a dried-out drunk passing a pub, I'm drawn, and every sensible argument against what I want to do can be countered with a perfectly rational vote in favour.

One won't hurt.

So I submit to whichever of the songs has called – in darkness, at full volume – and let it become all there could ever be. My life amplified, held up as an agonising truth for Judgement. Nothing is safe from the song. It is shrink, priest and conscience. It is poet, lover and friend. But, as any honest drunk knows, one *will* hurt, one is never enough, and it might be ten or fifty replays before numbness expunges the pain.

I phone Fenchurch again. The girl on the desk tries to fob me off but I tell her I know he's there. There's a pause, I sense her silently communicating who it is on the line. Common sense battles with intrigue. It loses and falls. He takes the call. I ask whether he has wider tastes than just *Plutonium* and he says of course.

"What have you got that's bleak, loud and long?"

He's trying to have this conversation in front of the girl and maybe he already knows where it's leading. He reminds me of Mervyn.

"Um, all sorts really..."

"I need to listen to some music. Tonight. I need to do this tonight."

There's a pause. He coughs out a laugh.

"Right. And would that be before or after I complete your paperwork?"

"Seven, in *The Drum*, I need a drink too."

He pauses again. Common sense tries to stand up. It fails.

"Okay, seven it is," he says.

a hard place

MALCOLM FENCHURCH removed the album from its dust cover, smoothing a hand across the exposed sleeve to wipe away non-existent grime. He'd replaced all his records with CDs some years ago but couldn't quite bring himself to get rid of the original vinyl. Album covers were an art form and their size did more justice to Chrissy Zook's photographic skills than a shrunken CD counterpart could ever manage.

The Rockies. In full sun and with the band at the start of real fame – Zak standing in the middle, naked and oiled from the waist up, head tilted back, hair half-way down his spine, screaming into the microphone with visible force. Malcolm wondered which song, which word, which exact *note* Chrissy had captured in this moment. Out of shot there'd be large canvas tents, electricity generators, trucks with over-sized wheels and heavy-duty tires, people with clipboards and tired faces and sweaty clothes. Then Chrissy Zook, slightly detached, focused, with her camera, her vision and her endless cool. He opened the cover and scanned the various pictures inside for any glimpses of these background mechanics reflected, perhaps, in the high polish steel fingerplate of a guitar, the mirrored lenses of sunglasses, or as shadows on the dusty ground. But there was nothing. Even these between-take shots were a fabrication.

He would ask her, later, to describe the shoot. Would ask about the R&R snaps, whether they were real, what it had actually felt like – to be there, to be part of that life, part of that success.

This particular album, *Rock and a Hard Place*, had been released in 1980. Malcolm remembered buying it with his birthday money. He was eleven. It was the first music he'd bought and the start of a lifetime's appreciation of *Plutonium*. Now here he was; twenty seven years older and getting ready for a date with Zak Zook's ex-wife. Life had never been so bizarre.

His mobile rang. It was Roger, wanting to know if he fancied a few beers and a curry later.

"Got a better offer, Rog'."

"Yeah? Who is she?"

He laughed. "You wouldn't believe me, mate."

But maybe it wasn't anything other than a drink, a bit of company. She was probably just bored, back here in Nowhere Land. Maybe he was the only person she could ask.

"Not that Zook woman?" Roger's envy was almost tangible. Malcolm left a suitably long pause. "Oh man, you jammy, jammy sod. What did ya do? Offer her free legals?"

Fenchurch laughed. "Sod off."

"Where you taking her?"

"Not a chance, Rog', not a chance."

"Bastard. Okay pal, have a good one… phone me tomorrow."

Malcolm Fenchurch was always prepared. The urge to be ready, for anything, was a personal tic he'd long grown used to. No need to rush around his apartment cleaning and removing unwashed crockery from the bedroom. He never consumed food there. No need to panic over a fridge containing no more than one pack of out-of-date yoghurts and a sole egg of dubious age. His kitchen was perfectly well-stocked. He had nothing more to do than briefly check there were two bottles of Chablis chilling on the second shelf, a selection of reds on the rack nearby. Malcolm Fenchurch had never known chaos.

He'd lived in this apartment for two years, having bought off plan to ensure he got the best view. For the first six months, he'd been sole occupant of *The Smokehouse* – a solitude he'd enjoyed very much. The place was now fully occupied, its communal spaces busy with the to-ing and fro-ing of holidaymakers alongside the permanent residents. But no matter. He was on the fourth and uppermost floor, out of the way. He had a large balcony which straddled the corner wall and provided what was probably the finest harbour and sea view in town. To the right he could look up the lane to the old redundant lifeboat house and beyond, out to sea and the fine line of the horizon. To his left, lay the harbour, restaurants, shops. Beyond a row of Victorian roofs on the far side of the harbour, peeped the spire of one of the town's oldest churches. Behind that, the sandier of two bays – obscured from his view, but for the silvery shine of water and another glimpse of that illusive horizon. The balcony spanned two walls of his apartment, jutting out at the corner point in mock ship's bow style, rails from either stretch curling forwards at the point they met. He liked to lean into this prow first thing each morning; breathe in the fishy, salty air, embrace the breeze of the incoming tide, listen to the clunk of boat masts in the harbour and stare outwards through the two stone pillars at its mouth towards the vastness of the sea.

He could not envisage ever moving. He was as trapped in this place as the generations of workers who'd scrubbed, gutted and smoked decades' worth of pilchards. Sometimes, when the odour of those years could be vaguely detected seeping from walls warmed by hot sun, it would remind him of his own choices, his own limitations, his own small place in this world. But he didn't welcome this sort of morose self-indulgence, though he had been aware of the odour more often of late.

The Drum was a peculiar choice of meeting place. It was an old fashioned pub, popular with the less upmarket holidaymakers whose taste in cuisine stretched no further than steak and ale pie with chips and high calorific puddings drowning in custard. It was certainly a suitable venue for a clandestine meeting if avoiding being seen was the order of the day. Given that Chrissy was a client, Fenchurch supposed the meeting did have an air of inappropriateness, although clandestine would be taking things a little far.

Maybe not.

But as his secretary had pointed out, socialising with a client was not something his father would have condoned during his reign at Boyd & Fenchurch. They'd both laughed, struck simultaneously by the thought of the other founding partner, Henry Boyd whose predilection for affairs with clients had bordered on the fetishistic.

"I'm not judging you," Rose said. "Not my concern. You deserve some fun. Enjoy yourself. Let's face it, your father's in no position to find out."

Malcolm could tell the old sod himself if he so choose and it would be forgotten in seconds. Charles Fenchurch was a barely-living confessional, now confined to a luxurious room in a private nursing home with only the Devil for company. Almost every memory the old boy once possessed had been stolen from him by Alzheimer's.

Strangely enough, he could always remember Malcolm's name though he could never define their relationship. In a way, it had always been like that. Malcolm checked his watch. Six forty five. Now was not a good time to think about his father. He ordered a whisky, large, and downed it in two gulps.

"Same again, please."

She'd probably be late. She seemed the type. The smell of chips was sickening. He drank the second whisky less greedily, queried the possibility of a bottle of champagne and a couple of glasses, and was surprised when the bartender produced a fairly decent brand and two champagne flutes.

When Chrissy arrived, Fenchurch was sitting at an outside table – located as far away from the kitchen fans as possible – and he waved as she lifted her sunglasses and peered at him, squinting against the low sun.

She moved like smoke. He had to glance down, check her feet were actually making contact with the floor. Effortless. He stood, pulled out a chair for her. She laughed.

"It's a dump inside," he said. "Thought we'd be better out here."

"Sorry," she said. "It's been a long time. It used to be the coolest pub in town. You should have said."

He opened the champagne, poured two glasses, handed one to her and sat down.

"So..." he said.

She laughed again. "You're wondering why."

But she didn't offer an explanation. Just pulled her sunglasses back down over her eyes, drank the champagne and relaxed into the hard chair as though it were the comfiest seat she'd ever encountered.

He asked her about *Plutonium* and Zak. About those heady days. She answered his questions but volunteered nothing beyond them. She said life on the road with a band, the money, the fame, was just the same as life elsewhere. That eventually a person realised this. That eventually a person saw how every situation could be broken into just two states: anticipation and disappointment. Then she laughed, less effusively, and asked him to refill her glass.

A family arrived and spread around the table beside them. A large man and woman with three bickering children. They argued over who should sit where and then, once finally settled, argued over the menu instead. Chrissy raised her sunglasses, looked at Fenchurch.

"Let's take this and go," she said. "Finish it on the beach."

"We can't take the glasses."

She arched her brows, challenging, teasing. "Yes we can."

But they didn't walk to the beach. Fenchurch

pointed out his apartment as they reached the harbour, his balcony jutting out to sea, and Chrissy suggested they go there instead, it was where the music was after all. He planned to take the glasses back to the pub tomorrow, and knew he would. He was also sure she wouldn't have bothered.

They finished the champagne, moved onto wine. Chrissy sat on the floor, flicking through Malcolm's CD collection, searching for something to satisfy the craving. Her selection played on a loop, its sound drifting out from the open doors. When she asked, he turned the volume a little higher. Tonight, for a change, it was his turn to piss off the neighbours. They talked, laughed and during certain moments, certain songs, she retreated into silence and he watched her. By the third loop of the album he could anticipate each lapse and when to break it.

"So. Is it true?" he said, as one silence approached its end. "You have Zak's name tattooed on the inside of your thigh?"

He reached out an arm, touched the hair he'd wanted to touch all evening, curling a length of it around his fingers. She turned, smiled, trailed a cool hand along his arm.

"Strange sort of lawyer who takes the word of a client as truth," she said. "I had you down as a man who'd check out the facts himself…"

death & sustenance

I COULD BARELY take my eyes off Alice's boots. They belied the fragility of her body, as though grim determination alone might be capable of halting the decay. Solid and thick, with treads that wouldn't be out of place on a truck, holding up her wasted frame, their ferocity tempered by a tender roll of wool against brittle ankles. She was wearing another saggy, miserable dress – a cheap cotton floral print, buttoned from neck to knee – a sunhat with faded stripes that looked like it had been crafted from old deckchair canvas, and a man's cardigan. Aged and bobbled, in an Arran knit, olive green, turned at the cuffs. Obviously far too big. Obviously not intended for a woman, even before the wasting. Maybe in the intervening years there'd been a husband.

Or a lover.

Or both.

She's a fighter, you have to give her that. Apart from that weak moment in the kitchen, she hadn't been needy. At this age, she probably loses a friend a month; you'd expect her to go on about it, old people generally do. Hard to picture how she used to be, to spot a brief memory in the muscles of her face, catch the remnants of a voice once richer, find in her movement any trace of the glorious flesh she used to carry. There was now so little of her left, she'd probably vanish before Death could grasp her. Maybe it was nature's intent – this gradual fading away. An evaporation. Maybe it's what makes the end bearable.

Even if it were polite to ask, Death at close range must be a subjective vision. That night, on the lifeboat house roof, it had taken the shape of suffocating desire; the utter embracing of purpose. The end had seemed the goal, the wanting far greater than the fear, and that, in the aftermath, was terrifying – to have desired what others so valiantly fight.

She's glad it's dark and she can't see the fall, only a moving shine on the water, blinking and shifting; a vague sense of the drop. But at the top, astride and facing Pat, she's big again, in control, safe. Like a giant in a fairy tale.

Her hands have gone dead. She can't even feel her legs or feet now. She wonders if she's still touching the tiles, or is actually lifting away from the roof. She senses this is the end, this is it, there won't be anything more and really, now, she just wishes it would happen. Close her eyes. Float away.

Perhaps it was like that for Alice too. Perhaps at the appropriate time, Death is a kinder prospect than life. But how aware is she? That this is it? The sum total? That there'll never be more than what has been? Does she think about that?

Are you scared, Alice?

She'd packed an oilskin tote bag – original, not retro – an item she must have possessed so long it had come back into fashion. She'd packed it with a precision John Albert Barker would have admired – sandwiches, home-made cake, apples and a flask of tea.

"No rush, is there dear? We can sit and have a bite up there, it's a beautiful spot."

She insisted the box go in the bag too. Wedged to one side by the foil-wrapped parcels, balanced at the other by the weight of the grey flask. Death and sustenance sharing space.

The exertion of packing seemed to have tired her. She suggested a cup of tea before setting out. I had nothing better to do and she did seem short of company. I suspected my mother might have been her last remaining friend. I hadn't seen any visitors. Her front room was sparse and I sat in the only spare high-backed chair, surprised at the lack of possessions. A small area of commonality, although I suspect for her it had more to do with poverty than philosophical belief.

"So, what have you been up to?" she said in her old teacher's tone. "How long has it been?"

"Thirty four years."

"Heavens, has it really?"

She knew about Zak of course, seemed to find it quite a thrill – hearing snippets of life on the road with a band. Obviously I kept details to a minimum. I doubted she'd be quite as titillated by the truth. She was less enthused about my later wanderings, even though I tried to recall as many amusing incidents as I could remember. The number of countries impressed her – I was right, she'd never travelled – but she didn't quite get the freedom of it all, didn't seem to understand the difference between exploring and drifting. In the end I gave up on the stories.

"What's been happening here then, Alice?"

I felt good. Fenchurch had proved a timely antidote.

"It was difficult when you left, dear. Your mother took it badly. But your father improved for quite some years. He had a new doctor, better medicine. They got on with it, you know. It's a shame you never called or wrote," she said. "She always hoped you would. Not my business, I know, you have your own life. But it would have made her very happy."

I did once try. In those slightly disjointed days, between the argument with Mervyn and the later reconciliation. It was something he'd said during that call – it obviously stuck in my head and I have a vague recollection of phoning, of being able to remember the number, of her voice, far away, answering. Anything I may have intended to say wasn't actually said, it just hung in the silence for a while and she said my name, asked if it was me. It sounded wrong – a stranger, another person's life, *Christine*'s life – and I knew I couldn't do it, shouldn't have tried, and whether I actually said that or whether it was just in my head I don't know, but I remember putting the phone down and sitting there for a while. Thinking it had been a stupid thing to do. A pointless effort brought on by one of Mervyn's ridiculous sentiments. *You only get one mother*, he'd said, *and when she's gone, she's gone.* For that brief moment, I'd thought it mattered.

So do I feel guilty? Do I wish I'd spoken to her? I don't see any point in musing it over. It's that warm glow again, the good deed for selfish return. For me, there would have been little point – my past is a life left behind, and for good reason, there could have been no personal benefit in a conversation with anyone from those times. But for her it might have mattered. For her it might have been worthwhile. So, yes, there's an element of guilt, but it would still have been there had I submitted. One phone call would never have been enough. Not for her or for Mervyn.

"Did you never marry, Alice?"

We were walking through town, away from the harbour, heading towards the beach and the narrow lane leading up to the cliff path. I didn't imagine she'd be offended. For her generation, not having married is the sort of anomaly that warrants an explanation.

"Good Lord, I abandoned that idea before you were even born."

She turned, smiled and winked to show she wasn't cross. I was struck sharply by an image of the Alice I'd once known.

"How old was my mother?"

"Eighty-eight, she would have been eighty-nine next month."

We passed the surfing gear shop, crawling with people who'll never step foot on a surfboard but who are drawn to shopping regardless of where they find themselves in the world. A crying child pushed past us, face ugly and stained, his father trying to both console and threaten simultaneously – out of his depth just days into the holiday – whilst the mother hung back, clinging onto smug detachment for as long as she could.

Alice struggles with her memory. As though the head fills up at some point and nothing more can go in until something is jettisoned. In this way bits of the past vanish and it becomes harder to retrieve what was once so accessible. She argued with herself for a few minutes over whether my mother's birthday was the third of August or the fifth. Eventually she remembered it was the seventh. When we got beyond the shops and shoppers we turned towards the beach, which was also full, and followed the pavement along the sea wall, away from town. The tourists thinned out as we climbed narrow steps cut into the hillside, past tiny fishermen's cottages on increasingly small ledges of earth; each jutting out towards the sea, their bleak windows serving as lonely vigil points for generations of worried women.

"I had a young man, once." she said.

We stopped and stood for a moment. She held onto the steel rail. To avoid peering into the kitchen window of a cottage, we turned and looked out over the sea. Alice breathed deeply, pronounced the view beautiful and told me she couldn't live anywhere else.

"For all your travelling," she said, "You can't beat this, can you?"

She was maybe wishing she hadn't worn the cardigan. I offered to carry it – I could push it through the straps of the bag, I told her. She said she hadn't warmed up enough yet. It was her old bones, she said, they feel the chill.

"So what happened to the young man?"

"Died at Dunkirk, dear."

We continued the ascent. There was a wooden bench at the top of the steps – a thoughtful later addition for a weaker generation of climbers. I tried to remember if there was another way to this spot that didn't involve a hundred and five steps – incredible I still remembered how many – but I couldn't think. We should probably have taken a taxi via the back road. Alice was wheezy and obviously tired and I couldn't see how she'd have the strength for the return walk.

The girl with the mousy hair reaches the top step first.

"One hundred and five!" she says, turning to her friend. Pat has dark hair and the sun makes it shine like a crow's feathers. "Wow, your head looks deep blue, like the sea, it's lovely."

"One hundred and five? Are you sure?" Pat says. "I think it's more. I don't think you counted properly. I think you missed some."

"I didn't. I counted carefully. A hundred and five."

The girl with the mousy hair frowns, looks back down the cliff steps, all the way to the bottom, the beach. The people are quite small, just colours and moving shapes. She loves climbing up the cliff. It's where she met Pat. It's a good place.

"I think I got it right," she says. She's not at all sure now. It's a long climb.

"We'll have to do it again. We have to be sure." Pat stands on the top step. They look down at their dusty sandals, feet together, toes pointing to the horizon. "Okay... one..."

Together they step down, the girl with the mousy hair concentrating hard on the numbers this time.

"Shall we have a cup of tea?" I said to Alice. "Rest up for a minute?"

"That would be lovely, dear."

We sat on the wooden bench. Alice sipped her tea contentedly, pointed to wild flowers and grasses, commented on the clarity of the sky. I wondered why the nicest people never have children, why it only seems to be the ungrateful ones who do. I wanted to know why she didn't find another young man, why she chose to spend more than sixty years alone, but I didn't ask. Maybe some anomalies don't need explaining after all. We'd come back to the song, to Love. There must be more dirges about it than all other topics combined. Its loss, its gain, its duplicitous nature, the longing, the loathing, the expectation, the futility. It's a human obsession. Songs do their best, but they all have the same starting point – an assumption of Love as Truth. People think they've got it covered, there isn't a lyric unwritten, but it all hangs on that acceptance of Love's existence, its form. Without that none of it makes sense. Where are the songs about Love's truth? That less aesthetic biological drive?

I imagine Alice spent sixty years alone because her heart was broken. She'd loved and lost and it was enough. If that wasn't the sentiment – if her choice had a more practical basis, an unwillingness to be hurt again perhaps – it still seemed an overly masochistic indulgence. The only way to tolerate the delusion is to accept that without Love, whatever we perceive it to be, we have no protection from the ultimate truth – our pointlessness. I know where that leads us, so I sing along with the rest. I love, I lose and I carry on, despite what logic tells me, because to give up would be to admit that final truth, and conceding to that would take me straight to the nearest lifeboat house to succeed where I'd failed in seventy three.

Their arms stretch into the darkness – elegant, unfurled, arced – and they glance down towards the source of the spray, the jagged bed on which their nest sits. Pat shouts "come on, let's do it. Let's fly. Just once."

Spencer knew all there was to know about the final truth and kindly imparted his wisdom to the rest of us, which isn't something you ever forget. We once stood at this very spot, looking out to sea. A day like this – hot, sunny, the beach filled with holidaymakers and happiness. But Spencer had no faith in first glances.

"Pointless, purposeless lives. Why do they not see it?"

"They're just enjoying the sun."

"Tell me," he said, "what you think you see?" He waved a hand, arcing it over the landscape of beach and people.

"I see families, enjoying the beach, the weather, swimming. Kids playing in the sand. The usual seaside stuff."

He laughed. Short, sneering, disappointed.

"What I see and what you'd also see were you to properly look, is the mindless repetition of a species too stupid to see their own futility. They look like ants, they behave like ants – pre-programmed to reproduce, pre-disposed to spend their brief lifetimes replicating the actions of millions before them. What they call *enjoyment* is a social construction to justify and soothe and make it seem a valid passing of time. They can't see their own stupidity because they don't want to see it."

I never looked at people the same again.

So I'm not now sure whether I see Alice as a higher being, a person of such moral strength she can face truth and look it in the eye without fear. Or whether she's just blind to her predicament, occupies the same vacuous space as anyone else and finds meaning in each ingrained repetition, never contemplating what her purpose might have been, what anybody's purpose might have been. Or perhaps she just craves pain. Some people do.

She said she was rested, we could carry on. She said the view further along was breathtaking. She sounded like an advertisement. She looks across that void and only counts colours, shapes, the lack of concrete. She doesn't hear the ancient screams lingering in the wind, doesn't feel the water's icy shock, the vile suck as life is dragged down into darkness. The water is not blue. The sky is not blue. I'm not even sure the hills are green.

"You know, Christine," she said. We were on the flat, it was a leisurely pace. "I think your mother would have been relieved, you being so independent – she worried, you know, that you might not be as strong as she imagined."

"She thought that? I was *strong*?"

Alice laughed. Again, a glimpse of the weightier Alice, the bouncy lady next door with toffee in her apron.

"We *knew* it," she said. "You were such a self-contained little thing."

She chuckled for another ten feet or so. To my right, the hedges dropped further down the embankment towards the edge of the cliff. There was a fence somewhere, overgrown now, to stop anyone walking out too far. The sea was just visible above the shrubbery, a vast stretch of nothing drawing the eyes to its illusion in the distance – water meeting sky, the thin line of apparent touch, the mirage of separate entities.

"An easy child," she said. "Content in your own company. But you never needed her, and she felt that, it was a shame."

She was talking about someone I could barely remember. It wasn't me, it didn't feel like me. It could be a story in a magazine – that little girl, that happy little contented soul with her dolls and her poking stick and her self-containment. But Alice was actually back there, in her version of my past, and confessed to often looking over the fence in the summer just to watch me – digging and mumbling she called it – *always something going on in your little head*. I wondered if she also thought my mother liked singing. If she remembers hearing that wobbly voice doing its best with the *Bye Bye Blackbird* for a man who was never going to find the rendition adequate. I wonder whether she ever once questioned her vision of self-contained happiness in the colder months, when that little girl was poking at the ground in the rain. But I suppose she never looked over the fence in winter.

drifting

A TEXT MESSAGE came in as we reached the sprinkling spot, the exact location Alice had in mind when she talked of my mother's favourite places. We were as high on the cliffs as it was possible to get along that bit of coastline. It was cooler there. Now the cardigan made sense. The wind stole away her muttering as I hung back and checked my phone. It was a message from Fenchurch – the paperwork was ready for signature. He signed off with an F and a kiss. I laughed. I'd called him Fen last night at the pub – told him Malcolm wasn't a great name – but hadn't called him anything later, in his bed, with *Battle of Evermore* filling my senses, his weight subduing the urge to soar, his penetration anchoring me to earth. A lover's name, like the prostitute's kiss, is not something to be expended lightly.

I thought about asking him to bring the paperwork to the house that evening. I contemplated taking him up to my bedroom to see if we could fuck away the past. I pictured my father's ghost, in morning suit and top hat, stepping down from duty, conceding to the insurrection of youth. But it was improbable. He would never bend. He'd be there, rigid as always – *sloppy, Christine, do it again* – and I thought now I'd damaged Fen as a lover and it was perhaps just as well because what I really needed to do was sign the paperwork and leave. There can be no insurrection of youth. Not now. I am roughly the age my father was when I last saw him. I am no longer sure which of us was the most damaged. I'd always assumed it was him. That he was the failure, he was the man without a life – all messy past and no future – and I was the one who had broken free.

But the skylight is like skin for a drum I'll never mend.

Perhaps having me so late had been the problem. I didn't notice they were old until Pat mentioned it. It wasn't a casual comment, a passing observation. Pat rarely said anything without force. She believed people should be like Native Americans – though we called them Red Indians in those days – who were quiet until they had something worth saying. We'd read it in a book at the library when we were waiting for my mother to finish work. Pat was hardly ever silent though. When I pointed out this hypocrisy, she said the Red Indian way didn't mean people had to say nothing, it meant they had to say important things. On this particular day we were contemplating the kids in school – who we liked, who we didn't. I quite wanted to be friends with the twins, can't recall their names now, but Pat detested them. She voted for Marion who I thought smelled funny, like she didn't wash her hair or clothes properly.

"Yeah, well she lives in a chip shop." Pat said.
"Well she smells of chips then."
"So?"

We chose Marion. That's how we became friends. We were probably about eight at the time, so my dad would have been in his mid-forties, something like that. The first time we went to her house after school we met this lovely man who showed us how to batter fish and said if we had any little brothers to get rid of, this was a good way to do it. Marion told us it was her dad. Pat didn't say anything at the time, but when we were walking home she said "He's better than yours."

"Nicer," I said.
"Funnier."
"Funny, just funny, 'cause mine isn't funny at all."
"Funny then. And not old."

I realised then.

Of course, Pat was easy in those days – we nearly always agreed – and we were naive. We knew nothing. It was a few years later before she decided to expand on her theory, telling me I must have been an accident. That my parents hadn't planned me. That they'd clearly not wanted to have children. We were teenagers then, things weren't quite so sweet – we weren't quite so sweet – and to disagree with her meant hours of argument. The Native American silence was no more.

So I ask Alice now – at the grand old age of fifty – whether I'd been an accident. It was mildly pathetic to hear myself but I need to know.

We took the container from within the box. It was a tight fit and not something you could shake loose. I turned it in a screwing motion, back and forth, pulling until it eased free from the cardboard confine. It wasn't even metal – it had that look but was actually some sort of plastic. The whole concept was incredibly tacky. I asked Alice whether she wanted to do the sprinkling and hoped she'd say yes.

"Well, we can each do a little, dear."

I let her have the first turn and she held the container close to her chest for a moment, half-burying it in the Arran knit, her pale fingers gripping tightly as though it might break free, sprinkle itself and spoil the ceremony. I thought about Judy's dog, all those years before, and hoped a sad monologue or prayer wasn't expected. I wondered if my mother was actually in there. There wasn't enough room for the ashes of a body and a coffin, surely. They must just scoop up enough to fill the urn and what's left is probably vacuumed up at the end of each shift.

Alice rested her chin on the lid. She closed her eyes and it made her sway a little. I thought she might tip forwards too far so I took hold of her arm – I could have wrapped my fingers all the way round if she hadn't been wearing the cardigan. She looked at me, two hollows of faded blue, and tried to open the urn. I had to help, it was fairly tight, and I dreaded it pulling free too quickly, the contents tipping onto our hands. I wasn't normally squeamish, but it was too vile a thought – it was windy; it could have gone in our eyes, our mouths – but I worked it free, handed the container back, held the lid by my side, not looking at it because I knew there'd be bits clinging inside, like cocoa.

"I miss you, Elizabeth," Alice said. It was quiet, controlled. A restrained whisper to the dead. "Your friendship, optimism, your faith."

She gave the canister a little tip, a gentle shake, and dust escaped onto the wind, some falling down, some spreading out, rising, making its way back towards town. She watched it go – I watched it go – and I wanted to comment on its fineness, I hadn't expected it to be so light, but we watched in silence. She handed the casket to me.

I didn't want to do it. I had nothing to say to my mother that wouldn't take an eternity – I couldn't edit it – and it seemed wrong to be forced into compliance just to make Alice feel the world was stable.

"Sorry, no, you'll have to..." I handed it to her but she didn't move to take it.

"She was your *mother*, Christine."

"I'll throw it, the whole damn thing, I will."

So she took the canister back, tipped the rest reverently and whispered something I didn't try to catch. I held out the box and she pushed the empty container back inside. I pictured a landfill site somewhere, intrigued seagulls. It seemed such a wasteful process. Then we sat on the bench and I wiped my hands on a tissue – I swore there was a layer of dust coating my skin – and tried to think whether I'd touched my hair or face or clothes. I wanted to take a bath.

"What did she ever do wrong?" Alice said. "Yes, I know he wasn't easy, I know that, but what did *she* do?"

She was trying to hold herself still, trying to hang onto that measured tone, but there was venom within. No reason why any of this was my fault, no reason at all. It was she and my mother who'd thought me strong, it was their vision, not my reality. I thought about telling her the truth, the absolute bleak truth of it. I had no obligation to protect her innocence, no compassionate urge towards the magnanimous gesture.

We sat a little longer. I wanted to call Mervyn but I knew he'd side with Alice, if I told him at all. I wanted to call Mervyn to hear his voice, to find out why I wasn't now needed in France, to find out why he wasn't retiring yet.

But I wouldn't. I never do call him when I really need him. He calls me. It's how I generally find out.

You'd have thought that now the job was done we could eat the food, if we must, and make our way back into civilisation. Alice might have thought the view justified a double-page spread in the tourist brochures, but I didn't. It's a desolate hell-hole frequented by nutters and poor sods who can't walk their dogs on the beaches in summer. There was a wooden signpost just a few feet from where we sat – stuck in the middle of gorse bushes – pointing out the town and two other nearby villages. Aged wood, carved in capitals, jutting out with the sort of importance that suggested it was a major throughfare. The nutters and the dogs know the way. They don't need a bloody sign. I said *can we go now?*

"You really are a selfish creature."

When she can move again, Chrissy says thank you to Jack and the landlady and the other helpers because tomorrow this will be all round town and her parents need to salvage something. She says she needs the toilet – "it's fine, honestly, I'm okay by myself" – walks steadily down the dingy corridor keeping her back straight, her pace even. But she doesn't stop at the entrance marked ladies. She walks through a side door which leads into the delivery yard, goes to Spencer's place because she knows he isn't there, breaks a window, opens the door, lets herself in, takes one of his cameras from the flat – it's his favourite – and empties the cashbox he keeps under the counter in the studio. Then she goes home, packs a few things, and just makes the last train.

Maybe I'd got it all wrong. Maybe people don't repeat a kindness to feel the warm glow, that self-satisfaction. Maybe it's only because once they've done one kind thing there's an expectation. They don't tip money into charity boxes a second time because it makes them feel good, they do it because if they don't they'll be vilified. I didn't have to be here. I could have thrown my mother's ashes out with the rubbish if I'd wanted. I could have said to Alice I know a spot, I know a lovely place in Lisbon or La Rochelle or Long Beach – and she'd have smiled and handed it over happily. Would have whispered a little something to the box, sat in her high-backed armchair and been content. It was good, it was done, Elizabeth Barker would drift in the sea breeze somewhere else, somewhere she'd perhaps have liked just as much.

"Me?" I said. "*I'm* selfish? You got your way, we did it here, your decision, your choice. What more do you want?"

She stood up and still looked small but I stood too. Her lips trembled, hands tugging at her handkerchief, twisting it, turning her fingers into reluctant shrouds.

"You never even asked how she died. Not once. Selfish, Christine. You haven't changed in all these years, still that sulky teenager..."

"I know how! You told me, Mervyn told me, she fell, she fell down the bloody stairs."

"The fall didn't kill her there and then. She was in hospital, I told you that too. How long was she there? How many hours did it take for your poor mother to pass away? Was anyone with her? Holding her hand? Was it peaceful? Was she in pain? Did she speak?"

"Oh for God's sake."

It was enough for Alice. She sat down again. I didn't. She extracted one set of fingers from the handkerchief, took off the faded sunhat and put it on her lap. She was trying not to cry. Trying to still the muscles of her mouth with a dry old hand. I should probably have sat too, what was said was said, it wouldn't need saying again. But I set off, back down the slope on the dirt track, following my mother's dust. I could see the roof of The Smuggler in the distance, one of the pillars at the harbour mouth, and a helicopter over the sea near the beach, performing a mock-rescue for entertainment. Alice's voice chased me from above.

"And yes, you were, what you asked before. And do you know what? She said you were the best mistake she'd ever made."

I turned. She'd followed me down the path

without the bag and had stopped, just staring, the handkerchief still wrapped round the fingers of her left hand. Her legs buckled, as though an invisible assailant had kicked the backs of her knees, and she dropped, lurching a few feet further on the incline where the momentum carried her, face first, into the dust.

distant horizon

MERVYN'S REVVING and he's going to make sure they rev too. Twelve hours before a deadline and he's their *bête* bloody *noire*. It's the only way. Shift the lazy bastards up a gear. He shouts to Jill *where's that coffee I asked for yesterday?* and she sticks out her tongue, puts down the nail-file and gets out of first. Danny would already be in fourth, if the stupid bastard hadn't broken his leg. But Danny always motors, which is why he's gone so far in the business and which, with a face like his, has got to be the right policy. He's never going to be a movie star. But Danny isn't here. And he's missed. Steve's about as much use as a chocolate fireguard. Even Jill is flagging, on countdown to her retirement at the end of the month. But Mervyn begrudges her nothing. She and Danny have been with him forever. The others come and go. The others need managing. Constantly.

He shouts through the glass to Annabelle who, like him, has been in since six.

"That idle tosser not shown up yet?"

She shakes her head.

"Where the fuck is he?"

Annabelle shrugs. No reason for her to protect Steve. Idiot's had it coming long enough. If you can't work with a hangover in this business, you're screwed. Simple. Jill comes back with a black coffee in a cracked mug. There's a picture of a fat pig standing on the letters M.C.P. and she puts it down in front of Mervyn, turns the handle so the pig looks at him, and says Steve must be ill. But then she would. She likes to keep the peace.

"Annabelle can cope," she says. "She's worth ten Steves."

"Yeah, babe." Mervyn sighs, motions for her to close the door. "Yeah, Annabelle can cope. Sod him."

He laughs, a weary sound, turns the cup round so the pig faces away, traces a finger around the rim. Jill watches. He lifts his eyes, peering at her from beneath messy brows, waiting for her to second-guess.

"You've told her," she says.

"Not exactly. I've delayed. Just till this print run's out of the way."

"Right. Just this deadline. And then what? You miraculously don't retire but take your supposedly ex-father-in-law's position as chairman... don't you think she's going to work it out?"

"It's not over till it's over," Mervyn says. "Nothing's definite. Yet."

"And how many more years will you wait? No." She raised a hand. "Don't answer. You're an old fool and you know it."

The thing was, he couldn't retire. His body wanted it but his mind resisted. It was the one deadline he feared. He and Jill had started together in this business way back, some forty years now. She was the most loyal assistant any editor could ask for and why she hadn't sought more, he didn't know, but some people are just happy to find something they're good at and stick with it – his own path hadn't veered much either. He'd seen to it that she got a good share option when *Meltdown* was bought out by the big boys. She'd done all right as far as working life went. But, unlike him, Jill approached retirement happily – eagerly – with plans and no regrets. One week from now she'd be bringing him the last cup of coffee she'd ever make in a mug that had somehow lasted thirty two years.

Chrissy had bought it, after a row, and Jill had continued to fill it, to wash it, to keep it safe. She knew it mattered. Ironic that this person who knew him better than four wives and a mistress did not now understand his reluctance to leave, finish, give up. Decline slowly in France. She didn't understand why he had to try one last time to hold on to Chrissy.

He'd realised in 1995 – it had really taken that long – there was only ever meant to be one Mrs Levy, but she was always a hand's length out of reach. Just beyond the fingertips. No matter how far he leaned she maintained that gap, the Mrs Levy that never was. He'd also realised at that point, when he finally found her again, saw the state she was in and willingly began the slow process of killing yet another marriage, there must be no more wives to hurt. So regardless of how many times she abandoned him for another adventure, another country, another crowd of wasters, and no matter how many potential fifth Mrs Levys he met during those empty years, he'd stuck to this promise. Until now, and the return of his fourth wife, who he still loved and who was, surprisingly, still fond enough of him. He was getting too old. He couldn't wait for Chrissy forever. He didn't want to retire alone.

"Ah but remember," he says to Jill, "that first day, when I found her."

Jill doesn't comment but sits down, leans onto the desk and pats his arm. He covers her hand with his own over-sized paw but doesn't look up from the coffee cup.

"You played your part," he says. "You helped it along."

"I know. Don't think I haven't regretted it."

Annabelle opens the door, sticks her flushed face through the gap letting in the clatter of machines, the ringing phones, takes in the scene and says *sorry, doesn't matter* and leaves again, closing it with a click. The buzz from the office subdues.

"She was lost," Mervyn says. He's said it a thousand times. "I *found* her. How serendipitous can love be? She had nothing. No-one."

"You were too good to her. You've always been too good to her."

He's wondered at what point he actually fell in love. He's thought about this many, many times over the years. Arguing with himself over whether it was at the train station, at six o'clock in the morning, seeing her slumped against the ticket machine, clinging onto a rucksack, looking scared, looking lost. The pimp approaching, offering her a cigarette, squatting down beside her with a practised smile and casual shrug. He'd been unable to walk away. Was it then? Or was that just the memory of the dead sister he'd never got to know? Maybe it was when he moved across, trance-like, pretended to be a friend, pretended to be late, thanked the pimp as though he were a Good Samaritan and took her arm, took the rucksack, took control. Was it then? The way she just turned herself over to Faith? Or their first night alone, together, months later, when everyone else decided on a club but Mervyn wanted food. The others left, Chrissy stayed, and he said *looks like it's just you and me, blondie. Like Lebanese?* She looked at him with those intense eyes and said *I don't smoke dope anymore.* It was the funniest thing he'd heard all week. Was it then?

"I've never understood," Jill says, "what makes her so special."

"I'm responsible," he says. This time he raises his head, looks at her. He'd introduced Chrissy to all the wrong people. The lifestyle had sucked her in. He should never have done it; should have known. He'd saved her from one fate only to consign her to its glamorous twin. A person doesn't walk away from that.

Marion and Pete didn't often argue. Unresolved differences were generally left to stagnate and eventually they too would drop and lie in a dormant silt of other pointless conversations that had never taken place. Arguing is unnecessary where compromise reigns. When they did disagree enough to warrant a digging in of heels, a temptation to stir the depths, it was only because each felt strongly about a particular issue. On these occasions, few though they may be, time had to be set aside for talking – for working at compromise, making an effort to understand the other – because marriage is not about the dominance of one partner over another. It's about compromise, love, respect. But time was likely to be scarce this week and Marion should never have brought the subject up because they were arguing in a dangerous, less controlled fashion. Now there was a queue of customers.

"We'll talk about it when I get home," Pete said for the third time, grabbing his white coat and hat, patting the pockets for the car keys.

"When? You won't be back till gone one, it's exactly my point. We can't manage."

She should stop. He needed to get to the other shop. Chris had phoned in sick and his assistant wasn't coping with the tea-time rush. Madness. They should just close early, give them time to think.

"I'm going. We'll talk later."

But they wouldn't. Not at one o'clock in the morning, both shattered after a double-shift. They'd muddle on, get through the next few days, and the issue would be gone when the work crisis was over. But it wouldn't rest for Marion. Not this time. She'd been thinking about it for months – their workload, voluntary responsibilities, the endless graft of it all. They should retire early, make the most of those savings, buy that little place in Spain. Actually go ahead and do what they'd talked about doing for the past twenty years. Now, whilst they were young enough to enjoy it. Now, before Pete went the way of her dad.

"I'll hold you to it," she shouted as he reached the door. He raised a hand without looking back, and was gone.

Marion looks nervous. The sweat makes Chrissy shiver. Pat shouts "on there, you and me, winner calls the shots, right?" and jumps the four foot gap, over a lethal drop onto teeth of granite and the sea's raking thirst. She's clawing at the frost and scrambling up to the ridge. Marion looks at Chrissy. She's terrified, you can see it in her eyes. But it's not as if they haven't been on there before. In summer, to watch the sunset. Sober.

Unless she does this there'll never be an end to it. One of them has to fall. One of them has to finally get the last word. It's perishing. The wind's getting up. The tide's coming in. Pat shouts again. Marion says "don't be stupid" as Chrissy climbs onto the wall, stands with arms wide to counterbalance the drink, the wind, the adrenalin.

"Oh my God, you silly cow, you stupid silly cow, oh Christ, I'm going for dad... don't move... I'm going for dad."

Marion runs round the harbour to the chip shop, while Chrissy cuts numb fingers on the edges of freezing tiles. She's glad it's dark and she can't see the fall, only a moving shine on the water, blinking and shifting; a vague sense of the drop. But at the top, astride and facing Pat, she's big again, in control, safe. Like a giant in a fairy tale.

Marion served Phyllis Evans, shifting the weight from right foot to left and dabbing a trickle of sweat from her forehead with a napkin. The heat had been unbearable all day and, despite the open door, there'd been little breeze from the incoming tide.

"Two sixty please, Phyllis."

Phyllis extracted coins from a worn purse,

one at a time, checking both sides before placing them on the counter tails up, poking them into an orderly row with a curled rheumatic finger. Marion eyed the queue, smiled apologetically and shifted back onto the right foot. Her ankles were killing her, feet swollen against the straps of her sandals, their flesh bulging out of the gaps.

"Two sixty you say, love?" Phyllis poked the coins again, recalculating.

It was a tolerable enough process in the winter months – this forgetfulness, this deliberate slowness, this belligerence – but not in summer when they were this busy. Marion had tried breaking the rules, passing Phyllis's fish supper over the counter with no more than a smile and 'there you go' but the damn woman would stand and wait to be told how much. She'd also offered, on several occasions, to count out the coins for her but that too was unacceptable. The correct action was to wait patiently, no matter how many hungry customers were inconvenienced.

"There you go love, that's right I think," Phyllis pushed the money forward and took the package with a shaky hand, working it into her string bag slowly. She turned, noticing the crowd behind her. "On your own tonight? Pete gone out?"

"He's at the other shop," Marion said. She'd already told her. "The manager's off sick."

"Sick? Oh dear. Hope it's nothing catching. Well, see you next week."

Marion served the next customer – a large, red-faced man with a skinny wife, two wet children and a well-rehearsed order – scooping and sprinkling, wrapping and folding, smiling and nodding with the familiarity borne of four decades' repetition. She watched Phyllis shuffling out of the shop. The old woman would have been in her thirties the first time Marion wrapped her Friday fish, though she couldn't remember it; she'd only been a girl herself.

"Twelve forty-five please," she said, smiling. "Looks like you've caught the sun."

The man passed a shopping tote stuffed with sandy towels and rubber rings to his wife and rooted in the pocket of his shorts for his wallet.

"He fell asleep," the older child said with a giggle.

"Daddy fell asleep in the sand," the younger one echoed.

"Mum didn't wake him," the first child said.

The father glared at the mother but she looked away, biting a fingernail, her bony shoulders hunched. Marion guessed they were just a day or two into the holiday. She wondered sometimes why people bothered. You saw it all here, year in, year out; the tensions, the unsatisfied expectations, the absolute *reluctance* of folk. Too much misery. The world was full of unjustified complaint.

The sky was turning a burnt orange, the sun finally dropping. Soon the teatime rush would be over and she could close up, have a cool shower, pour herself a long gin. She'd definitely got the better deal – Pete would be hard at it until midnight. They'd stopped doing the late shift at this shop a couple of years ago – there comes a time when you start to recognise thankless slog for what it is.

Phyllis was still outside on the pavement, talking to Joe Scott. Her dinner would be getting cold. They were probably swapping obituary notices. It's how conversations go at their age, death and illness the topics of choice. Compelled to speak of negatives, to think themselves old. They were in their sixties, not eighties, the road to death was still a distant horizon and they were fools to focus on its hazy shimmer. She'd seen it happen to her mother. But they'd known each other all their lives – Phyllis, Joe, and the rest – here and nowhere else, growing, maturing, reproducing and ageing together. Inevitable they'd now be fascinated watching each other die. Once, they'd gathered together in a noisy huddle to count coins with grubby fingers and buy sweets from a shop long gone. Now they clustered neatly on a Thursday morning, a tidy queue of old friends, to collect their pensions, shared lives simultaneously heading closer to the grave with each passing year.

Marion shifted her weight again and turned her attention to the next person in the queue.

"Hello, love, what can I get you?"

dung & death

HOME. To me it had been so many things.

Here, and that childhood of difference and indifference, of avoidance and retribution. Escape into shared lodgings plucked from an evening paper – disputes, compromise, democracy, a voice. Later, a single bedsit in a cheap part of the metropolis, an invisible landlord, a standing order at the bank – a place where I answered to nobody. The magazine had been home too. Mervyn's battered office, the banter, the warmth of strangers' beds. Freedom. In the best of days, of course, home was Zak, the crazy run of hotels and cities, the comfort of appreciative crowds, the tightness of the tour bus. Schmoozing, calculating, pushing him forwards. I'd worked so bloody hard while he trailed behind like a sulky toddler who thinks Christmas is taking too long to arrive. But home had never been more than a moment in time. A brief stay, a long stay, a stranger's spare room, a friend's sofa, a lover's arms.

I was tired. I'd come full circle.

I stuffed bundles of papers into black plastic

rubbish sacks. It had all been checked, nothing of value found. To put it back in the cupboards would be to perpetuate my parent's inability to recognise and let go of the pointless. Why did people cling onto this stuff? Old bills and receipts, no longer of use or interest, if they had ever been so at all; letters from dead people, talking about events long past and inconsequential – faded echoes of a life once led, a purpose once in evidence. Someone had to declare it junk.

It was hard to gauge whether the furniture was less or more ugly when empty. Either way it offended and needed to go. The place screamed mundane at a level even the two radios and their staggered output could not drown. I thought about Spencer and Pat. How incongruous they would now seem against this backdrop. How very real their dismissal of the traditional journey had been. I thought of other rebels I'd met along the way – never quite the same, never quite as valid as Spencer and Pat, but better than this. I was drawn to them. I was one of them. I'd always managed better than this.

But had I escaped? I was here after all.

Spencer is in full flow. He raises his glass, his voice too. He doesn't care who hears him – in fact, the more the better. He doesn't often have a large audience.

"Look at them!" he says, "Fools! Two weeks away from their mundane lives and what are they doing?

More of the same! Repeating those same old boring routines, but in a different location. With sunshine. Why not eat dinner for breakfast? Breakfast for lunch? Stay up all night and watch the dawn? No, no. They eat their cereal as usual, stick to the same old same old. And why? Too stupid to see the truth. Routine doesn't stave off the inevitable end, regimented ritual does not deter Death... though it may, of course, make the prospect of that final breath all the sweeter – I don't know, I've never tried it, oblivion already holds enough sweet promise for my palate."

"But if it's all pointless," Chrissy says, "then it doesn't matter either way – how they live, I mean. It can't, can it? They might as well just do what makes them happy."

"We should all do what makes us happy!" Pat shouts from a distance. She's climbing the plinth at the harbour entrance again. "Scream! Swim in the sea, naked! Light a fire on the beach and stay there for days, reading poetry, making love, mocking tourists!"

"Happiness," says Spencer, "is another Lie."
And he downs the remainder of his drink.

I've long felt that in the event of a viral epidemic – a selective bug targeting mundane thoughts and behaviours – the bulk of the population would disappear overnight. The virus would invade, multiply and thrive in wanton bliss. When it had replicated itself into extinction, what remained of the world would take stock.

I liked to imagine I'd still be around, albeit one of the walking wounded, with perhaps a limb missing or a slightly weakened immune system – some sign I'd not been as interesting as I'd thought. But people like Spencer and Pat would be unchanged. They would have given the virus nothing to grab onto; not one brief moment of promise.

So it was inevitable that now, in this world, neither would be there. I had to face that fact. Spencer and Pat were always destined to be brief, glorious flourishes of colour on life's canvas. Too much time would have diluted them. They were flashes. Sparks. Fireworks. Intended to be unique memories.

Pat probably did jump off the lifeboat house – it was the sort of mad thing she'd do. Spencer's nihilistic bent would certainly have seen him off years ago. These things must be seen as fact. Looking at this detritus – this awful pastiche of normality – only validated such mavericks. They had a point. Living *just because you can* is more bizarre than leaping into death to *feel* it. Spencer's colour field canvasses were as valid a world view as any other, and Pat's rash, crazy urge had been truly inspired. There was a definite symmetry between the two, despite their opposing views. The only fly in the ointment had been me – failing to make an impact, failing to know which side I was on. *Sloppy Christine, do it again.*

For Pat, anybody could be anything – it was

a matter of want. But for Spencer, want was all we'd ever have. Everybody was nothing. There was no *anything* to be had. He was fluent and persistent when speaking of this illusion, and Pat believed what she believed with fervour. To be stuck between the two was to be confined in the tightest of spaces. It was bound to end badly – we were all far too sharp around the edges.

I'd needed to leave. They'd needed to die.

They'd both been right. Standing here, amidst the remains of my parents' lives, it seemed Spencer had been more right than Pat. No matter what can be achieved – no matter how much of *anything* can be gained – we are nothing in the end. Gone. No more than a good idea, a fleeting muse. Even the mavericks. Even the creators. It doesn't matter what the *something* was when all that remains is debris – the image of a burning guitar, a smooth granite orb, words that will never be fully understood. It's all debris in the end.

In my parents' case, there wasn't even tangible debris of any worth. They had achieved nothing. They had been nothing. They were solely detritus of the most useless kind – a few bags for the charity shop, a handful of photos, and vague, dimming memories in the heads of others destined for the same fate.

They might never have existed.

I'd always tried to cling onto Pat's version of life. That anything was possible with want. But

I'd kept moving. I'd realised quite quickly it was the only way. To keep on finding the unexplored, the potential. To keep on walking. When each landscape looks different, you can believe you're somewhere new. Time to move on when you realise you are actually nowhere new at all. That each turn, each fresh length of road is merely what has gone before in a different disguise. Every step on a new adventure is a repetition of someone else's dream, someone else's anticipation, someone else's disappointment. And behind you are more itchy feet waiting to echo the tapping steps of your own. The start is the end and vice versa. A timeless, immeasurable cycle. Dung and death.

The danger of starting to think like an old person increases when faced with youth in control. Two nurses, fresh of face and lithe of body, started at one end of the ward, moving between beds, one either side, taking turns to lift each patient forward whilst the other plumped up pillows. They did not appear to notice it was visiting hour, moving between the cramped plastic chairs as though the occupants were not there. Nor did they seem aware that not all they touched was inanimate. Person and pillows blended into one set of repetitive movements, before they pressed onwards, to the next bed, the next person and pillow.

I squeezed Alice's dry hand, leaned forward to speak in her ear. I wanted her awake when they reached us. I wanted to look them in the eye as they talked over her. Wanted to force them to see us, to acknowledge we were there.

I hate hospitals.

It's a rational fear. Illness comes suddenly for people like me who have lived to excess, who have never feared life's end. Death slinks into view with enough time for regret, too little to atone, and one day it will be me in this narrow bed, being hauled forwards in silent indifference, placed back down onto freshly plumped pillows to gaze again at the strip lighting and wait for the inevitable.

For Alice this moment was both life and death, the two no longer quite as distinct as they had once been. For the nurses, it was life and work – and a failure to see that each is merely a way of keeping busy enough to ignore Death's creeping advance. Too far in the future for them to fear. Death to them, for now, just a set of repetitive tasks to clear the space it had occupied.

"I've been thinking about my mother," I said to Alice as she woke and registered recognition.

"Have you? That's good."

"Why did she stay with him?"

Her gaze moved from my lips to my eyes. "Well it's what our generation did, dear."

Nothing can be predicted – not life's turns, not death. Journeys cannot be anticipated with any level of accuracy, regardless of what we assume or hope. Roads have a way of suddenly bending, throwing the horizon out of kilter, and what you thought could be is so easily changed. Take Alice. Take every Alice. Their lives a series of interconnected events they could never have predicted, all of them out of their control. Someone pushes in front of an Alice in the supermarket, takes her place at the checkout, makes her five minutes late for the bus. She crosses the road to sit in a café and wait, but gets hit by a car, which is there at that moment because its driver had a row with his boss and is speeding home on anger. On the pavement, a child sees the old woman hurled over the bonnet, landing with a cracked skull on the kerb beside her small feet. It's an image she'll carry in her nightmares forever.

These are the pieces that make up life's jigsaw. Handed out randomly by the gods, sections at a time.

The nurses had reached the bed next to Alice. They'd spanned almost the whole ward in ritualistic procedure. It must be boring, this endless routine, and probably not what they signed up for. Maybe they too had dreams of marrying rock stars. Maybe they too wanted excitement and variety. But if everybody's lot were improved who would do the shit jobs?

The plump blonde was talking about her forthcoming wedding. Some of the old dears smiled as they listened, though she didn't notice. Her friend, a little older, perhaps slightly more life-worn, urged her to choose the most expensive of everything.

"It's the best day of your life, you'll remember it forever."

"Rod says it's a waste of money, champagne, and we should just do sparkling wine. Most of his lot can't tell the difference anyway," says the blonde.

"That's men for you. Tell him. It's an important day and if he loves you…"

A game. We are all just part of a cosmic game. At the mercy of vengeful, petulant gods warring with human life, tit for tat. Is it any wonder we grab what we can?

"I remembered something, Alice," I said, touching the bone of her arm. Eyes that had closed against the harsh ward lighting opened again and looked towards me. I think I saw love in them. Patience, certainly. A level of tolerance I did not deserve. "I remember going to the zoo. With you and my mother. And Pat. I remember. It was a happy day."

"I've forgotten, dear, but I'm sure we did go to the zoo."

There'd been a monkey. An ugly creature with blue face and sunken eye sockets, sitting on a log close to the glass, watching the watchers. A polite notice beside the window warned us not to imitate its facial expressions. So Pat and I tried. But no matter what we did we couldn't offend the creature, gleaning no more than a dismissive stare – a few million years of knowledge in its black eyes. Perhaps it recognised captivity as less degrading than paying to gawp, perhaps such impassive scorn came with the boredom of daily taunts. Either way, like a parochial native faced with a foreigner's clumsy attempts, it had snubbed us.

The nurses were now upon Alice, lifting and plumping. She maintained a stoic silence; the humility of one who knows she is a nuisance. When did we forget what other animals still know? It had been our common language, before the liberation of speech, before the ability to truly converse. Such freedom had proved a fallacy. Humans, able to discuss at length the vagaries of the weather, write coherent posters warning people not to imitate apes, but rendered, in the process, oblivious to the miniscule twitches and flickers of another's facial muscles, the minute dilation of another's pupils, the lightest flush of another's skin. What had once freed now ultimately constrained, and what had been lost was irretrievable. All these people now – nurses, patients, visitors – their faces perfectly composed masks of normality; smiling, talking, making eye contact, sitting close, touching even. Yet each as lost as the next, and too evolved to notice.

"When can I go home, dear?" Alice asked the older nurse.

"Oh, we'll have to see doctor for that."

"It's nearly tea-time now," the blonde said.

"Yes, won't be tonight, Alice," the older one said with a smile. "Maybe tomorrow, eh?"

Alice clearly needed to get home. She couldn't waste time in hospital. Each day was stripping segments from the end of her life; eventually time and its terminus would meet. She needed to keep the world in the sort of shape she recognised for as long as possible, before reaching the point where she'd succumb to the ministrations of others. She must be scared watching her generation die. Even for the seemingly invincible contenders in life's race, the advance of the finishing line must be a terrible sight. To die in hospital – in a public ward with a flimsy curtain around the bed and the sound of the dinner trolley clattering up the corridor – was too great a horror to contemplate.

As the nurses moved away, swaying arrogantly with the flexibility of youth as though it were theirs forever, I wanted to shout and tell them *you'll be like this one day.*

Marion's trailing. She just can't keep pace. But Chrissy has never felt so alive – she's sharp, edgy, and can walk all night if she has to – she's not even cold. She's just alive. Vibrant. She's waiting for Pat to really start, and she doesn't give a damn because this has been coming forever. Pat's at the top, she looks elated. "Come on then, bitch, if you're brave enough." It's no longer about Spencer. It's about every challenge levelled since she was six. Unless she does this there'll never be an end to it. One of them has to fall. One of them has to finally get the last word. It's perishing. The wind's getting up. The tide's coming in.

"That's the easy bit." Pat's voice hacks across the icy gulf. Her hair's whipping around her face, going into her mouth. "Now we sit. Now we fucking wait."

I phoned Mervyn whilst running a bath. I needed to hear life. The radios were not enough. They hadn't been enough since I arrived, they were certainly not enough now.

"Hi Merv."

"Hi." He sounded tired again.

"How's it going?"

"Busy. You know how it is."

"I hate it here."

Silence.

"Did you hear me?"

"I heard you."

"So, tell me something."

"What?"

"I don't know. Anything."

"What's this about, sweetheart?"

"Everything. Here. Life. Small towns. France. You. Me."

I heard him sigh. Thirty two years is a long time, even at distance, even with absences – that sigh was worth a hundred words. I knew every one of them.

"Merv?"

"What?"

"I'm scared."

"Of?"

"Getting old. Being alone. Being like Alice."

"You don't have to be alone. You know that."

"But I'm scared of France too. Not sure I'm ready."

Silence. Here, the sound of running water against the pointless waffle of third rate DJs filling space between tracks, wasting time on meaningless nothing. There, the muffled clatter of work – voices, laughter, telephones – the same nothing, just louder, and a slow, deep scratching noise. Maybe he was doodling, maybe he was gouging lines across his desk.

"Merv?"

"You'll never be ready, sweetheart. Never."

I climbed into the bath, sliding down until my nose was the only part of my head exposed. Water blocked the outside world, replacing it with a womb-like song against which my heart beat, its sound coming from within my head. Maybe this is how it feels to drown – a peaceful, musical process if you don't struggle. These things needed due consideration. Everyone should have an escape plan.

I'd always known what I didn't want. Humans are selfish creatures, driven to satisfying our own needs under the pretence of communal effort. We claw our way through life, striving for complexity, craving simplicity. We want to do it all, and yet we want to do so little. When we realise we can't keep trying out different lives, seeing which one fits, we echo the mistakes of our parents instead, and live with what we know. I'd never wanted that. I'd never wanted to settle for nauseating togetherness. The fusing of two into one to a point where identities merge, dependency becomes the norm. Life's events jointly captured and recorded. False history. The parts we want to remember photographed, painted, written down. Immortalised before they become distant, their reality forgotten; a last sleepy thought at bedtime.

I needed to get out of here.

I thought about Mervyn and France. Whether the years in between could be obliterated, as though neither of us had a past, together or apart. As though we could rid ourselves of all those snapshots; strangers who'd been and gone – our many selves, our persistent evolution. Or whether we could be content to be the briefest of touches where two lives meet; neither ever knowing the other's whole, neither holding the complete album of the other's life.

There was too much baggage.

We had both shied away from the only real point of existence – reproduction. Was it through fear or a feeling of superiority that we'd escaped the mundane? Did we think that we, in barren frivolity, were somehow more evolved than everyone else, had more purpose, would look back on our choices and feel we'd done something more worthwhile than merely creating little selves? In truth, we were no more purposeful than anyone else. Possibly less so. We hadn't reproduced. We'd failed. Because no matter how we distance ourselves with faith, marriage and the dignified marking of death from thousands of lesser species, we humans are nothing more than upright carnivores who captivate, copulate, replicate and die. The complexities with which we pass the time, justify our presence, convince ourselves we're different, are a delusion. When we take off our elegant clothes and lie on our high-status beds, we fuck and grunt like all the other animals. It's the only purpose we've got.

deconstruction

The distant past advanced. Familiarity grew daily. I was no longer a visitor, the decades were receding. I picked at the wallpaper whilst talking to Fen on the phone – a loose flap, stiff and curled, three steps up the staircase. It itched, an irritating scab, and I hooked a fingernail underneath, watched the seam open, willingly surrendering its hold, the past coming away from the wall, embracing freedom in a sospirando rush.

Another decade lay underneath.

Uglier, a forgotten picture, a garish pattern of brown and beige – still there, still waiting for release, stretching in all dimensions, shrinking the tall, weakening the strong.

"I've got to go," I said.

I couldn't help but pull some more. Peel back another segment. It was there. It was all still there. I held the phone between shoulder and chin, grasped at the curled seam, tugged and scratched and clawed. I needed tools; the seventies were holding fast.

"What's that noise?"

"Wallpaper."

"You're decorating?"

These were the snapshots that didn't make the album but were never thrown away. These were the snapshots that lay in a dusty drawer, in an old shoe box, in the folds of paper scraps that now meant nothing. These were the snapshots you had no reason to keep but no strength to discard. These were not history's rooms, these were keys; each opening another door, another lost place. The longer I stayed, the more I would be consumed. By Alice, the past, by Fen. Lovers do that. Absorb you – ink into blotting paper – until you no longer exist in any external context. People are too needy. The sharing of innocuous facts leads to self-dissolution – you a strand of someone else's life, they in turn a strand of yours – the mixing of time and place and purpose and expectation weaving tighter, closer. Drawing and seeping two lives into one. Beginnings can look so very beautiful.

But it's a human compulsion to pick things apart. To look around every corner, into every crevice, examine and question, find its core. Become resentful of independence, frustrated by mismatched edges, critical of imperfections. Put it back together in a better way, as part of a bigger whole, edges matching. A two-piece jigsaw, its beauty absorbed and contained. Tighter. Tighter.

Grow bored.

Disappointed something so special could become so mundane.

And it really doesn't matter whether you're the blotting paper or the ink – whether you consume or are consumed – the damage is the same. You will never again be free. I knew this and yet I was still here. The longer I stayed, the longer I'd be expected to stay. But I was here. Still. Uninspired, uncharacteristically static, held fast by the Something Else. Here, still, because if I left, what would happen to Alice?

I was already dissolving.

She hadn't asked me to stay. But there was an assumption, at the hospital, I was somehow responsible. As close to next of kin as was necessary. Imagine, eighty six years old and alone. Eighty six years old and scattering the ashes of your last friend.

You must be scared, Alice.

I'd checked on her that morning. She was fine – *no need to fuss, dear* – she was up and dressed but hadn't eaten. The bread was mouldy, the milk sour. I shopped, cleared out the fridge, swopped her library books, did the laundry. All the time she said not to fuss, not to trouble myself. All the time I wondered how many other Alices had woken to mouldy bread and sour milk that morning.

There was a new shabbiness to my parents' house. A fresh, clean shabbiness. There were sections of wall I couldn't reach – high above the staircase – but Fen was borrowing a friend's ladder and a steam machine. Like a cobra, he was luring his prey; drawing me into foolish advance, soothing all logic with captivating eyes and a steady sway.

The hall wasn't enough. I tore paper from elsewhere, room to room, ripping and dropping, kicking through the debris like a kid in an autumn wood. As each layer of history fell, I was consumed and released and consumed again. As each layer of history was compressed into plastic sacks, the floor emerged to defend the past – *I am still here, we are all still here.* So I pulled up the carpets too. Another decade gone. By the time Fen arrived, with ladder and steam machine, the front door couldn't be opened. He came round the back, past the heaped furniture on the paving, and we stood in the kitchen, surveyed the plunder. He said I was crazy, there was a right way and a wrong way, and I laughed – high on victory – but I knew it was only one battle in the war.

I checked on Alice while he cleared a path through the slaughter. I told her we were going for a takeaway, we could bring her something back. She'd never eaten Chinese food, but yes, she said, she did like rice. She wanted to know what the noise was, why there was furniture outside, had we got a leak? Was it rats? She pulled her cardigan close, pressed her knees tight, sat forward in her stiff chair and glanced at the connecting wall, afraid of the unknown.

"I'm decorating."
"Are you staying?"
"People want plain rooms."

They're no longer soft, pliable bodies but grotesques cut from Parian marble. Hard and permanent, shaped around the frozen ridge tiles, stiff hair etched across their faces. Feelings are muted beneath the chill; shrunken by the vast blackness around them. She knows she could fly, really fly – the measured dipping and rising of her dreams – higher and higher. Defeating the cold, abandoning her body to its worldly limitations, soaring warm and easy, fast and slow, zooming in, zooming out.

Pat looks up. She's had the same thought. It happens. Her fingers uncurl and she forces unwilling arms to spread, to move up and down jerkily – not the smoothness of dreams – and Chrissy watches in catatonic wonder. She unhooks her own clawed hands from the ridge, wipes the hair from her face with a shaky movement, stretches out her arms. She's trying to hold her teeth together, grimacing in a way that could be pain but could be laughter and her chin bobs up and down with the effort. It's laughter. She's laughing. Pat is laughing too. Their arms stretch into the darkness – elegant, unfurled, arced – and they glance down towards the source of the spray, the jagged bed on which their nest sits. Pat shouts "come on, let's do it. Let's fly. Just once."

The answer to everything. Disappointment,

Futility, Pain. To soar greatly, just once, must surely be enough. They force dead legs to life, squat like fledgling chicks, facing across the void, bonded but mistrustful. Filled with Love and Hate but no strength for either, they call to each other in voices raw and broken.

It was just as well Fen was there for the aftermath. When the adrenalin subsided, the purpose faltered and the remains lost their crisp hope. When we lay close on my bed, his hand trailing my shoulder, and I saw another small remnant of history trapped between the wardrobe and the wall – a brief fragment of pattern, an echo, and yet enough to fill the space again. When I remembered what was underneath this carpet, in this room. When I remembered the poems.

We'd started our new school. We must have been eleven or twelve. A huge living beast, wide bright corridors and walls littered with instructions, schedules and past glories, where generations of girls were forced into a duplicitous mould of sharing and competing. A place of limited stillness or sanctuary, my father's rule mimicked by the Antaean head who fixed herself daily to a solitary point on the assembly hall stage and regurgitated the past. Girls filled the space below in obedient rows, sitting and standing in unison, shoes squeaking on the high gloss of the floor – praying and singing in Cocytian harmony as her eyes checked our faces for dissent. Any anomalies previously overlooked were now magnified there, in that cold mass of confidence and worldliness. The other girls were evil, their ranks somehow formed before they arrived and now defended tightly against intruders. They talked of horse riding and skiing, called their parents 'mummy' and 'daddy', had brothers, sisters, cousins and friends. This was where the good girls went. This was where brains and effort took you. This was the reward.

"I can't do five years."

"They're bitches, they're all bitches."

"I hate it."

"We should run away."

But we didn't run, although I know Pat meant it. I was always the weak one. We served our five years slowly. The only time we stood at the bus-stop and egged ourselves into truancy – the only time I ever remember Marion being off sick – we got caught and my father collected up my magazines and posters and burned them in a brazier in the garden. He said until I behaved like an adult I would be treated as a child. I said *that'll make a change from being treated like a dog.* So he took away my record collection too. But he couldn't burn Pat. We sat on the floor of my bedroom and vented our anger – school, the other girls, parents, the world. We wrote poems. They would still be there, under the carpet. If I carried on deconstructing the house I'd find them.

breathing

THE CRISIS with the shops had been resolved but the difference of opinion it had generated between Marion and Pete had not and it hung in the hot, greasy air between them. Too exhausted by the symptom to debate its cause, they fell back instead on the comfort of repetition – daily routines performed without words, without argument, without even conscious thought – the unspoken issue of Chrissy filling any remaining pockets of air; the atmosphere behind the counter compressing in slow suffocation.

"Christ it's unbearable," Pete said, tapping surplus fat from a scoop of chips before tossing them into the serving tray. "Too bloody hot."

"Only on this side of the counter."

"Take off if you like, rush's over now."

But that was not what she meant. An hour or two in the sun and sea breeze was not enough this time. The air was too thick, the unspoken too belligerent; no longer willing to lie in the silt and be forgotten. She wanted to discuss their future but knew he wanted to hear about the past. For the first time in their marriage something alien had risen to fill the space between them, expanding with every laboured intake of breath.

"Why don't we close early?" she said. "And both take off?"

"But I've just done these." He pointed the scoop at the freshly cooked chips.

"For once, love, eh? Let's sit in the sun with a drink and enjoy it like everyone else."

He'd always been cautious with money. They both had. They weren't in the habit of frivolous spending like some people they knew and neither were they keen on generating waste. Running your own business taught you a thing or two about the value of earnings. This, as with most things, was an issue on which they both agreed. Yet, as her grandma Ethel had always maintained, there are no pockets in a shroud. All well and good saving for the future, but a person needed to know where that future started. They had initially – and tentatively – imagined it started with children, and the early years had been geared towards saving for that happy event. But it wasn't to be. The future became the expansion of their business with a second shop, modern equipment, a better car, new carpets and furniture for the house and, as the years passed, a far more distant horizon – retirement. Somewhere in the midst of such practicalities dreams are lost.

In compromise they closed an hour early, left the last of the cleaning until morning and walked down to a neighbouring pub where they sat outside to watch the evening harbour activity and enjoy a cool beer. Pete glanced back periodically, as though expecting irritated customers to be clamouring outside the shop. He seemed more anxious than pleased when this wasn't the case.

"Stop looking," she said when he turned for the third time.

"Can't help it. I feel guilty."

"Remember," she said, not looking at him, not taking her eyes off the horizon, "when we made our decision? The things we said? Our dreams, our plans for the future?"

Pete sighed.

From the corner of her eye she saw his perspiration, the redness of his skin, the tightness of his collar. Just like her dad. Stature mimicking success, growing fat, growing comfortable, growing, growing, growing. She could blame Chrissy for her dad's death – she always would – but the truth was more complex and the quiet voice in the far recess of her mind knew this. Just like she and Pete, her dad had worked too hard. No time to look after himself – a vanity – no time for hobbies and leisure activities. There was only time for the repetitive cycle of work, eat and sleep. The result, an unstoppable expansion of the self, a burgeoning of the outer shell whilst the inside rotted.

"We're unfit," she said.

"This doesn't help." He raised his beer and laughed.

"We're always working."

"Oh. That again."

"Yes, that again. Why can't we talk about it?"

He shifted in his seat, glanced back towards the shop, towards the comfort of routine. She'd long accepted his ways – his abject horror of confrontation, his unwillingness to talk about emotive issues beyond what was absolutely necessary. There was an upside: she had a husband who didn't pick fights. Not many couples were so lucky. In any case, marriage wasn't a permanent courtship, the honeymoon was rightly a brief phase. To know, twenty or thirty years on, each and every foible had been an anticipation she'd relished when they first met. Any fool can fall in love, it's perseverance that counts.

But the reality of marriage, the subconscious learning to live with unimagined normality, it's a progressive condition. There is no fixed reference point, no *norm*, just a constantly shifting baseline for good and bad. Ask anyone with chronic arthritis – today's unbearable pain is tomorrow's respite. There were times she wanted to grab him by the shoulders and force a reaction – *for once in your life say something, do something, contradict me, tell me no, disagree, anything* – but the most to which he'd ever commit was a quiet sulk. Perhaps close a door with slightly more force than usual, leave a room without comment, slope off to bed without a goodnight kiss.

Even back then, when they made the decision

not to pursue infertility tests, not to force themselves into a situation whereby one party might have to live with the guilt, when they chose childlessness to preserve love, it had been her suggestion. He had merely acquiesced. The path of least resistance. She'd never been sure he fully agreed.

"So?" She looked at him, catching his eye.

"So?"

"The future, Pete. It's now. This is it, can't you see? Those plans were for *now*."

People travel a long way on autopilot. Some keep going until death. Most, in fact. Marion knew this – she spent many hours with the elderly and their regrets, she was under no illusion as to the futility of effort if you chose to see it that way. But this was where faith helped. Yes, life did sometimes seem futile but the trick was – and she had always tried to hold onto this – to make the time on this earth as productive as possible. To contribute. To see beyond the self, to view the whole. To recognise each cog as vital to the smooth running of the mechanism. Each cog matters. Anybody reaching old age only need look back and see their good deeds, the smiles, the friendships, the kindnesses, to validate their time, no matter how brief, as part of that whole. Those still unconvinced need only take a peek into the Good Book to be reminded that this was, indeed, all that had ever been required of them. To live and love, to care for each other. It's not without reason that Faith prevails. Even in a society choking on its own greed.

Yet she had long battled with a small niggle which, left unchecked, would periodically expand and grow in her mind like a tumour. She compressed it regularly with work, effort, Faith and usually this was enough. In its more persistent moments, when additional strength was required, she'd contemplate the eremitic Christians and scorn her own weakness – feel ashamed she should perceive her pathetic struggle as difficult when others were engaged in far greater efforts. The tumour would shrink once more, the niggle go away, conviction be restored.

Since Chrissy's return, nothing was strong enough. Not work, not effort, not Faith. Not even thoughts of those locked in perpetual daily struggle against their own failings. The tumour was growing and this time it was winning.

"We haven't done anything," she said. "Half way through our lives. More than half way. I mean, *think* about it – work, work, work – and it's much more than half, isn't it? Way more. The good years anyway. What've we got left? Twenty? Thirty? How many of those will be pain and dribbling? What have we *done*? We're over half-way through our lives and what difference have we made? We could have done less, nothing, something completely self-serving, and still have arrived at the same meaningless point. We've *done nothing*."

"Whoa." Pete put down the pint glass, reached out a hand and touched her arm, his fat fingers strong and warm against her skin. "What the hell's brought this on?"

"We could have done so much more."

"I dunno what's wrong, love, but you're not you and... hey, come on."

"Jesus Christ, *I could have done so much more.*"

When her dad died and Chrissy ran away and she saw how little was left, Marion's own dreams died. She'd figured there must be a reason. It hadn't been the initial thought, of course. She'd railed against it for months. But later, when she and her mother had found a routine that worked, when the business was ticking over again, when the regulars had stopped mentioning their loss, when the world stabilised and life went on, she'd imagined there must have been good cause. Then she'd found it. In Pete, the church, the business – in this little fragment of the world. Her thoughts had clarified. She was part of a wonderful community and it needed her effort. It's not enough to keep gardens neat, say hello to neighbours and always pick up dog waste – more tangible commitment is required. She still believed this. Without that tangible dedication the common good is replaced by fences, net curtains and an inability to distinguish stranger from kin. The elderly rot alone within their own four walls, post offices and primary schools close, people are forced outwards, further and further, until everyone commutes, returning tired at night to a place called home, curtains drawn, privacy guaranteed. And nobody remembers how to care beyond the needs of their personal cocoon. Once dampened, community spirit is difficult to rekindle.

She'd known then she would remain. Would turn into her own mother, drink hot chocolate at nine o'clock, sniff disdainfully through the evening's television, perhaps even share the space with her own daughter and son-in-law. Another section of family history would traverse the spiral, ending, beginning and continuing simultaneously. But it had seemed right, this on-going sameness, generation to generation. It was life. Change is a miniscule transition, an imperceptible, gentle easing towards the future. You only had to look at the town itself, how it had slowly morphed over time. Lack of radical alteration is what draws in the tourists, provides a haven for retired city executives, helps maintain the common good. Pete had felt the same. They discussed it. Together, they said, they'd be a force for that common good.

"What is it you *want* to do?" Pete asked, reaching into his pocket, pulling out a crumpled tissue. "What exactly? What? Tell me, love."

She took the handkerchief. Held it to her face, pressing into her eye sockets until they ached, but shook her head, unable to answer.

"Is it kids? Do you wish..?"

"No," She said, the fabric muffling her voice. "No, not that."

"Well, what then?"

It wasn't the lack of children. That disappointment had long since turned into a blessing. Of sorts. When they'd found out they wouldn't have any – that there'd never be a daughter to share space with – it had merely confirmed what they already believed. Their purpose was wider than the personal cocoon. Their purpose was the common good.

When they buried her mum, Marion again briefly glanced back and was mystified as to why she'd ever wanted to leave. A foolish teenage dream – university, big city, adventure – that's all it had been. Nothing more than a foolish teenage dream. Over the last decade, the memory had become an even more distant ethereality, someone else's foolish teenage dream, any momentary recollection of it so fleeting and painless she no longer recognised it as ever having belonged to her.

Then Chrissy returned.

Something changed.

And now it was fighting relentlessly with all Marion held true. She still believed in the community. Still believed their efforts had been worthwhile. She did believe that. She could still look back and see good deeds, smiles, friendships and kindnesses and know that she had, in some small way, made the lives of others brighter. But that foolish teenage dream was no longer opaque and obtuse. It was sharp and vivid again and it jostled with her conviction – taunting, resisting compression – *what if, what if, what if…*

She woke late, heard Pete in the bathroom, the repetitive scraping as he shaved. Sunday. Church. She unravelled her hands from a quilt held tight against her chin, touched stiff fingers to her eyes, felt the puffy lids and sighed.

Nothing had been discussed or resolved. She'd had her chance but the words hadn't come. She couldn't acknowledge this weakness. Couldn't permit the tumour to win. Pete had eventually raised his hands in defeat, settled to watch the late news, left her alone with her thoughts.

Sunday. Church. Perhaps she'd find new strength.

She heard him cleaning his teeth. Then silence as he combed his hair. The splash of aftershave into his palm, the clink of the bottle as he put it down, the rubbing together of his hands, the *slap, slap, slap, slap* against his face. In twenty eight years she'd never known him deviate from this order of grooming.

driftwood

A STRING OF coloured bulbs lights a safe path round the harbour in darkness, its sharp hues too brash for the faded woodwork of the boats below. The shadows cast make the small seem big, distort the familiar into the strange, bleed colour out of the world. Once again I'm struck by the oddity of hating silence but loving the dark.

But it is not silent yet. The night is still young, and this is the best time of the day. Pubs and restaurants compete for the lucrative summer trade with colourful chalkboard menus offering home-cooking, casket ales, families welcome. The air is rich with the smell of cooling seaweed, beer, food. Doors open periodically; laughter, music and cheerful goodbyes emitting from the yellow glow; a cacophony of accents of those well-fed and softened by alcohol. Car doors slam, engines rev and behind it all the rhythmic beat of the retreating tide breaking gently against the outer harbour walls.

Pat and I used to love hanging round this part of town on Friday nights. Before Spencer. Before we thought we were old enough to be in that yellow glow ourselves. We'd sit on the edge of the harbour wall, dangling our legs and listening to the slow chug of cars down the narrow streets, live music drifting on the summer breeze, tourists calling out loudly – as though everyone were on holiday, as though none need rise at dawn to face a working day – whilst locals sighed, took the money, tolerated the intrusion.

We both liked and despised them. The visitors. We were never really sure.

When Pat was around I didn't fear silence, though it was rarely present. There wasn't a topic we didn't discuss, at some point, over those years. At least that's how I remember it, though the individual conversations themselves are gone. I remember fragments more than anything, and the sense that they represented the norm. We talked. It's what we did.

"What are you thinking about?" Fen asks.

I laugh, though the question irritates. I can see the imbalance clearly at these moments. I know he would like me to stay.

"Just someone I knew when I was here."

"His name?"

I laugh again.

But his question makes me think about Spencer and I don't want to do that. I want to think about Pat. To work myself up to the point where I can perhaps walk up the lane to the lifeboat house. Can perhaps go where I know I must eventually go.

Though not yet. I'm not ready.

But thinking about one invariably conjures up the other. It isn't fair to blame Fen.

"She. Pat. A friend."

"Ah. Does she still live round here?"

This is how it goes. The start of destruction. I'll tell him about Pat – I need to tell someone – and he, in turn, will tell me things I want to know but shouldn't. We will explore the depths, the most intimate secrets; will pick each other to the bones. Then we will realise there is nothing. And I will feel this first, because I am expecting it. But it matters not. I'm leaving anyway.

It's funny but I've never told Mervyn anything. Thirty four years and nothing. Nor has he pressed for detail. Maybe I always knew he was for keeps, in some form or another, and so was worth the effort of discretion. But, as I say, our edges are irregular and he too practical a man; solving problems when all that is needed is an ear. He would have tried to *find* Pat, at a point when I did not want her found.

But I want her found now.

Fen is a practical man too. So I tell him. I explain how life is when you love and hate in equal measure and with a passion which destroys everything it touches. How the aftermath of such intensity is endless. How this is obviously my interpretation. This is what I see. What I feel. This is neither true nor false – it is a perception; a photographer's view of the world.

I tell him what I think Pat did. Jumped. Flew. Whichever.

The silence is tangible.

"She must have died," he says, eventually. "You realise that? Nobody could survive falling onto those rocks, into that sea, and in the winter."

We walk to the beach. It's darker there, although the moon is almost full and the sky clear. If I was here alone, in silence, more of the past would be audible. I need Fen to keep talking. I don't know why. I wonder what forgotten thing is waiting for me – what it is that I just cannot reach out and touch. Did I push her? Is that the horror I can't now recall?

"Do you think I might have pushed her?"

He squeezes my hand. "I don't know, but I can find out."

Ahead we see a large shape on the beach, a piece of driftwood in silhouette against the shine of the sea. Fen says it looks like a person climbing out of the sand, one arm raised, pulling on an invisible rope. I say it looks like someone sinking into the earth and waving in desperation, hoping anyone passing – maybe us – will hurry forward and grab its hand. Then we walk another twenty paces or so and it no longer looks like either.

"What are your plans?" he asks. "Once the house is finished, on the market?"

I shrug. I tell him I move around a lot. I like finding new groups of friends, creative types, where there are few rules and even fewer expectations. He asks where I was before coming back, where I think I'll go from here, whether there's a lover waiting somewhere. I can hear the creaking and cracking, though he cannot. I don't want it to end just yet.

"There's nobody," I say. "Let's not talk about this now. Let's make love, here on the beach, near the sinking man."

Fen is a meticulous lover. It would be easy to stay, to enjoy his touch, his company, his thoughtfulness. But as with Mervyn, there's too fine a line between want and need. The point at which anticipation becomes expectation and so morphs into disappointment does not take long to reach. I can already sense his need. For me, too, this sharing of facts – the unburdening of soul – is a new experience that threatens like a drug. I've resisted its cunning lure for so long and now, after one brief and already regrettable slip, I'm in danger. I could hurt myself. I could so easily hurt Fen and, in turn, Mervyn. In any case, if there is to be any settling down, any embracing of oneness, then it should be with the man who has waited three decades. He called today. Mervyn. An ultimatum, delivered in hesitant voice. I have until the end of next week to decide about France. He's never tried to force my hand before.

Pat's at the top, straddled across the ridge tiles, hair blowing. She looks elated. "Come on then, bitch, if you're brave enough." Unless she does this there'll never be an end to it. One of them has to fall. One of them has to finally get the last word.

"Oh my God, you silly cow, you stupid silly cow, oh Christ, I'm going for dad… don't move… I'm going for dad."

"That's the easy bit." *Pat's voice hacks across the icy gulf. Her hair's whipping around her face, going into her mouth.* "Now we sit. Now we fucking wait."

Jack's glancing from one girl to the other – he can't be in two places at one time – and shouting "ROPE GET ME ROPE I NEED ROPE" *and somebody must already have it because it appears near his feet just seconds later.*

Just as Pat takes off.

The moon behind Fen's head is blue white, his face distorted by shadows. He looks angry, though I know he isn't, but the force of each thrust driven by this illusion of rage excites me. I want him to be angry. I encourage him with wordless sound, hold his eyes fast in my own, and for a time it feels like real passion. Like Spencer.

But afterwards it's Fen again. He kisses me gently. "You could always stay on here for a while, if you have nowhere specific to go."

I know he is falling in love with me and that I should leave, sooner rather than later.

"The other friend," he says, as we walk back towards the harbour. "Still here, you say?"

"Running the family business, apparently."
"Are you going to see her? To ask?"
"Maybe. Yes. Tomorrow perhaps."

Then the strangest thing. He asks me for Pat's surname and I start to answer, to feel the forward momentum into speech. But nothing comes. I can't remember. I should know – it feels like I do know – and yet each time I try to envisage the letters, scan them from left to right, form the word and speak it out, there's an empty space. I mentally recall the others – Alice, Marion, Spencer, even some of the awful girls from school – and find their surnames as attached as they ever were, paired up automatically with forenames, clearly etched in my mind by forgotten years of repetition. But for Pat, nothing.

"Christ. I can't remember."
"What was the year?"
"Seventy three."
"Okay. It'll probably be enough, but let me know when it comes to mind."

I suppose when you look back, sometimes things do get muddled. I've known a lot of people. It's been a long time since I was here. If it was just the name it could be explained away like this – the sheer volume of people, of names.

But it's not just the name.

I realise now I can remember very little of the incidental detail – the sort of thing that never gets forgotten. Inane facts that come to mind without effort of recall, regardless of whether they are wanted or not. Like Marion's gran was called Ethel; her pet rabbit, Micky; her first boyfriend was Oliver Roberts, a geek from the boys' grammar who took her to see *Cabaret* and didn't even try to put an arm round her. How can I remember so much of the periphery and nothing of the core?

Spencer. Spencer Greene, flat 3b, Wheelwright's Lane, birthday fourteenth June. I haven't needed that information in thirty four years, but it's still there. But Pat? Nothing. Where did she live? Why can't I remember something as simple as that? We were together most of the time. We must have spent some of it at her house. This is how I remember it. Pat and me. Together.

Again I wonder if I got it wrong.

Perhaps the intensity of the friendship is an afterthought – a false memory – and the reality may be that it was nothing. That Pat was nothing. She may even be no more than a conglomerate of other people I've met, compressed and amalgamated during the darker times when edges blur and clarity is out of reach. Or it could be down to the force of her personality, the absolute madness that was our friendship, rendering detail pointless, able to slip from memory and leave only the essentials – that we loved and hated with an equal passion. You don't have to know where that sort of emotion lived. It doesn't need a surname.

fragments

PETE FED peeled potatoes into the stainless hopper, trying to maintain a steady noise level – the grinding of the slicer as blades connected with starchy flesh, the dull *thud thud thud* as cut chips dropped into the steel bucket below. The more rhythmic the sound, the clearer his thoughts. At the other side of the preparation room Marion was filling a steel bowl with ready-mixed batter from a large plastic container. Her father had always made his own, as had Marion initially, but time and commercial pressures had eventually colluded and they'd switched to the pre-mixed stuff sometime in the late eighties. Only a few of the old regulars had noticed, and they were long gone now. Nobody else gave a damn.

Marion looked at her watch. "Best open up."

He grunted and tipped in the final three potatoes. The grinding noise dissipated, the last chips falling into the bucket to bring the level exactly to the rim. You don't do a job like this day in and day out for twenty five years without becoming an expert at gauging quantity. He wiped his hands, switched off the chipper, its background drone instantly halting, leaving a thick silence broken only by the sound of Marion sliding the bolts on the shop door.

Another day, another dollar.

Pete carried the bucket through to the shop, filled the wire mesh waiting beside the fryer, plunged it into the hot fat and heard the angry rush of disparate temperatures meeting.

"Did you get the fish out?" Marion asked, glancing at the bare worktop, answering her own question. She walked through to the back room, a stiff waddle almost, her feet shuffling more than lifting.

"You okay?" he said as she returned with a large tray of naked white fish.

"Fine." She slid it across the work surface towards the bowl of batter, leaving him to dip and coat each fillet whilst she returned to the prep room to get the pies.

No matter how hot the day – and today was going to be another scorcher – people wanted their fish and chips. He savoured the feel of cool batter on the ends of his fingers, looked up at the large wall clock and made a small bet with himself that the first customer would arrive in exactly five minutes.

The minute hand clunked from one black marker to another. He dropped the battered fish into the hot fat, moved to the next fryer and gave the basket a shake, checked the colour of the cooking chips, glanced back at the clock.

"You haven't switched the fans on," Marion pressed past him, flicked the switch on the wall and the ceiling fans groaned into action. "You're not with it this morning."

No, he wasn't. But she seemed more cheerful, though tired and clearly still not herself. He wasn't stupid, he knew he couldn't avoid the retirement debate for much longer. It wasn't as though he was against the idea, in principle. They'd always said they'd buy a little place in Spain – Tarragona or Vinaròs perhaps – and early, before they were too old to enjoy it. She was right, maybe now was the time, maybe they'd done their share, worked hard enough, given their best. Maybe now would be an appropriate point at which to do something for themselves.

But it wasn't the only thing bothering her. And it was this that now concerned him. They'd always been a team, both in and out of work, a strong and solid couple. They'd lived a decent life, had a good marriage, they'd been both lucky and diligent – neither under the illusion that either element was superfluous. Marriage, just as with business, required effort, a willingness to bend and a measure of luck. He sighed.

He looked towards the door and saw Jack Crozier crossing the road towards the shop, his bandy legs striding out with the energy of a man half his age.

The clock's hand jerked onto the fifth bar.

"She wants us to sell up," Pete said.

Jack scratched his chin, his hand thick and weathered. "Sell up?"

"Buy a place in Spain."

"Spain? Wha's in Spain that don' be here?"

Pete laughed. He tucked the edge of the wrapper into its own fold, pushed the hot package across to Jack who counted out coins in his rough palm.

"Wall to wall sunshine," Marion said. "Peaceful warm winters. We like Spain, been going for years."

"Aye but where else youm been?" Jack winked at Pete. "Might be summat else be better'n Spain and then wha'll you do? Can't keep upping and offing. An' where be fit fer holidays when youm in Spain always?"

"We won't need holidays," Marion said with a laugh.

"Wha'll youm do all days?"

"Nothing," Pete said, "we'll be retired, Jack."

"We'll relax," Marion said, "potter, do what we like."

"Way I sees it," Jack said, picking up his parcel, "Ain't much point goin' half-way round world to do nothin'. May as well stay where youm knows folks an' do yer nothin' here."

Marion gave a snort and turned to stir the curry sauce. Pete watched Jack leave the shop, jauntily cross the road, heading back to his boat. A woman with a camera stood on the pavement just outside the door, also watching Jack, staring intently as he made his way back down the harbour steps until he dropped out of view. She didn't look like the average tourist but neither was she local. The camera looked expensive and proper. Likely she was a professional photographer, there were plenty here in summer, taking snaps for postcards and brochures. She didn't seem the type to want chips that's for sure.

The woman turned and looked into the shop, staring first at Marion and then Pete, with the same intensity as she'd watched Jack.

"What does he know," Marion said, putting the lid back on the curry pan. "Silly old goat's never been away from here."

"He's got a point though," Pete said, shifting to face her. "What would we do?"

She didn't reply. He turned back to check on the woman, see if his assessment was wrong, see if she was a chip eater after all, but she'd gone.

Neither of them had much of a past. At least this was what Pete had always believed. They got together in their mid-twenties, though they'd already known each other for a couple of years – introduced by a mutual friend who'd thought, quite correctly, they were made for each other. They'd both had other relationships, brief, nothing serious, or so he'd previously assumed. He wasn't quite so sure now. This business with the Christine woman had confused his certainties somewhat. Marion had never mentioned her and yet clearly she'd been significant. Neither had he known how much his wife regretted missing out on university – until the other night, down at the pub, when she had her little breakdown.

That in itself had been a revelation. Not once in twenty eight years – even when they went through all the infertility upset – had he seen her like that. Weeping in public and either oblivious to onlookers or unaffected by their stares. Not that he'd been embarrassed. Well, perhaps a little, though his loyalty had quashed such petty worries. But it was unlike her to succumb to such a fatalistic view of the world, let alone do so in public. The whole outburst had left him stunned.

Actually it had shattered him more than any other event in his life to date, which possibly indicated she had a point: he really hadn't done anything of importance. In the days since, he'd felt he was moving through a heavier, more solid air; under threat of an impending storm and powerless to do anything other than anxiously await its arrival.

"That woman with the camera's back again," he said, noticing her standing outside, almost hesitating on the doorstep. "You think she wants to photograph us? You know, for a brochure or something?"

"Go ask her," Marion said, turning to see. "Oh God."

Having been spotted, the woman – presumably the mysterious Christine – stepped over the threshold and walked towards the counter. Pete glanced at Marion, her stiff stance, mouth drawn tightly closed, hands pressing against the warm steel counter. He looked back towards the woman. Her expression was not as confident as her walk but still she moved towards them without hesitation.

"Marion?" she said, when within two feet of the counter. A curious accent – not easy to place – but a strong voice and a manner that suggested she was used to being heard. "It's Chrissy. Chrissy Barker. Alice told you I was in town?"

"She did." Marion said. "Didn't think you'd have the gall to come here though."

Chrissy tried a smile, but didn't reply. She looked at Pete, then back at Marion. Pete gave the wire basket a shake, more to generate a sound than because it was needed. Marion stood stoic and silent.

"Is this your..?" Chrissy indicated him with a nod.

"Husband," Marion said. "Yes."

"Pete," he extended a hand over the counter, Chrissy took it in cool fingers and smiled, gratefully he thought. "Nice to meet you."

"You too," she said.

"Is it?" Marion looked at him.

"Why don't you pair go through to the house?" he said, lifting the hatch on the far end of the counter and beckoning Chrissy through the gap. "I can manage, it's still quiet."

He could feel Marion's eyes on his back but didn't look round. He pointed out the way and Chrissy walked down the corridor without checking to see if Marion was following.

"What the hell did you do that for?"

His wife was clearly furious but, Chrissy having now vanished into the sitting room, had little choice other than follow.

Marion's back with her dad. He's a bit thinner than he once was but he's still too fat to climb so he runs into The Smuggler and brings out a few strong men. One is Jack Crozier who used to fish but now takes tourists round the bay. It's Jack who gets onto the roof. It's solid and almost dry. It doesn't dip and twist with the wind, doesn't keel over and make a man pray. It's a pleasure trip.

"His idea, not mine," Marion said. "I don't have time for this, we get busy lunchtime."

Chrissy. Like a stranger, garish against the faded decor – too modern, too polished, for this traditional backdrop. Yet there was also a weird familiarity to her presence. She was neither one thing nor the other – both known and unknown.

"Oh, I remember those," Chrissy said, pointing to the ornaments along the mantelpiece.

"I didn't think you'd stick around..."

"But the furniture's different. At least I think so, I really can't remember much."

Chrissy looked at her, gave another of those irritating shrugs, that artificial smile. It probably worked on half-drugged rock stars but it wouldn't wash here. What Chrissy seemed to forget was that Marion was no stranger to her manipulations – no stranger to the wiles and artifice of the unreliable pretender. No stranger to the complexities of this unstable mind. For almost a decade she'd played fool to the endless apologies, excuses and fantasies of Chrissy Barker. Not now. She was no longer the ignorant child she'd once been. She took a deep breath.

"In fact, I hoped you wouldn't come because I really don't think we have anything to say to each other."

There. It was said. She'd rehearsed the line multiple times over the past week, never quite sure she'd be capable of such rudeness when the moment came. But she'd done it. Had said what she wanted to say.

Silence. She could swear her beating heart was loud enough for Chrissy to hear but if it was, she didn't register any sign.

"You must hate me," Chrissy said, breaking the quiet. "And I wouldn't have come, but I need to find out what happened."

Marion laughed. She heard herself, shrill and artificial. Typical of Chrissy to try and play the victim – hadn't it always been that way? Pushing and pushing until she'd almost shoved a person too far and then concocting some elaborate excuse, something so outlandishly tragic only the hardest of hearts would have been able to reject it. Marion's heart had never been remotely hard. She'd given in every time. She'd had several decades to relive those moments and now knew how many times she'd been fooled.

"You've got a bloody nerve," she said, her whole body quivering with the effort of denying a rage that wanted release. "Just go. Get out. There's nothing for us to talk about. Nothing."

Marion says "don't be stupid' as Chrissy climbs onto the wall, stands with arms wide to counterbalance the drink, the wind, the adrenalin. "Oh my God, you silly cow, you stupid silly cow, oh Christ, I'm going for dad… don't move… I'm going for dad." Marion runs round the harbour to the chip shop, while Chrissy cuts numb fingers on the edges of freezing tiles.

I guess I should have expected Marion to have changed, to have become the sort of person who could eject an unwanted visitor from her home without stuttering, the type who ends up running a business and a half-wit husband single-handedly. The signs had been there. That quiet prissiness – subdued but stubbornly present.

Inevitable a few years sitting on every committee within a ten mile radius, making petty local decisions, would have brought it to the fore. But I can't believe she asked me to leave. Maybe there's a chance I remember her incorrectly. Perhaps she always was a bossy bitch. But no, the old Marion would never have dared to speak like that. She'd occasionally grumble, quietly, but when her back was tight against the wall she'd hunch down and submit before she'd ever start kicking. Funny, but I'd maybe like this new Marion.

"I don't get it," Fen said, tugging the small mattress out of the room. "I mean, yeah, obviously what happened was grim, but it's been more than thirty years. Bit of a harsh reaction. Sure you've not forgotten something?"

Well of course I might have forgotten. Nothing was clear, nothing was complete. It was highly likely the argument itself contained insults and hurts of which I clearly have no recollection. Maybe she'd taken Pat's side – maybe she, too, had thought Spencer a fake – although it wasn't as if we'd been particularly close by then. When Pat and I started college, Marion slipped off the radar somewhat. She was still at that hideous school for her A' levels whilst we idled afternoons away in cafés, smoking and pontificating with other artists and dreamers. In the evenings we rarely saw her either. She'd be at home cramming. We'd be in local pubs, hanging out with Spencer and his friends, taking drugs and learning more about life in one year than we'd done in the previous ten.

We grew up. She remained a child.

"Was she closer to Pat than you?" Fen asked.

"No way. Marion was the butt of our jokes. Pat had even less in common with her than I did. I don't even know why she was there that night. Nobody was closer to Pat than me."

Or maybe I did remember why she was there. If I let myself contemplate the meltdown that led to that night, it'll come back. Because what I do now recall, in a vague whisper that given a moment might return in more solid form, is how when everything I held true and important began to implode, it was Marion who tried to rescue me. In that quiet prissy way.

"I don't know what's real anymore."

"What do you mean, real? This is real – you, me, this table, today. What's happened? Is it those people you're with? They're too old, you know, they're freaky, dangerous, Chrissy. Have they been giving you drugs?"

"The world, me, everything around, it's not real, none of it, it's all lies and it just goes on and on. What am I going to do? I'm not like you, I don't know what I want and the more I look, the more I see none of it's real anyway."

"Of course it's real! You've just lost confidence, that's all. Think – you're young, healthy, clever – you have your whole life ahead. You can do anything!"

Marion didn't understand. But she had tried.

Pat kept saying Spencer didn't really love me. She, it seemed, could tell. The more I challenged him to prove himself, the more it seemed she might be right. It's hard to accept that level of Truth – to find you've been deluding yourself. To find that nothing is as you thought. I figured at the time, the easiest thing to do was reject Pat, get rid of that nagging voice of reality, lose myself once more in the intensity of delusion. Everything with Spencer had felt so good, surely it could be so again. So I tried to avoid her, but she'd turn up. It was her crowd too – she knew where we'd be. She'd appear, sit beside me, mutter and frown and make everything he said seem duplicitous.

By the time that last night came, I'd been arguing with the pair of them for months. I was exhausted. Everything that had mattered was in question. Every movement, every word, every gesture, hung in a cloud of tension, a perilous balance that had me second guessing, reading between lines, anticipating, questioning everything. Pat claimed to have my best interests at heart, but I no longer believed that. I no longer believed anything. It was then I turned to Marion. I went to see her one night, perhaps a week or two before that last time. I didn't tell her it was Pat – I wanted a generic response – so I just said I had a friend, at college, who was trying to split up another friend's relationship because she thought it best and I asked Marion what she thought about that. She was always a good person to ask these things. She liked people – more than they ever liked her – and she was logical, always thought things through. She wasn't the sort to act on impulse or irrationally. What made her boring also made her invaluable.

"A real friend wouldn't do that," Marion said. I'd known it was what she'd say, I just needed to hear it. "A real friend would stay quiet, supportive and wait for the inevitable."

"Do nothing?"

"No, not nothing. They'd be there, ready, with tissues, sympathy and encouraging words. It sounds like the interfering friend has a separate agenda."

"Like what?"

"Maybe she's jealous."

Together Fen and I move the wardrobe, I try not to look at the remaining wallpaper behind it. We drag it carelessly across the floor, banging and scraping against the door frame as we heave it onto the landing. I'd like to just take a hammer and smash it into pieces, throw them down the stairs, but Fen says it's easy enough to get it out in one piece. His friend is coming with a truck, whatever can be rescued is going to some charity or other, I don't know. I just want it gone.

There's only the carpet left in my room. Fen

thinks we should go shopping, buy a few things – a proper bed, a quilt, a little table for the dining room. He's got it all planned out in his mind. I suppose he thinks if we make it nice enough I might stay. I ask him to rip away those last segments of paper. I can't bear to do it myself. I keep my back to him, hear the tearing, the stuffing of yet more unwanted past into plastic bags, and I stare at the carpet. There are sections barely aged, other areas worn almost to the floorboards. Once over, this carpet was new, proudly installed by my father – though not for me. I'd never been anticipated. This carpet was installed for guests who never came.

To put yourself into something – give of yourself – only to see it destroyed, is a painful thing. It can scar a person forever. Were my father here today he'd be hurt to see his hard work torn apart, strewn over the garden, crushed into rubbish sacks. Were he standing here right now, after all the effort and will he put into the few achievements he'd had, he'd feel as though we were ripping out his own innards – would literally experience the twisting and pulling in his stomach, the grasping heaviness on his heart.

That's how it was to lose Spencer and Pat. To know I'd lost them even before it actually happened. It was a real and physical pain. In those final few weeks when we collided and fragmented, breaking what we'd thought unbreakable with a will that was not our own, I'd known it was the wrong thing to do. Maybe they did too. But I couldn't stop by then, even though I was breaking myself in the process.

The girl wraps a strand of mousy hair around her finger. She winds it tightly and the flesh turns red at the tip.

"If you loved me, you'd say it." She hears the whine in her own voice. "It's simple enough, but you don't, so you mustn't. That's how it looks to me."

"Jesus, this again – why?"

He touches palette knife to canvas but his concentration has been disturbed and he makes a mistake. No big deal, oils can be corrected, but it annoys him. He scrapes, wipes the knife with his thumb, wipes thumb to rag. It's wrong. He's made it worse.

"I just want you to say it," she says.

"And that'll make it all right? How? I say it under pressure, it's even less believable than if I said it of my own accord. And for what? Love? What the fuck is love? My perception? Yours? It's a word, just a word, it means anything and nothing."

He throws down the knife. He can't work like this. It's a fucking mess. He'll have to start again. He turns to the girl, he can barely look at her. "Just go. Leave. I can't fucking do anything with you here. Just go."

The girl is spiralling. She leaves, but she doesn't want to leave. She hates, but she doesn't want to hate.

She loves. She's not even sure she wants to love anymore, not like this, but she doesn't know how to make it feel good again.

Later, Pat says, "See? I told you. He doesn't. He's not worth it – all you've done for him, he doesn't appreciate you. He's not worth it."

"Just fuck off! Stop putting all this crap in my head." Everything's swirling now – her head, the view, the thoughts, the individual words.

"You're only mad at me because you know I'm right," Pat says, "He doesn't love you. He's a shit. It's like I said."

I tug at the edge of the carpet, just beneath the radiator where my father cut it to fit around the pipes. It pulls away from the gripper with a glorious sound. Dust, old and stale, wafts upwards and catches in the back of my throat. I'm breathing with my mouth open, I know what's under here, I need to see it. There's a section of wall – maybe a foot or so – with no gripper. This is where we stuffed the poems, pushing them further with a bent coat hanger. As I pull the length from the wall, the tearing sound pauses but the carpet still comes away. This is it. This is the spot.

They are there. Un-faded, though covered in a layer of dust. There are fewer than I remember. I count the envelopes, eight. I'd thought we wrote more than that. Each is sealed, I don't know when we thought we might look at them again, if ever, but imagine we perhaps planned to do so when we were very old. She should be here, to see this.

Fen carries the plastic sack downstairs. I pick up the eight envelopes. Each is labelled with one word, the title of the item it contains. I read the first, *Bastards*, slide it to the back of the bunch. That was the one about school. We wrote that together. The second reads *Love* – I think that's one of mine. A poem it about Spencer, though I seem to remember Pat wrote one with the same name about me. I flick through the remainder. There isn't another called *Love* – maybe both poems are in the one envelope.

My handwriting has changed a lot since I wrote these. I barely recognise this neat print. Far messier now, but I guess it's been a deliberate evolution born of thirty four years freedom from anyone standing over my shoulder criticising.

Strange to hold these fragments of the past. To know what's inside – how much of the me that once was is lying on scraps of paper folded over and sealed for three decades. Now I've rescued them I'm not sure I want to open them. I came here to grab what was mine and leave but have somehow become entangled in the past to the extent I cannot simply move on. The Something Else draws ever closer, its opaque mystery gradually regaining some of its original colour.

The erasing of my parents from this place is helping. There was too much clutter – both real and figurative – too much history, too many memories, and now there are fewer. Now I can focus on finding Pat.

She's here somewhere.

I can feel it.

the dead

I TAKE BACK what I said about Judy's dog. The ceremony in the garden was a necessary part of its life and death. The finality of saying goodbye to a section of freshly dug earth is important. I tell Fen – about Judy's dog, about not having experienced anything like it for Pat.

"Bit of a difference, burying a dog and burying a teenage girl," he says. "But yeah, I see where you're coming from. They call it closure, you had none."

I try to go along with his theory of her having died, but I'm not convinced. A part of me still thinks she flew. I don't tell him this. He wouldn't understand. For me, the ability to conceive of the inconceivable comes from having artists as lovers – and since Spencer there have been others. I'm drawn to them. When you've lost yourself for hours in the abstract of an artist's mind, have seen within random brushstrokes more clarity than is ever apparent in the real world, you reach another level – a place where common perception and reality are often quite disparate, a place where all things are possible.

"Art isn't about giving people what they want to see – it's about showing them what they can't see. When the crowd is looking west, it's your job as an artist to turn and look east. You can do that, Chrissy, you have the eye, the heart, the understanding. You, my love, have the soul."

I probably couldn't argue it eloquently enough to convince someone like Fen but I believe Pat flying is as valid a potential outcome to that night as anything else. Spencer would understand, though he isn't likely to get the chance. I walked down Wheelwright's Lane yesterday and saw how his flat and studio – that warm and wonderful womb – is now a holiday rental. Swimming costumes draped over the railings of the tiny balcony, the sound of harassed parents and squabbling children coming from the narrow French windows. It was all wrong. Hearing anger in that place of love.

He draws the dry brush down her chest, its sable hair soft against her skin, curving it under one breast, tracing the line back and stroking a curve under the other. She barely breathes, so captured is she by his focus, his concentration. She's never felt so naked, never felt so delicious, so observed, so loved.

"When I paint you," he said, "it'll be inside out.

You won't recognise yourself – you may even hate it at first. But you can't have this, you can't have what you see in the mirror, what would be the point? You know that view. I see something else and I'll paint what I see so you'll know it too. You are beautiful. Do you know that? Do you? Maybe not, but you will."

Though I'm obviously choosing to ignore the arguments he and I had, towards the end, when Pat had done what she'd set out to do, when momentum took the destruction further than was ever desired. When I lashed out with words and fists, and he mocked and goaded and pontificated on how bloody right he'd been all along. It was ugly. Yet it was of equal passion to what had gone before. We did nothing without passion.

"Don't think you own a part of me. You don't. I'm free, you're free. Go do something else for a few days, I need space, I'm trying to work here."
"Maybe I'll go fuck a stranger."
"Maybe you should."

Spencer had always openly hated commitment. It was one of his favourite discussion points – and I'd been happy to follow the same principle. It didn't make a difference to us in any case. Neither was seeing anyone else, knowing we could was the important thing. But Pat thought it worrying. That a person could expect love and yet deny verbal commitment of it. She'd bring it up again and again, imprinting it on my mind along with all her other theories and gut instincts about him, the validity of his love, the reality of his beliefs. By the end I no longer knew which thoughts had been hers and which my own, so when I lashed out I did so with conviction – even though her vision had never been my religion. What Spencer said about commitment was right. I've never wavered from that belief in all the years since. But for a short time, under her guide, I abandoned my own grail to undertake hers and it cost me everything. Though is it really fair to blame her for what happened when I can't actually remember?

Fen has to work. I'm getting tired of staying at his place and so I return to my parents' house and drag the single mattress back upstairs. I find a lamp, one of the radios, a lightweight blanket and a pillow. The simplicity is refreshing. It's quite spiritual. I think I'll be far more comfortable here than at Fen's. But I pace around for a couple of hours feeling something isn't quite right, something else needs to be done. It's the floorboards – various shades of brown, stained in places. Too dark. There might be paint in the shed.

Therein lies another of those horrifying realisations. The ones you can't believe you ever forgot. The shed. Alice had even mentioned it, that first day when she lost herself in memories of the war. How my mother couldn't bear to go in there. How she had to hire a man to do the garden after my father died. It was where he killed himself, which explained my mother's avoidance, but it was so much more than that to me.

As a child I wasn't allowed in. I've never been in there. There'll be a key somewhere. Maybe Alice knows. As a child, I was threatened with punishment if I was even caught trying to see into the tiny, cobweb-covered window, let alone enter the place. The structure took on an evil form. I was terrified of it. I had no idea what was in there, why it wasn't right for me to go in, why my father guarded this private space so fiercely, but I was quite certain he'd make good on the threat if I let curiosity guide me. But one day I saw the door was slightly open. This was before I knew Pat, I must have been very young. My father was, I knew, at the side of the house, looking at a section of guttering that had been leaking and staining the wall with damp. I snuck forwards, I couldn't help myself. I thought maybe I could just peer in for a second and see what was there. He must have seen me. He crept quietly up behind me and put a hand on my shoulder. He gripped far more tightly than was necessary. He didn't speak. He just took me inside, made me bend over the bed and hit me with his belt. Once for having disobeyed him, once for being within the thirty-six inch restricted area and once for having looked inside the shed. But I hadn't actually managed to look inside. That last belt lash was completely undeserved.

Later, when he'd gone back in there and I'd stopped crying, my mother told me it was where he painted his miniature soldiers and that he liked to be left in peace. I'd only ever seen the soldiers in the house when he lined them up on the table before he made my mother sing. It was some sort of ritual, I didn't know what, I just got out of the way. His bringing the soldiers in, beginning the meticulous process of setting them out in rows along the table, was my cue to go outside and into the garden where I'd dig and scratch at the soil until it was over.

Pat claimed she'd been in the shed once. She said there were canvasses – paintings depicting headless soldiers, limbless civilians, all blood and bombs and fire and weeping women. It might have been true. My mother once said he'd been at art college before the war, though I never saw him draw or paint anything and it wasn't something he ever spoke about. I wonder now whether the canvasses are still there, or whether they existed at all. Pat wasn't always honest.

I won't go into the shed today. I go to the local hardware store instead. Buy a wide brush and a tin of white paint that's supposed to be for garden furniture but which will dry quicker than gloss and do the same job. I get to work on the floorboards, the aura of the room lifting as sullied wood lightens and the space fills with an alien scent.

It's strange how memories can return. Just fragments, snippets of what once was. When I first came back I could barely remember ever having lived here. Now, after clearing out the house, talking with Fen and revisiting a few childhood haunts, things are starting to clarify. A little at least. But the Something Else still evades me and I dread the results of Fen's searches – that he might discover I pushed her. I haven't remembered anything else about that night, have had no enlightening dreams of violence, but it remains an obvious possibility.

Of course when a memory does return, doubt is never far behind. Am I recalling an actual incident or inventing whole moments from mere fragments? Am I remembering what happened or what I wished had happened? More and more I see happier moments with my mother. Was it so? Or do I just wish it were so?

I still recall nothing positive about my father.

But I'm feeling pretty good. The bedroom looks pure and unthreatening. I leave the paint to dry, propping the small mattress against the balustrade on the landing, folding the blanket, stacking it and the pillow to one side with military precision. John Albert would perhaps have approved.

Because I'm feeling inexplicably bright, I decide on a walk around town. Visit some more places where I went with Pat. Maybe even a few where I went with Spencer. He has been on my mind. I guess I'm preparing to leave Fen.

My primary school is still there. It looks quite different – much bigger now – but the old buildings are easily identified, though the gates are locked and I can't get close enough to look through the windows. School wasn't the happiest place for Pat and me. Not this one and certainly not the one that followed. The high school is out of town, I have no plans to visit it, but I pass the bus-stop where we waited each morning, returned each afternoon, and can only picture the dark, damp, winter days.

I look for the sweet shop down Candlestick Lane. Not that we ever had much money to spend there, neither of us having any grandparents to offer shiny coins in return for a kiss. Marion did. It was generally her money we spent. The shop building is easy to spot. Same architrave but recently painted and with a gaudy, modern sign above the window. It sells swimwear and flotation devices. Kids presumably get their sweets from the supermarket now. I stop near the train station, sit outside a pub which overlooks the children's play area. We went there a lot, as children and teenagers. There's a family on the table next to mine and I know the man has recognised me. He keeps twisting round, turning back, leaning over his table and muttering to his wife. The two teenagers are uninterested, though at some point I hear one ask *who?* and the other one laughs.

Eventually he leans across to where I sit.

"Excuse me, are you Chrissy Zook?"

He's about the right age to have been an original fan of *Plutonium*. He's about the right age to now be obsessed with reliving his youth. There's a look in his eye as he asks the question that suggests were I to confirm it was so, he'd fill the rest of the afternoon with his memories. I'd hear details of every concert he saw and who he went with and what drugs they took. I'd be complimented on each album cover I shot, or he'd take the opportunity to tell me where I went wrong. He'd want his wife to take a picture of us on his mobile. He'd send it to all his mates. If she wasn't listening, he'd want to let me know how much he fancied me when he was young and slim enough to have been able to do something about it. If brave enough, he'd wink and tell me he's still up for it if I play my cards right.

"No," I say, "But I'm always being told I look like her."

"I told you it wouldn't be," his wife says.

I'm not feeling upbeat as I walk out of town. The incident with the guy at the pub was irritating. I've wasted an hour thinking about Zak and the band, the years leading up to it, the years that followed. And while there are some fantastic memories – life on the road, the crazy after-show parties, the frivolity of spending other people's cash – the time sandwiching those days is dark. At least the parts I can remember. I then end up thinking about Mervyn and I want to speak to him but can't get a decent signal on my phone.

Things are compounding again.

I'm spiralling. Again. There are moments I struggle to recall my own name, and when it comes there's no context. It's a word – Chrissy – it conjures nothing. Who am I? What am I? Where am I?

Around me are people and I love them all but I don't know why. The air is warm, humid. I'm somewhere hot but its name doesn't surface. I don't even know if the voices are speaking English. I recognise the sounds, it may be a language I know, but nothing will hold still long enough for me to compute.

I hear the sea. I hear the sea in my head and its sound does not match the tranquil air of the day. It's an angry sound. It's a cold sound. I shiver and feel the tips of my fingers ache. My thighs clench around nothing but I recognise the frozen touch of the lifeboat house roof – can almost believe, if I looked, it would be there.

I can see Pat. I can see Pat so clearly in my mind – wet, furious, terrified – and even when I open my eyes, see the bright sunshine, the musicians and poets scattered around, leaning against vine-covered stone, smoking and drinking, singing and talking, I still see her. Pat. In the dark, the cold, the wet. I can still feel that chill.

I want to reach out and touch something real. It might help. But the artists and lovers are all out of range, sitting against their warm walls, lost in the beat of their own happiness.

Was I with them just then? Before?

Now I am here. Ten yards that may as well be ten miles.

Pat's white face still haunts me, goading me to close my eyes again. But I won't. I'll refuse sleep and, as soon as my arms and legs cease this rigid inertia, will walk over to the sunny walls and join with the drinking and singing.

A woman comes towards me. I hope she comes close enough to touch, to talk. Lucy. She's called Lucy. She carries the phone, its wire dangling behind, beginning to tighten. She makes it to me before the limit is reached and holds out the handset. Her mouth moves but I can't follow the sounds. She laughs, strokes my face, says "You gone, baby?" English. She's speaking English.

"*For you, a call.*"

I take the handset with fingers too numb to feel.

"*Chrissy? You there, sweetheart?*"

The voice – a sound I know exquisitely – loosens

my limbs and I unfold, warm, sit forwards, hold his comforting tones to my ear and try to speak.

"Merv..."

"God, babe, you were hard to find this time. Do you know how much you cost me in private snoops? Why the fuck can't you call, leave a number, send a note? Jesus, hon, you'll be the death of me, you'll be the fucking death of me."

"Merv..."

"How are you? Doing okay? Marrakech? What's that about then? All drugs and meditation, I guess, huh?"

"Merv..."

"Don't know why I'm calling. Shouldn't be. How long's it been? You were on my mind, I just wanted to know you were okay, you're doing okay?"

"Merv... oh, Merv."

Independence means solitude. It means not having anyone to share things with. I've spent decades telling people I don't need this but it's a lie. I was just never going to have another Pat. It doesn't mean I haven't needed someone. Someone completely on my side when it mattered, someone who put their all into our friendship. What were the goading and arguments if not just Pat watching my back? She was generally right about people. She was generally right about what was best for me. I *survived* with her. I can't say I'd have lasted as long without her as a kid. I know I wouldn't. Because I know where I was and what I was thinking of doing when we first met. Six years old and far too young for such bleakness.

But it's not something I think about.

I know over the years since I left, I've made bad judgements. Mistakes I would never have made had she been around. Those first eighteen years, when I forgot, are no clearer than the ones following my argument with Mervyn and the recollection of that night – of her – but I know how many errors I made during that time. Even after I remembered her, even after I awoke to my past, it wasn't enough. It wasn't the same as actually having her around. I still fucked up. I still do. Fen is a perfect example. Would Pat have thought it a good idea to get involved with a too-sweet guy in a town I have no intention of adopting as my own again? Well, maybe on a bad day. She'd have thought it a laugh to screw with his head. But overall she'd have said it was a stupid thing to do; I wasn't going to stay, so why waste the effort in pretending I might? Why give myself the problem down the line?

And she'd have been right.

If I'm honest, I think the flying theory has more to do with guilt than reality. We were both supposed to do it – that I do remember – but I didn't. I don't know why, I just didn't jump. That hesitation, that fraction of time, gave Jack Crozier the chance to grab, to save me, bring me down from the roof, down to life again, down to where I did not want to be. In the years since, I've been left with a feeling of flight, a sense that at any moment I could just jump. A part of me is still there, waiting to finish it.

For a time after I'd left, during those first eighteen years, I suspect I didn't think about Pat in solid terms because I could sense her in ethereal ones. Now, looking back, I think I half-expected to see her at some point. It was never a distinct thought, just a sensation that I was still whole, despite how disjointed day to day life could be. At a subconscious level I was waiting for her to eventually catch up with me, be part of the creative sphere I'd found. And maybe during those years my eye was occasionally caught by a flick of someone's dark hair, the deliberate sashay of a distant stranger's hips, the raucous laugh in a crowded room, but I never coherently linked those things with her. They merely added a layer of reality to the unspoken assumption, the feeling I wasn't completely alone. I carried on drifting through life as though she were still around, somewhere. Still trying to catch me up.

Yet now, back here, it feels the closest I've been to losing that sense of her being out there, somewhere. This is presumably why I'm heading for the graveyard. To find out for certain.

It isn't until I get to the church I remember it's where we started drinking on that last night.

We bought a bottle of vodka – I've no idea where the money came from, but we did buy a bottle – and we sat in the stone vestibule and got drunk.

Now I'm here, standing looking at that same spot and being assaulted by an invisible wave. Looming and threatening, growing taller and taller before crashing down, deliberate and exact. I should be soaked, but I'm not. I'm dry but very cold, as though the wave was there just then, it did actually happen, and yet had been formed from air rather than liquid and had left behind nothing more than the chill of having passed through me.

I can almost feel us. Those two teenagers. Drunk and wanting to fight. We thought we'd learned so much yet we knew nothing of what would come, nothing of what would seem important in the decades that followed. Buoyed up by the flexible energy of youth, taking issue with everything and nothing. Fighting when we should have been still, hating when all that was needed was love. And oblivious to how little time we had left together.

We must have stolen the vodka. We couldn't have afforded to buy it. These are the petty details to ruin every memory. Nothing is complete, nothing is clear. I wonder if I go nearer, sit in that vestibule, more will return. But I'm not sure I want to get that close. She isn't there, I'm not there, the moment has passed and its echo will not be enough.

I don't know how long I stand. Staring towards the vestibule, mesmerised by the sharp diagonal line of sun meeting shade, splitting it in two. The stonework is not to be trusted; it says one thing in the shadow another in the sun, such duplicity mocking the supposed Truth contained within. Or perhaps that is the Truth. Dark and light, side by side, neither able to overcome the other. There is no right and wrong. There is no good and bad. These things are as intertwined and dependent as the oak, the ivy and the cool dead bodies beneath my feet.

The church door opens with a movie-grade creak. A woman emerges, conservatively dressed and wearing the thin white line of duty around her throat. She's carrying books and papers, moving forwards with her head down in much the same way Marion used to walk – a shyness, a lack of self-belief, an unwillingness to seem pushy or bold. But the vicar clearly senses my presence and raises her face to smile, nod and wish me good afternoon as she passes.

"Excuse me," I say as she hunches down again and moves to scuttle by.

"Sorry." She stops, glances up, looks me directly in the eye and hugs the books close to her chest. "Can I help?"

"I'm looking for the graves of people buried in nineteen seventy three."

"Ah, rightie ho." She's more confident when she speaks. "Well, burials here ceased in the late seventies – before my time – ran out of room. It's what happens with these ancient churches, of course, so nothing beyond seventy eight, seventy nine, thereabouts, but seventy three... hmm... I think if you were to aim for that far wall, see the one? Over to the right? And come down, let's see, maybe three or four rows? That would be as good a place as any to start."

They're near the old lifeboat house. Pat has the vodka and she's not sharing anymore. She swings the bottle towards her mouth, misjudging speed and direction, her arm numbed by drink, anger and cold. Now her cheek is doubly wet. She's ahead of them, walking backwards so she can see their faces – "I hate you" – then turning, staggering on, up a narrow road that leads nowhere. They follow because they knew this would come. It has to be seen through. Even though it's freezing and she's hogging the booze.

Marion's trailing. She just can't keep pace. But Chrissy has never felt so alive – she's sharp, edgy, and can walk all night if she has to – she's not even cold. She's just alive. Vibrant. She's waiting for Pat to really start, and she doesn't give a damn because this has been coming forever. They reach the lifeboat house. Pat stops, as though this was always the destination, leans against the wall, dangerous, reckless. She's smiling, but it's twisted and ugly. It could go either way from here. There's a part of her that wants to be stopped.

Chrissy says "are you going to share that bottle, or what?" Marion gives her a look. Pat stops smiling. She says "want it, bitch?" and throws the bottle over the wall.

Pat's at the top, straddled across the ridge tiles, hair blowing. She looks elated. "Come on then, bitch, if you're brave enough." For Chrissy, it's no longer about Spencer. It's about every challenge levelled since she was six. "Can you stand on one leg? I can. I bet I can do it longer than you."

Can you sit on a cold roof?

Unless she does this there'll never be an end to it. One of them has to fall. One of them has to finally get the last word. It's perishing. The wind's getting up. The tide's coming in. Pat shouts again. Marion says "don't be stupid" as Chrissy climbs onto the wall, stands with arms wide to counterbalance the drink, the wind, the adrenalin.

People always say graveyards are peaceful places, as though that peace is born of something spiritual, something sacrilegious. But I believe what we experience is the essence of humanity released from care – a collective atmosphere of vanquished stress. For all our concerns, the serious and the mundane, for all the years of fretting over situations brought on by ourselves in our endless quest for advancement, for all the years of thinking These Things Matter, we are, in the end, gone. And in that instant, with that very last breath, our worries and fears vanish too. This is what the living sense amongst the dead – the evaporation of concern. The conversations about you after death, the accusations you'll never defend, the inaccuracies you'll never correct, the missed questions you'll never answer – they don't matter. You are now without burden.

So walking amongst the dead is bound to be peaceful. It's only a shame we can't soak up some of that essence whilst we're still alive. But our minds continue to buzz with the importance of our times – which route to take on a journey to avoid the rush, the right way to make an omelette, whether a lover's words have hidden meaning, how many regrets we've amassed along the way. Yet still we fear death. As though it's somehow worse.

I search for over an hour. She was right, the vicar, and I find seventy three without any trouble, but I don't find a gravestone for a teenage girl called Pat. I search the other rows, just in case, but nothing. I go backwards as far as nineteen forty, forwards to the last person interned, but I still find nothing. Maybe she was cremated. Or her body was just never found.

Or maybe she actually did fly.

removing all trace

Alice stared at the pile of unwanted furniture on the lawn. Sixty years of Elizabeth Barker's life. Some of the pieces had lived elsewhere before coming here. The dining room dresser was at least as old as she was, but where they'd end up now was anybody's guess. Christine said they were going to charity. That was something at least.

There was so much stuff out in the garden there could hardly be anything left in the house. Christine said dark furniture wasn't popular anymore. She was only trying to make the place look good for potential buyers. But it was a pitiful sight, stacked tightly together like that, as though it were a bonfire waiting to be lit.

"Are you coming in?"

"Yes, dear, just navigating the furniture."

She'd always been steady on her feet, a keen walker in her day – had been president of the local ramblers' association from sixty-six to sixty-nine. But each year brought a new state of disrepair with which she must learn to live. Injuries took such a time to heal. Her left leg and arm were still heavily bruised from the fall ten days ago. The dark stains would eventually fade, purple to green, green to yellow, but she wasn't sure the anxiety that now accompanied every step would be quite as short-lived. Her legs just couldn't be trusted anymore.

Christine brewed a pot of tea, pouring boiling water from what looked to be a new electric kettle. Four unfamiliar mugs waited next to an open bag of sugar and a spoon. The radio was on low, tuned to a station with jangly adverts and presenters who speak too quickly. Other than these few items, the counter was bare. Gone were Elizabeth's cookery books, egg-timer and windowsill knick-knacks. Gone was the wall hung utensil rail, the pine kitchen roll holder and the wall calendar. Most curiously, at the far end of the worktop run, the cooker was draped in a white sheet.

"Why have you covered it up?" Alice asked.

"Can't stand the sight of it, but Fen needs to disconnect the electrics before it can go."

Malcolm and his friend, Roger, arrived in a large truck, reversing with difficulty up the narrow drive. Christine poured the tea and asked Roger whether he wanted sugar. He stared at her but didn't appear to notice she'd spoken. She laughed, held up the bag and spoon and he blushed like a teenager, *oh, sorry, yeah, two please.*

"Wait, dear," Alice said, reaching to open a cupboard door. "There's a bowl for that."

But the cupboard was empty. Gone were Elizabeth's beautiful tea cups, gone was the matching sugar bowl and lid, the milk jug, side plates, dinner plates, dishes. Everything gone. Apart from a few escaped sugar granules where the bowl had once stood there was no sign of her china ever having existed.

Except in Alice's memories.

The floor of the sitting room was awash with black plastic sacks, cardboard boxes and lengths of ripped tape, all filled with the contents of cupboards and drawers, wardrobes and shelves. Once the boys had cleared them out this room would be completely empty. There'd be nothing left at all. The hall was also bare, the cream telephone sitting pathetically on the floor, its cable curling round in a loose circle mimicking a side table no longer present. Two dark holes on the wall near the door marked where the coat rail had been. Gone. Everything that had said Elizabeth and John Albert Barker was gone.

"What d'you think?" Malcolm asked Roger, nodding towards the boxes and bags. "Start with this junk?"

"Nah, let's do the furniture first, while we're firing on all cylinders."

Christine popped her head around the sitting room door. She was carrying a plastic bucket filled with water and a long handled mop. Red, shiny, new. A strong scent of floral disinfectant emanated from the steamy suds.

"I'm going upstairs, Alice," she said. "To mop the floors. You coming?"

Alice shook her head. There would be nothing up there. Nothing but empty rooms, bare walls and floorboards, naked windows and the ghosts of what had been. She walked around the pile of clutter. Books, crockery, pans, pictures and ornaments crammed into boxes, waste bags stuffed so full they were beginning to split. Goodness knew what was in them all. She poked one. Soft. Pulled at the gathered top where it was tied, stuck in a finger and tugged a section of fabric towards the gap. Clothes. Elizabeth's clothes. She clawed at the opening of another bag, bedding, another, more clothes, another, curtains.

There was a clatter outside as the boys dropped a piece of furniture, a metallic clang as it presumably hit the truck. One of them swore, the other laughed. Above, the *slop slop* across floorboards. There was a sound missing. It took a few moments for her to realise it was the wall-clock. It had a distinctive loud tick and on the hour a small door would click open and a wooden bird come out and cheap the relevant number of times. She glanced over the boxes, scanning for its faded paintwork, listening for its muffled tick. Nothing. Perhaps it was already in the van.

"Where's Chrissy?" Malcolm stood in the doorway, flushed and sweaty.

"Upstairs, dear, mopping the floors."

He shouted up, said he and Roger were taking the load, should be no more than an hour. The slopping sound paused and she called something back, but Alice couldn't quite catch what. Her eye had been caught by an item sticking out from one of the boxes. A photograph album.

"Why are you getting rid of everything, dear?"

Christine poured the dirty water from her bucket into the sink. She looked over her shoulder to where Alice was sitting at the kitchen table looking at the photographs.

"Oh, you found that."

"You can't throw away memories, Christine, it's not right."

Alice turned the page and tapped a finger on a black and white snap – aged, faded to a barely distinct range of greys – a car with a woman posing against it, just about visible against a backdrop of similarly hued hedges and sky.

"Look at that, dear. Your mother, their first car. Do you recognise that lane? You should. Come and look, tell me where you think it is."

Christine put down the bucket, removed her rubber gloves, leaned briefly across the table, glanced at the photograph and straightened up again.

"Could be anywhere, no idea, one lane looks much like the next to me."

"No, dear, no, you're not looking properly. I mean, this was before your time but it hasn't changed much, not really. The hedge is taller now of course. But look closer, you should know it. What can you see in the background?"

"The sea? Sky? I don't know, nothing, it's old, faded."

"Behind the hedge? There, in the distance."

Christine sighed, leaned forwards again.

"Don't know, a signpost or something?"

"Yes. That's it. And where *is* that signpost?"

"Signposts, lanes, hedges, they're everywhere."

"It's where we scattered your mother's ashes, dear. That's the lane behind the cliff walk, her favourite spot, her favourite view. And look at her smiling. *Smiling*, Christine. She's out with your father and she's smiling. They were happy then."

"Yeah, well, it was before they had me."

Christine was wrong if she thought she was the cause of her parents' situation. Alice remembered John Albert's first breakdown and it was some years before Elizabeth fell pregnant with her daughter. Of course it wasn't his first, just the first he'd had since he got back. Discharged from military hospital, declared mentally fit and well, he'd made his way home to reconnect with the young girl he'd left behind. They readjusted over the coming months, getting to know each other again. Two new people – he a more serious John Albert, she a more competent, patient and mature Elizabeth. They married in 1948. He was almost thirty four by then, she twenty nine. Their lives ahead of them and yet too much past behind. To think a person could have been broken so young, could have died inside before they'd even had time to live. Though at least he'd come home. Others hadn't.

This particular photograph was dated August 1949. It was probably their happiest time together. Before he became ill again. In fact – Alice now peered closely at the snap – that headscarf was a birthday present from John to Elizabeth. Here, in this photo, she's holding its tie in a gloved hand, as though fearful it might blow away in the cliff breeze. Maybe this was taken on her actual birthday, her touch reflecting a delight in the scarf's newness, joy that the man she loves has chosen such a beautiful object for her.

"He had a good eye for colour."

"What?"

"Your father. He was an artist, you know, before the war." She tapped the picture again. "He bought your mother this scarf. She loved it."

It was probably in one of those bags, now, in the sitting room. Scrunched up with everything else by someone who didn't know how special it was. A year or so after this picture was taken he started to behave oddly. They'd have a pill for it these days, but not then. People just got on with things as best they could or they got locked away. He wouldn't see a doctor, didn't want to end up back in the psychiatric hospital, Elizabeth thought they could cope, and so they muddled on. One night she'd found him curled in a ball under the dining table, spit and tears dripping from his face, trousers soiled and fingernails torn from where he was trying to claw through the carpet. He was in another place. It took until morning to coax him out, calm him down enough to see there was nothing in the room that could hurt him, nobody else there but her. It was the first of many such incidents and the end of the honeymoon period.

"She told me that," Christine said. "And Pat saw some paintings in the shed once. Did he do that? Still paint? Did you ever see them?"

"Yes, dear, he did, but they're gone now. Not the sort of things to hang in a home. She had them all destroyed."

When she can move again, Chrissy says thank you to Jack and the landlady and the other helpers because tomorrow this will be all round town and her parents need to salvage something.

Malcolm and Roger came back with pre-packed sandwiches and cakes. They all sat round the small kitchen table to eat, pressed close together in the humid, musky air. They'd worked hard, were hot, tired and sweaty. They needed a breather before sorting out what they called the 'junk'.

"Some could go to charity shops," Alice said.

"I'm not going through it all again," Christine said. "Just chuck the lot."

"But the clothes," Alice said, "the sewing machine, all those books. Surely they're of use to someone?"

"I'm not sorting through it again."

Malcolm turned the pages of photographs with one hand whilst eating Alice's second sandwich with the other. Appetite faded with age, for nearly everything. The only entities of which an old person could never have enough were good health, hugs and friends. Everything else generally came in far too big a portion.

"Hey, look at this," he said turning the album so the others could see. "You?"

"Yeah," Christine said, "happy smiling me."

Roger leaned in for a closer look.

"You had brown hair," he said.

"Mousy. I was a boring-looking teenager." She closed the album. "Stop being nosy, it's junk, should be back in there with the rest for chucking if Alice wouldn't keep trying to rescue things."

"It's not junk, dear, these are memories and you shouldn't throw them away. You'll regret it, mark my words, you'll regret it when you're as old as me."

"You keep it then. I certainly don't want it."

They started to load the truck with bags and boxes. Christine even helped this time, perhaps worried if they didn't get it all out of the house quickly enough, Alice would start to sort through. Roger picked up the sewing machine, its plug trailing along the floor, catching on a plastic bag and snagging fast.

"No, dear, not that," Alice said, putting a hand on his arm. "Not with the rubbish. Please. It's a perfectly good machine. She saved a long time to buy it."

Christine sighed, unhooked the plug from where it had caught and wafted him out of the room.

"Stop, wait, listen to me, dear. It's not right to throw away useful things. Someone will want that, someone who can't afford a new one. Have a heart, Christine."

Roger hesitated in the hallway. Malcolm put a hand on his shoulder, "Just put it on the left, mate. Left for charity, right for junk, okay?"

"Are you sorting it, dear? Oh, you are good."

Christine rolled her eyes. Malcolm leaned over, kissed her cheek and smacked her gently on the bottom. He winked at Alice over her shoulder.

"Shall I make some fresh tea?" Alice said.

She goes to Spencer's place because she knows he isn't there, breaks a window, opens the door, lets herself in, takes one of his cameras from the flat – it's his best one – and empties the cashbox he keeps under the counter in the studio. Then she goes home, packs a few things, and just makes the last train.

"What happened?" I said. "That night, when they realised I'd gone?"

"Well they didn't know straight away, dear, your mother was late back from the hospital. The nurses couldn't get your father to settle and asked her to stay, you know, until the medication started to work."

"Oh. They kept him in then. Thought he'd just gone for a check-up."

"No, it was a new treatment. He was bad at the time, I'm sure you remember. Had to stay there a week in the end. Then they let him home and he saw a therapist every fortnight. He was good for a while, he took his medication properly. You'd have been surprised, you know, he was a different man."

I can't picture this different man, can't see anything other than the cold bastard who haunted the house late at night, the maniacal, unpredictable nutter who'd emerge from a prolonged period in his shed to force my mother into his twisted view. A rare memory of allegiance with her – the unspoken understanding we had when he locked himself away in that private space. We knew what was coming and she'd often slip me some cash if she could time things right. Suggest I go out, meet friends, go to the cinema or something. It took between five and seven days for him to build up steam, reach the point where he'd bring in the painted soldiers and make her sing. It would generally be finished twenty four hours after that point.

As a small child, I'd gone into the garden – of my own accord – but as a teenager it was better to get away from the house completely. He and I were too similar in the end.

"So what did she do?" I asked. "When she realised?"

"She waited till morning, phoned Marion's parents. That's when she heard about Jim, his brother was there by then and Sylvia wasn't in any fit state, or Marion, but your mother got the gist of what had happened from Jim's brother."

"Marion's dad? Why what happened?"

"Don't you know? Hasn't she told you? He had a heart attack, dear. He died there, in the Smuggler that night."

Mervyn called. He's coming down tomorrow. Wants to see me. Whether this means he wants to help me make up my mind before the Friday deadline, or whether it means he's changed his and wants to tell me in person, I don't know. But it's odd. I'd felt good for a few days. Not feeling quite so bright now.

No wonder Marion hates me.

I dial her number. The husband answers. I can't remember his name. I ask for her, tell him not to say who's calling, tell him I have to say something, I need to speak to her, he must get her to the phone.

"Hello?"

"Marion, it's me, Chrissy, don't hang up."

There's a silence. She wants to cut me off, but she's curious. I speak again, quickly so she has to listen, has to hear me out.

"I'm sorry, God I'm so sorry, only just found out about your dad, I didn't know, truly I didn't. Shit. No wonder you hate me."

Another silence. This time I wait.

"Don't try for pity, just don't do it," she says. "Don't try and turn this into your pain."

"I'm not. I promise I'm not. Just wanted to say sorry."

"It's not enough. It'll never be enough."

And she hangs up.

a fleeting truth

MERVYN STOOD at the kitchen door, leaning out and breathing deeply. Christ, it was good to taste clean air. Nothing to beat it – the smell of the sea – made him feel like a kid again. As did seeing Chrissy. It had been a long time. The combination of her and the seaside in one hit was almost enough to persuade him to sod work, sod France, sod everything. Just stay here, run away, do what she'd done in reverse.

"So did you just fancy a day at the beach, or what?" she said.

Most men spend their lives in one of two states of being: kidding others or kidding themselves. It's probably fair to say a proportion of them exist in both modes simultaneously. The majority of his adult life had been spent that way, no argument about it. But he took comfort in knowing he wasn't alone.

"Came to see you, sweetheart."

He walked around the kitchen, opening cupboard doors and peeping in, moved into the hall, glancing up the staircase, into the sitting room, eyeing up the walls and windows. Pacing it slowly, feeling the empty space.

"Thinking of buying?" Chrissy said, following him. He laughed. Moved towards the window and opened it.

"Listen to that, just listen to that."

Seagulls. Made a bloody change from city pigeons. There was something about the echo in their voices – seagulls – the way they repeat that squawk until it sounds like it's coming from miles up and bouncing off every surface on the way down. Probably drives a person insane after a while, but he couldn't get enough of it. A good sound to wake up to that, and waves hitting pebbles but you couldn't hear those from here. It was a downside to the French place too. Mrs Levy had wanted to be close to Paris – no, had *insisted* – so they'd had to opt for rural rather than coastal. After she left him, he thought about selling it, unfinished, buying something by the sea, but he'd been too busy with work. Always too busy with work.

Or had he been kidding himself then too?

"So," Chrissy said, with a wave of her hand, "as you see, I've been working hard. Not much left. Nowhere to sit other than the kitchen, but it's better now. Total dump when I got here."

"Not sure the ripped lining paper effect'll catch on," he said. "I take it your folks had outdated tastes?"

"Hideous. My room hadn't been redecorated, same shitty paper as when I left."

Now, of course, it could turn out fortuitous not to have sold the French place. If he did end up retiring there with Mrs Levy. It was highly likely. Chrissy was never going to come with him to France, he knew that. He'd hoped she might – still did – but if he were honest there was more chance he'd wake tomorrow morning to find himself five stone lighter and with the sexual impetus of a twenty year old.

"What do you want to do then?" She moved closer, touched his arm.

"Sorry babe, miles away, listening to the gulls."

"Fancy walking to the beach?"

He coiled a length of her hair round his finger, hooked it gently over an ear, looked into eyes he'd known forever and felt the seconds tick, the minutes stack up, the hours queue to pass. So few left. How had it come to this? They should be touching, kissing, making up time, not wasting more. Like all the other long-awaited visits, time was vital, a life to be lived now, not wished for, not remembered, but felt and lived in this moment.

She leaned forwards, pressed her lips briefly onto his and he pulled her in, her face falling into place against his neck, arms curling round with familiar ease, warm through the fabric of his shirt. Still. A snapshot. A memory for each of his senses. Breathing, tasting, touching, counting more seconds as the melancholic coastal tune squawked on through the open window.

"Merv?" Her voice sank into his skin. "Why did you really come?"

Not now. Not yet. It was early. There was still time.

There is still time.

"Fancied a change. Come on, show me that beach."

I know how close love is to hate. How they live side by side – light and dark, like the diagonal line on that old stone church vestibule – interlinked, dependent, validating each other. I know, too, how they echo each other in intensity. How one cannot shout louder than the other. How they begin in parallel, converging as they peak, and I know that point at which they touch and cross. It is a tortured place where the world becomes surreal and from which it is impossible to return, to ever separate the lines and see again the simplicity of those strands. When love and hate are fully grown they are one.

I wonder if there's now a part of Mervyn that hates. There must be. He's loved so long and hard, the lines must surely be touching. But I don't see it in him. I see a broken Mervyn. I see a man too afraid to say what it is he's come to say, and so of course I know what it is he has come to say. It's not what I want to hear and yet it is what needs to be heard. Someone must end this. But it can't be me and I'm not sure it can be him either.

We head for the beach, making our way through the noise of town. The act of being surrounded by others relaxes, the normality of those we pass soothes, and for a time I forget why he has come. He smiles too. Laughs at the gulls stealing food from unguarded hands, peers into the windows of art galleries and points and contemplates. To anyone watching we are an ordinary couple, on an ordinary day – a holiday perhaps – and for a while we can pretend it might be so.

"Is there somewhere decent to eat?" He asks.

"Are you hungry?"

"Not really. But we should, shouldn't we? Have lunch?"

"Okay, we'll eat."

But the sky is darkening. Storm clouds block out the sun, yet the air doesn't cool. Humidity clings fast, the pressure intensifies. People leave the beach, restaurants and cafés fill. Everyone wants to eat now if it's going to rain anyway. The first large drops fall in ominous slow motion. We squeeze into a corner of the nearest café, between wall and window, surrounded by the complaints of children dragged away from their sandcastles, the irritated snapping of their parents, too many people, too little space. I wonder if here would be a good place for him to say it. Quietly, where there can be no fuss. Then it will be done.

Mervyn scanned the menu for the third time

but failed again to register the words. A mother on the next table rocked a fretful baby, her movements increasingly desperate, jaw tight, eyes focused on the window. She moved to push a messy strand of hair away from her eyes, stopped the rocking to free up a hand and the baby screeched as though dropped. She glared. At anyone, everyone. Daring someone to tut or roll their eyes, sigh or frown.

Fuck it. He wasn't even hungry.

"Do you actually want to eat?" he said. "Should we just get out of here?"

Chrissy shrugged, pointed to the window. The rain was now heavy and vertical, bouncing off the pavements, filling gutters and drains, pouring relentlessly down the glass, subduing the squabbling voices within. A rumble, a flash, momentary quiet in the café; a collective appreciative murmur as the sky finally cracked and split.

The baby stopped crying.

Its mother visibly sighed. She smiled. At him. At anyone.

A waiter came to take their order. He left again.

They sat, crushed into silence by the proximity of others. Mervyn watched Chrissy peel an edge of plastic from the menu. He checked his watch, counted more minutes.

When you work in a high pressured world, waiting is a fraught inevitability. Even now, when essentially on holiday, it's not easy to switch off, to stop seeing the slightest delay as a problem. The café was busy, the staff harassed, it was probably chaos in the kitchens, and the atmosphere – despite the weather's release – was still charged. People were labouring in this. Those merely idling had no justification for complaint.

It would take years to learn to relax.

Retirement was, from this side of the finishing line, just another anticipated stress. He wondered what those first few days, weeks and months would be like. Chrissy had sensed what today was about. It was obvious from her silence. She wasn't going to ask him outright. Not again. Not her style to push. But what he needed most, what he really *wanted* her to say was *okay, let's do France*. Those first few steps into that unknown would be tolerable then. If she wasn't prepared to say that, the least she could say right now would be *okay, so I guess it's over*. Because he didn't think he could. But someone had to.

My cheese sandwich sits on the plate untouched. Mervyn ordered ham and that, too, now dries and curls and will be thrown away. All this noise and waiting and tension will have been for nothing. He isn't going to do the deed here. He wants me to do it for him. We've known each other too long. It seems forever. Time only really started then, at that railway station, when he found me. I don't remember that morning, but he's told me, and it's as good a starting point as anything that followed. He doesn't need to say it's over. I can feel it.

"You're not eating," he says.

"Neither are you."

"Wasn't really hungry."

The rain eases and stops. The air lifts, just a little, just enough to combine with the re-emerging sun to raise the mood of the other diners. The children no longer fret over the sandcastles they left behind and they think, instead, of the new ones they'll build. They giggle, heads together, pulling silly faces and opening their mouths to show each other half-chewed food.

The crying baby is asleep.

I realise what sound is absent. Mervyn's phone hasn't rung since he arrived. He must have switched it off, a measure of how definite this is. How absolute. We're killing time unmeasured whilst he gathers strength, disconnected from his world. Just him and me, and us.

"Still want to go to the beach?" I say.

"Yeah, yeah, let's take a walk."

I lived in France, briefly. Arrived in the heat and knew the place already, lost in the beat of a lover's guitar. Ultimately I loved the music more than its player and stayed only till the last sunset of the season. I wouldn't go back there. It's not wise to visit the same place twice, what's gone cannot be chased. But the life Mervyn paints could be anywhere. He always said it didn't have to be there, that house, that town. I wonder whether there's another place, worth a longer stay than one season, or whether we could move on together, follow the heat, keep finding the unexplored. But he's tired. He wants to stop. Pull up a chair and relax. I don't, and yet nowhere else is calling, nobody else is waiting, and this is clearly the final boarding call. After today I will be here and he will be gone and all remaining chances will have been depleted. I don't know what that will be like. Mervyn has always been there. There's only one way to keep some sand in the timer. What else is there to do? More of the same – lovers, freedom, space to breathe, and the absolute nothing I've been outrunning forever. There's not enough time to think, yet it will soon be time to talk.

Mervyn had known nothing but deadlines for more than forty years. Time in short supply was the core of his working life. He loved it, the challenge, the office buzz during those final few hours – the anger, the humour, the camaraderie. Each month his magazine became a ticking bomb and he the cool-headed hero to defuse it. But this deadline was something else. It went completely against his moral principles but he did wonder whether he could extend it – adjust the clock by a few years and try harder this time. He no longer trusted the steadiness of his hand, no longer felt quite so sure he was cutting the right wire.

The sea stretched out towards his other end point. France, retirement, the future. He and Chrissy paused in their walk, leaned against the promenade wall to scan over the heads of dedicated sandcastle builders now returned to take advantage of the wet sand and out towards the horizon. The storm clouds had blown past. Blue sky touched blue sea once more.

"Look at that," he said, turning to face Chrissy. "Fucking glorious."

"Should have brought Alice," she said. "She likes to bang on about it too. In fact, if you fancy a *real* walk, go up there, her and my mother's favourite view apparently."

She pointed in the direction of the cliffs. He followed her finger, traced the imagined vista from cliff to horizon. Yeah, it would be magnificent from up there. Houses pressed into the grassy walls of the hill, their white walls reflecting the sun's touch. He could always just stay here. It was an option as viable as any other at this moment in time. They could sell Chrissy's place, buy something with a view of the sea, one of those little white houses – they didn't need much space, just the two of them – or something higher up, maybe there was something substantial right at the top.

"I could live here," he said.

"It's not always sunny," she said. But she linked her arm through his and they leaned again on the wall to face the horizon.

I shouldn't have mentioned Alice. Thinking about her whilst under this cloud of finality depresses me. Even if Alice wanted a lover now, she'd be hard pushed to find one. Most men her age were dead or dying. Anyone younger would be searching their own age group or lower – unless, of course, she were secretly loaded, which she isn't. But she's a tough old bird, could have another decade in her. Realistically she must anticipate spending it alone. I don't know what I'll do when it's my turn to grow old and unloved.

Mervyn is thirteen years older than me. These things must be viewed with long-term vision. I'm in better shape than he, my life expectancy is already greater, there's a strong chance I'd still be alone for that last decade or so. Fen is fifteen years younger, a more sensible option. There till the end, give or take random unexpected accidents and illnesses. And he is, of course, a meticulous lover. But he needs too much already. Mervyn, for all his decades of desire, has never tried to bend my will, to mould me to his ways. I am as I am. I continue to be me. Such freedom cannot be dismissed in favour of the flex of a well-maintained muscle, the placement of a skilled pair of hands, the brevity of an urge that will one day cease to hold any fascination. Not now. Not when contemplating the Alice years. Christ. Planning ahead is almost as abhorrent as the backward glance.

I should go with Mervyn.

France, anywhere. Just go, now, before the sand runs out forever.

As they pass a gallery window, Mervyn sees a painting of an old fishing boat, its wooden cabin faded and chipped, a seagull perched on its roof, glaring towards the viewer with a reddened eye. It's a good picture. It has soul.

"I like that," he says. "It'd look good in my study. Let's go in."

"Look at the size of it," Chrissy says. "You can't lug that back on the train."

But he insists and she concedes. He spots the gallery owner straightening a picture on the far wall, attracts his attention to ask about the large painting in the window. The man turns and smiles, starts to walk towards them. Chrissy lets go of Mervyn's arm and he senses her moving away, back towards the door. The air is stifling, the guy needs to install a fan.

"Hi, I'm interested in that large painting…"

I'd assumed him dead. I'd no reason to believe

him gone other than having known how little life was important to him – death, to Spencer, had always offered more – but I know it's him. Thirty four years of wear and tear cannot take away the essence of a man. I would have sensed him there had I been led in blindfolded. I watch them through the window, talking about the large painting of the shabby boat. Now Mervyn is distracted by other large paintings, other shabby boats, and together they walk the gallery walls – Spencer, long and lean, pointing out features of each, drawing new pictures in the air as he speaks, Mervyn listening, nodding, shuffling alongside.

I remember a touch, a connection which transcended words. I remember it. I was there. It happened. It formed the root of perspective for my life, the benchmark against which all else had been – and continues to be – compared. It was the curse to hinder all that followed, an ache I will never lose, a craving I've longed to satisfy. It's him, Spencer, alive.

His arms create arcs through space, eyes fixed on Mervyn's face, checking he is being heard, is being understood. He's no longer his younger self, pacing naked across the wooden floor of his studio, running one hand through long, untidy curls whilst the other paints his visions in the sky, but it's close. I can't hear them through the glass but I have the echo in my mind, as clear as though words I'd once heard were being spoken now, in there. But they're not. He isn't talking to Mervyn about the pointlessness of human existence, the fleeting glimpse, the sheer bloody nothing that is our lot. He's talking about painting old shabby boats and how best to catch the light.

And I am sixteen again.

loose ends

MARION STEPPED out of the shower, wrapped a large towel around her body and sat for a moment on the edge of the neighbouring bath. She looked down at her feet, their unpainted toenails in need of a trim, a fine edge of dry skin wrapped around the base of each heel, yet otherwise intact. Toes neat, unblemished. They were attractive as feet go, not yet swollen from the day's efforts, not pitted or mottled or calloused. They were smooth, compact, almost childish in fact, the way her toes snuggled together in incremental size. And she had good skin. She'd always had good skin. There was just a hell of a lot more of it these days.

It takes time and effort to keep a body in order. Trimming and painting toenails is an indulgence that can't easily be factored into the busy working day, not without taking away from something else, something more important. Stealing time is what turns pampering into a vanity. But when they moved to Spain – if they moved to Spain – she'd paint her toenails every day, let the varnish dry in the morning sun whilst she reclined on a padded garden chair, or maybe a hammock, a good book in one hand, a cold drink in the other. In Spain, she'd grow her hair into a neat bob, let it dip and bounce freely on bare shoulders. She'd bathe in fragrant potions, lavender, rose and lily-of-the-valley, with no futile war to be waged against the smell of frying fat. In Spain, she'd catch their scent again and again throughout the day, each floral echo reminding her how hard she'd worked, how hard they'd both worked, to reach this point. If that was a vanity, perhaps she'd now earned it.

Pete was still in bed when she walked back into the room, firmly wrapped in her thick fleece dressing gown. He was sitting up, alert, awake, and yet showing no signs of getting up.

"Shower's free."

"I've been thinking," he said, making no move to get up. The curtains wafted slightly as warm air crept in through the open window, sunlight flashing with each flutter, lighting up the faded wallpaper. "We'll call the agent today. Let's just do it."

"Sell up?"

"Yep. Sell up. You're right, it's time. Let's get this lot on the market, see the season out and then take off. Spend as long as it takes to find ourselves a nice place. Let's do it. Let's go to Spain."

Marion sat on the bed, half-waiting for Pete to shake himself out of this momentary aberration and say *no, good God what was I thinking? No.* The flashes of sunlight hit her naked feet, those untrimmed, unpainted nails sitting in their neat line patiently waiting. For time. Time and leisure and rays of sun which didn't come and go on the whim of a breeze, the flutter of a curtain, but which shone relentless and true from dawn to dusk.

"I mean, you're right, what's it all for?" Pete said. "Get up, shower, dress, work, undress, shower, sleep, get up. It's all we do, on and on."

"But *wha'll youm do all days in Spain?*" Marion said.

Pete laughed. "We've done enough. You were right, Jack was wrong. It's time for us to relax. This has all just become a habit, hasn't it? All this working, this getting up and dressed, slog, slog, slog. And maybe that's what was holding me back before but now I'm thinking about how good it'll be to have time for stuff and, yeah, time for nothing too. Warm all year, pottering around… hell, maybe even taking up a hobby…"

"Hobby?"

"Yeah, why not? Haven't had a hobby since I was a kid."

He reached out and put a hand on her shoulder and pulled her gently towards him, wrapping one arm around her, the other sneaking into the folds of her dressing gown and circling her naked flesh.

"Get off me, you silly devil," she said, trying to wriggle free.

"Maybe," he said, "we'll just stay in bed *all days in Spain.*"

He peeled open the fleecy layer which was denying desire its aim, his hands stroking her clean smooth curves, his breathing growing heavy, his grip insistent. Daylight blanched her exposed self, a shameless glow.

"Pete…" she tried to pull the gown closed, "We've still got a business to run, you know. I need to get dressed, you need to get showered…"

"There's loads of time," his voice was muffled against her breast. "God, I want you, I want you always, so beautiful, so damned beautiful…"

Marion enters the hallway. She glances round at the walls, neatly papered in geometric print. A small round table sits in the corner at the foot of the stairs holding a cream phone, its wire curled neatly out of the way. The girl with the mousy hair says "So, this is it. Here's where I live. Happy? Can we go now?"

The girl's mother appears in the hall. She smiles at Marion, introduces herself, wiping her hands on the apron tied to her waist, pushing a strand of hair from her flushed face. She's cooking dinner. The steam from the kitchen hovers at ceiling level, creeping into the hallway. The mother pulls the door closed behind her. "Hello" she says, "You must be Marion. It's lovely to meet you at last."

Pat stays back, leaning against the banister like a gangster's moll. She sniggers at the mother's pretence.

The girl with the mousy hair gives her a look.

They listen – the mother, Pat, the girl – to Marion as she answers politely, tells the mother how well her parents are, and that business is good, and yes she's looking forward to starting at the grammar school after the holidays. But also they listen – the mother, Pat, the girl – for the father, his footsteps, which might, at any moment, sound from the kitchen. He's in his shed. The girl with the mousy hair glances at the kitchen door and waits.

The mother tries hard to be kind to their guest. She even invites her to stay for dinner but the girl quickly says "She can't, they're expecting her back and I have homework to do."

Marion says "I could phone them" but the girl repeats "I have homework to do".

Partly this is true. Woebetide her if she's tardy with homework and her father finds out. But mainly the girl with the mousy hair wants Marion out of the house and away. She's only let her come to put an end to the asking and if her mother would just stop with the niceties and act more normal, it'd be enough, this glance, this proof there is a house, there is a mother.

"You'd better go now," she says to Marion and ushers her back to the door.

Mervyn sits on the sitting room bay windowsill, one shoulder pressed against the pane, staring out as though there were a view. Chrissy raises her camera, focuses on his profile, shadowed, caught between the light of the window and the dimness of her parents' living room. It's a noble profile, strong chin, a hint of jowls to come, firm Jewish nose and long-lashed hangdog eyes fixed now on a future in which she won't exist. It is the profile of a man who copes, a man who will survive.

"For a minute, back there, on the beach," he says, into a room whose sparseness amplifies his quiet pain, "I thought you'd decided to come with me."

She lowers the camera. A pause. A brief silence. A last moment to look left, look right, survey these two clear paths, a final chance to choose.

"Yeah. For a minute, I thought that too."

"What changed your mind?"

She raises the camera again, crouches down to the floor, zooms in once more on the face of a man who is part of her, as fixed in her life as he is, now, in the lens. He turns, the machine obscuring his view, filling the space between them – a heartless interloper – protecting her from the urge to just wipe this sadness from his eyes, to comfort, soothe, to quell the sheer finality, turn it all around, make it good again.

"Don't look at me, look back out, it's a good shot."

He obliges. Stares back through the glass, at something. For a moment she tries to work out what, but professional autopilot takes over and she grips, twists, adjusts distance, time, focus, snap, snap. Still he looks, still his proud profile obeys, defeated, strong, snap, stronger than any man she's ever known. Snap, snap. Colour is wrong for this, it needs to be monochrome, warts and all, his skin as it appears, aged, large-pored, the slight shine on receding brow, lines drifting out from the edges of his sorry eyes, as though wiped, stretched, gently teased into melancholy curls by a loving finger. The lens is her eye now, safer that way, and he, Mervyn, this man who's been present forever, an object, a view, a composition to be perfected and stilled.

"I love you, Merv."

"But not enough…"

He's the father she's never had, the brother, the constant friend. He's been there, always there, solid and true and, despite how others might view his appalling track record with wives, he's her a hero, dedicated, true, a committed lover. He's been prepared to give her everything. And it's still not enough.

The girl with the mousy hair arrives and sits on the edge of the harbour wall. She sneaks a glance at Marion who's smiling, gazing dreamily into the murky water below.

"*I don't think Pat's coming,*" *the girl says.*

Marion's smile falters. She looks up from the water, turns her gaze onto her friend.

"Good." It's almost a whisper.

The girl with the mousy hair says nothing. In a way, it's better that Pat and Marion hate each other. In a way, she enjoys knowing they aren't ever there, behind her back, having fun together without her.

"Well?" she says to Marion. "How did it go?"

The smile returns.

"It was lovely. We went to the pictures, saw Cabaret, fantastic, you'd love it."

"And then?"

"Came back on the last bus, sat here for a bit actually, talked for ages, about all sorts. And then he walked me home."

"And?" The girl wiggles her legs like a kid and tugs on Marion's arm,. "Come on, tell! Did you… kiss?"

She hisses out this last word and nuzzles her face into Marion's hair. They giggle, and now the girl has completely forgotten the disappointment of Pat's absence, there's nothing ahead, there's nothing behind, there is only this moment and it feels good.

"Yes," Marion blushes, "Just once. It was lovely."

Forever had never been closer than there, in town with Mervyn. Had he not spotted that painting, in that window, at that moment, I'd have said it. Yes, to France and the future and settling for all that's comfortable and safe. Yes, to the cessation of moving on, thinking momentum is somehow progression. I'd almost said it. Yes.

Then Spencer. There. Like Beelzebub himself. Now Mervyn has gone, back to London, forward to his future, and I have never felt quite so alone. It's right that he patch things up with Mrs Levy IV, she's waited long enough, he's waited long enough. Together they'll head into the winter of life. They'll be okay. Most people are content to be content.

For me, it's autumn and I'm grasping out to catch leaves on a windy day. All the half-hearted attempts at happiness, all that drifting, have come together in a frenzied peak where everything that is, is not, may be, could have been, once was, is spinning past and I'm just grabbing. Grabbing, with no clear vision of what I want to catch, yet knowing I've got to catch *something*.

I'm still that girl with the mousy hair.

I'm still that scared child, too afraid to love, too afraid to *be* loved, too concerned with pinpointing the exit door. There would have been no exit from France. There would only have been forever, increasing expectation and need, and the doors would have closed one after another after another.

Alone.

I'm not sure it's such a bad thing. It was always too easy to know Mervyn was there, where he'd always been, a bolthole, a place to run when *alone* began to compress. He deserves more.

It's time to stop grabbing.

Time to let life's leaves fall where they will.

It's right that people pass out of your life. Not all will stay. Some come for a brief moment, like Fen, and perhaps what we take from them is the strength to move forwards. Others, like Mervyn, come for longer, appearing here and there as if there'd been no gaps. From them we learn who we are. Like it or not, that's what they teach us.

I've thought about my mother. My heart breaks to accept how little I gave her, how much I took away. I look at Alice now with my mother's eyes and see a reason to stay. My mother, even in my absence, was there for me, always. She was one of those constants. It's late, but I think she's teaching me who I am. But my father. He was a fleeting presence and yet I've carried his effect with me always. Time to let go. Time to see him as the brief moment he was and steal the strength to move forwards. Time to banish his memory and focus on the future.

The shed door is still locked.

The man at the hardware store makes a joke he's probably made a thousand times as I pay for the crowbar and heavy lump hammer. He asks if I want a SWAG bag too. He laughs. I laugh too and buy an empty petrol can instead. His eyebrows raise slightly but he obviously doesn't have any jokes left, so takes my cash and wishes me good luck.

I won't need luck. Just fortitude and a prevailing wind.

Breaking through the timber door is easier than I imagined. The wood is dry, neglected, and once I've made the first indentation, cracks away in long splinters with each jab of the crowbar. It seems to welcome the destruction, as though it's held its secrets too long.

Wrenching off the first full timber board releases the door, which leans towards me, thick fusty air escaping through the gap. I yank it wide with the hook of the crowbar, kick it back against the shed's outer wall, pin it open with the lump hammer.

I stand for a minute or two, unable to enter, unable to look away. The years evaporate and I feel I should be shrinking, reverting into that small girl with mousy hair who peeks into the dusty gloom, moments away from her father's cold grip. I glance round, as though he might be there, creeping round from the side of the house, but he's not. And I don't shrink. I am not that girl. I am a grown woman in her fifth decade, dirty and sweaty from hacking at the door of a shed that now looks small, unimposing, and empty bar the dusty workbench, a few old tools hanging on nails, and twenty years' worth of cobwebs.

It's easier to demolish from the inside, to push the walls out, though the air is dry and hot and makes me nauseous. But I daren't stop to get water, cannot break this momentum, and so I lash out with the hammer. Each strike cracks through brittle planks and I swing in wanton fashion, hitting, just hitting out, revelling in creating air holes on all four walls.

I stop.

Catch my breath.

Wipe sweat from my eyes.

Then I begin again. Systematically forcing nails to give up their grasp, release those walls, panel by panel, let the past fall away and litter the ground, let it lie where it falls, covering the grass in wanton disorder, an insignificant pile of junk.

I gather it up and I burn the lot.

beyond the muse

SPENCER COULD TELL within the first twenty seconds which customers would buy and which would just piss him off for half an hour before leaving with nothing. He was rarely wrong. Beyond this, buyers could be broken down into two sub-sets. Those for whom the desire to spend was the main focus – they were easy. Irritating, but easy. A group loved and targeted by marketing departments everywhere – sale offers, two-for-ones, limited editions. People on whom the words 'bargain', 'new' and 'reduced' had been clinically tested, measured and subsequently inflicted. Gluttonous consumers for whom acquisition alone was the primary force. A drug. A buzz. A high from which they wished they'd never drop. These were people whose attics and wardrobes bulged with unwanted excess. The trick with this mob – already of a firm mind to spend – was, of course, to persuade them to spend more.

It passed the time.

The second group was trickier, but more interesting. These were the cautious buyers. They had money to spend, they were prepared to spend it, but they wouldn't do so recklessly. They were above obvious manipulation. These people considered themselves intelligent, savvy. Once in a glorious while knowledge did lie behind their deliberations, but more often than not they were the same ignoramuses, wearing coats of pretention. The parting with cash/receiving of goods deal was not quite enough. In return for their custom they wanted to leave with the item and the satisfaction of an intellectual battle won.

Customers were a fucking pain.

This guy, today, was of the latter kind. Well-groomed, angular, in deck shoes and casual trousers, a sharp crease pressed down the length of each leg. He carried himself stiffly and was accompanied by a cool, detached-looking woman to whom he addressed his genius.

"No, no, the light's all wrong, darling. The artist was clearly having an off day." He steered her away from the painting which had caught her eye and stood her in front of another. "Now, take a look at this. See? Superb balance, sublime colour, glorious light – puts me in mind of Hockney."

"Perhaps so, Giles, but it won't do at all for the library."

"Well, yes, of course, I *know* it's not suitable for the library – though one might argue the room must not dictate the art – I'm merely saying one must consider the work with a *discerning eye.*

We're not selecting cushions, my sweet. One does need to understand what it is one's looking *at*."

A quick scan of the walls and Spencer upped the guy from the five hundred pound work he was now contemplating to one of greater aesthetic merit – and cost – a few feet further round the gallery wall. Delicate handling was required. Timing was key, pleasure coming, as it did, from the execution of the challenge rather than the sale itself. Though he did feel today he might be in line for the double.

A better morning than he'd anticipated.

"Ah. A *connoisseur*," he said, approaching the couple, placing himself between them and artwork. "A desperately rare quality in a client, and certainly one to brighten my Tuesday morning." He held out a hand. "Spencer Greene, Artist of Occasionally Off Days."

"Gosh, how clumsy of me," the man said, taking it. "My apologies."

"Not at all, not at all, a valid and insightful point. Fortunately for me, others do not have your informed eye and will merely be attracted to the essence of their holiday caught and contained on a four by two canvas, fortuitously priced."

He pressed gently against the woman's arm, gravitating her forward, back to the original picture, the man instinctively moving alongside. Stopping in front of the painting, he paused for their attention, looking first at one, then the other, before settling his eyes on the woman's.

"Most are only looking for something pretty to hang on the wall," he said. "To catch an echo in their minds, the faded glory of a history they misremember. To experience the auditory recall of standing out there, in the sun, viewing the craft in question, alive, real, creaking and leaning into the harbour's arms as the tide sucks at its hull."

She maintained eye contact well. An intensely sexy trait. He looked away, broke the spell. The man shifted position, the squeak of his deck shoes interrupting the pause. He coughed. Spencer waved a hand in slow arc across the painting, stopping at a point to the left: the flaw, the blemish on his otherwise immaculate conception.

"Most do not notice this."

He looked at the man. The woman's silence was beautiful. Another attractive quality, and a depth not immediately apparent when she'd entered the gallery. The man straightened, features expressionless but eyes bright with satisfaction.

"Uncle on my mother's side," he said. "Art historian. Many a happy summer spent at his place in Oxford, learning, listening. Had no son himself, you see, think he rather hoped I'd follow his line. Alas, I was seduced by law – a tempting mistress – yet a fragment of my heart will always remain with that first love. One keeps one's hand in where one can."

The morning's promise blossomed, the

challenge unfolding with each tick of the clock. Spencer wondered whether to set himself the additional goal of a deadline or allow the experience its chosen span – enjoy the moment for its natural length. These days were few, such pleasure a diminishing luxury. How many years now? Twenty five since he first put the key in the lock, another to amass the first stock of this crap, and a long twenty four spent turning out more of the same, standing here second-guessing each purse or wallet to cross the threshold.

"I see what you mean," the woman said, still staring at the flaw. "I truly hadn't noticed, but I do see it now. You were right, darling."

Spencer caught the smug twist of the man's mouth, there for a second before it was corrected. The woman had such wonderful skin – another weakness of his – and a tempting promise in her eyes. Spencer considered upping the stakes. Going for the triple.

"Are you staying locally?" he asked.

Twenty five years ago this had seemed the right thing to do. The only thing if he were to survive, financially and mentally. There was an argument to validate the choice he'd made – a good living, a comfortable life – but he'd long since ceased to debate it with himself. He'd sold out. Nothing less. Every cell in his subconscious knew it. There was no effective counterargument late at night, in the dark, alone. To despise these people was to despise himself, only a fool could think otherwise. He created the shit, they bought it – one could not be scorned without the other. But it passed the time to believe he was somehow still removed from the frivolous concerns of the masses. Even though tonight, when he turned the key in the lock for the nineteen thousandth time, it would strike him, as it always did, he was one of them now. He'd been one of them for a long time.

Being one of them required him to play the game. No point dragging his feet through a mire of regret and finishing last. He'd made his choice, he lived with it, and would continue to do so. What else was there?

He'd walked the couple through most of the gallery. The window display was an ever-changing range of his work from all price bands, but the gallery itself was split into three distinct sections. In the first third, paintings up to two hundred pounds, affordable by most who ventured in. The second, in the middle of the room, displayed works ranging from two hundred to six hundred. But it was the third section – at the rear and beautifully lit – to which he now manoeuvred them. His prime display. No visible price tags here.

Giles, for all his irritating qualities, provided the sort of intellectual workout Spencer had grown used to doing without. Giles was it seemed, when he relaxed and ceased to be quite the lawyer, a man of many interests. His knowledge of art was comprehensive. Clearly his first love had been influential – the law must have been one hell of a mistress to compete and win. There was no urgency, Spencer moved them slowly through the gallery, allowing conversation due space.

"I must say you're one of my more erudite visitors," he said. "Tell me, what possessed you to choose law over art?"

Giles smiled. "*Ius est ars boni et aequi.* I took it to heart."

Spencer laughed, placed a hand on Giles's back, steered him towards the intended purchase. Amazing how good he'd become at this over the years, recognising what a client *wanted*. Almost instantly. Almost as soon as they'd entered his domain. Despite its flaw, the man had been drawn to the first painting – a rotting gillnetter, lying in low water, waiting for the returning dawn tide. It had been the first thing to catch his eye, as well as his wife's, when they'd entered the gallery. It was always important to watch them as they came in. But of course this astute customer had noticed the imperfection almost immediately, and so had moved on. The painting onto which he moved had certain similarities.

As did this one – the one they would ultimately buy.

"I'd be interested to hear your opinion," Spencer said, stopping in front of it.

"Ah." Giles paced and paused and paced again. "Yes, yes, *marvellous*, absolutely marvellous. Take a look at this, darling."

His wife was looking a little bored now, though it didn't distort her beauty. Possibly she was thinking ahead to lunch, perhaps contemplating the evening's entertainment. They were hosting a small soiree at their place on the cliff top, she'd told him. *A few select friends and acquaintances, nothing formal, we're very easy when we're here, aren't we Giles?* She'd started to say more, but her husband had finally remembered the name of his old master and was keen to know if Spencer did, indeed, know the chap. He was fairly certain she'd been about to ask him to join them.

The triple was still a possibility.

Timing was now critical. Leave them alone too long and one might distract the other, focus on the purchase could be lost. Rejoin them too quickly and they'd feel rushed, may even spot the manipulation, and the game would be over.

Through practice he'd discovered the time taken to go to the store room, find wine and glasses, open and pour, place on tray and return to the gallery was ample. Perfect even. Not least withstanding that having accepted the offer of a glass, they were unlikely to leave before he got back. Although this had happened. Twice. But that was years ago. He'd perfected his approach since then.

He returned with the drinks. As anticipated, the timing was perfection – they were discussing exactly where it should hang as he approached. They turned to smile, take their wine and tell him yes, it was perfect, exactly right for them. The men shook on the deal, the matter of price quietly stated by Spencer, brushed away as inconsequential by his client.

"Caroline and I were wondering," Giles said, "whether you'd care to join us this evening? As she said, just a little get together, very informal. A few people coming I suspect you'd find interesting."

A woman came into the gallery. She looked expensive, though her sunglasses hid any immediate reaction to the artwork on the walls, which was a pity. He didn't like to miss that all-important first minute. But he was keen to wrap up this deal and only half-watched as she walked the room. She seemed in no hurry.

"I'll be with you shortly," he called. She waved a hand in acknowledgement but didn't turn.

It's easy to spot the long-married couple. Just as it is to see which of them is the dominant partner.

The long-married have a way of affirming individual comments that cloys. Speak to one and you find you're speaking to both, a habit borne of too many years as half of their whole. The constant verification bounces between them like a tennis volley, sustaining their adopted roles.

"It would be lovely if you could come," Caroline said. "Wouldn't it, Giles?"

"Absolutely. Though we mustn't press, darling, I'm sure Spencer is a busy chap and we don't want him to feel in any way obliged."

Giles and Caroline had clearly been married decades. Perhaps they'd each gone into the relationship as equal, with little expectation beyond happiness, and had merely drifted into their respective roles. Or maybe they'd recognised them in advance, willingly evolving into them over time, to a point where they no longer felt any connection with their independent younger selves. It was possible they no longer even remembered having been anything but one half of that whole.

"It's very kind of you," he said. "I'd be honoured."

"And partner, obviously," Caroline said, "if there's somebody you'd like to bring..?"

The long-married don't understand, until it's too late, the contradiction between how strong they feel as two halves of a whole and how vulnerable they actually are. Somewhere, in the recesses of minds conditioned to recognise their situation as a healthy normality, lie the remains of that younger independent self, the remnants of being discovered as such, desired as such, pursued and claimed as such. As with anything, it's a matter of timing. One momentary meeting, one intriguing stranger who looks beyond the couple to see its separate entities, one direct stare into one set of eyes, one considered comment addressed to one receptive mind, and either half of any whole is reminded of the individual they once were. It can be a dangerous realisation.

Time to clear the room of this unwittingly fragile couple. Too great a pause had elapsed since his new customer had walked in. She had ceased moving around the walls, did not appear interested in any specific painting, and had walked over to the counter where he and the couple were still standing. She looked familiar, though people did. But her hair and sunglasses covered much that could be recognisable. It was hard to say. There was *something*. The way she moved, for one – smoothly, comfortably, like a cat stretching on a warm windowsill. It reminded him of youth, its fluidity, its lack of pain. Not until a person becomes older do they realise how glorious the body once was, how easy it had been to live inside young skin, move supported by flexible limbs, think through a mind that did not forget. But there was something else. She was almost *too* familiar. Her scent, perhaps? An aura? *Something* was niggling.

He'd probably slept with her once.

It happened. A surprising number of lone women came during the summer, thinking they wanted solitude. Somewhere to recover, perhaps, from a broken heart, yet really they were looking for more of the same, another opportunity to screw the wrong man, notch up another regret. Some women were compelled to keep repeating their mistakes. This he knew. He'd spent decades enjoying them.

He was left alone with her now. Asked if he could help, had anything in particular caught her eye? She didn't answer. Reached into her bag instead. A large soft canvas pouch with drawstring top, the sort of thing you'd see on the continent – relaxed, practical, and yet still smarter than the garish accessories of choice closer to home. British women are careless with the detail. She was clearly from elsewhere. European, granted, but definitely not here.

Her mouth. He knew that mouth.

She took out a camera, placed it on the counter.

A vintage Hasselblad.

A familiar camera.

His camera.

The memories of youth clicked. Clear, focused, a series of shots – one, two, three, four, five, six, seven. Her, him, the old studio in Wheelwright's Lane, the darkness, the light, the love, the frenzy of living, working, breathing, believing. It was all there, caught in the space between them – an almost tangible inspiration, the sort he'd once known. A compulsion, a consuming force to drive the crafting of the absolute. To capture it before the image evaporated, the muse retreated.

"Jesus Christ."

He touched the camera, picked it up, turned it, examined, felt its weight, admired the angles afresh. She removed her sunglasses. She still hadn't spoken, she just stood, watching, waiting, whilst he reconnected with the past.

It wasn't her past he could now see. Nor the past they'd shared together, those exhilarating months of passionate belief. It was the space between her leaving and her being here now. He stared at her face – those eyes, that mouth – and saw the gallery without even turning to look. Its walls of commercial trite, the colours all wrong, all wrong. And backwards, years of this shit, to a time far gone when art had been just that. Christ.

She'd seen the creations of that tangible inspiration. Had once seen inside his mind. No wonder nothing here had caught her interest.

last year's man

I'M WAITING for him to tell me this isn't his work. That he's just helping out, this is some sort of artists' cooperative and he's merely doing a stint at the till. Upstairs, maybe, is the real art. Upstairs, maybe, is where his work is displayed. Or that it's an intended joke – some kind of ironic statement – this trite spectacle, this abhorrent farce. It's an installation, a statement on commerciality, a mockery of the masses. Yet I know he isn't going to say this. This is his work. This is it. This is what he now does.

It's not awful. The paintings are skilled, the subjects much loved by the buying public. This is not tat, but it is not the work of the man I knew. Now, confronted by him, this awful reality, these harsh conflicting truths, I am without words. I walk the walls again, perhaps hoping to find a hint, *something*, a tiny brushstroke to echo past brilliance. But there is nothing.

"Is all this yours?"

It's the first thing I've said and the sound comes from elsewhere, somewhere deep, somewhere long past and if I sound alien to myself, how must I sound to him? He shrugs, doesn't take his eyes off the camera, holding it, turning it, feeling the quality, admiring its bold shape.

"It still works," I say.

"As it should. You've cleaned it regularly, I presume?" he flicks open the view finder. "These beauties will go on forever with the right amount of love."

I can't keep getting the snapshots wrong. He did exist. This is not false memory. The first night with him, as lovers, has remained in my mind forever. It seems implausible now, looking at all this, but I know it was true – that girl, that life, that artist, that room. Lying on a silk patchwork, thrown over an oversized sofa – third or even fourth hand, it doesn't matter now – the dirty blue woodwork, ochre walls, the lack of furniture. The badly fitting curtain at one end where he had his dark room, where he worked in a red glow that lit up his face like a devil's whilst I sat, back tight against the wall, peeping through the gap to study his shadows. I went there many times as a student. On the night we became lovers, he wasn't working and I wasn't observing. Though I was, in many ways, forever his student. The curtain to the dark room was ajar and he motioned me to sit on the sofa. He rolled a joint.

"It'll relax you."

He handed it across. I inhaled, exhaled too quickly. He laughed.

"No, no. Like this."

He held in the smoke, his eyes closing, head tilting backwards, before exhaling slowly, smiling, eyes re-opening lazily, focusing on me. Only on me. The memory is clear. It couldn't be clearer. It cannot be a falsehood. He'd been almost too beautiful, a person needed to avert their gaze. He was like a fallen angel.

His old studio is more real than any other memory I have. I loved that room, the time we spent there as lovers in that large womb lit by candles, infused with cannabis and sex. The most delicious combination. But a fleeting truth. Eventually I would go home, the odours would fade. Eventually it would never have been. Yet I do remember it. Perfectly. As though it *had* somehow been captured, without need for camera or pencil or brush, and had not been allowed to fade and die as other memories do. It had sustained me to know I had once loved. There'll be no faith left if it proves to have been a lie.

He studies the camera again, points it at me across the gallery, gazes down into the view finder. A press of the button and the shutter moves with a firm resonance. It is the finest of cameras, he must have missed it. But that click, glorious and purposeful as it may sound, is worthless. There is no film inside, there will be no stored memory. This moment did not therefore exist, is gone forever, or will be poorly remembered in days, months, years to come, or mixed up with another memory, another lover, another place. This has happened before. It's not possible to trap things tightly enough. Perhaps all the memories are wrong. Perhaps my vision of us as lovers is as much a lie as it seems a truth. Once more, I know nothing for certain, only that this second, now, is here, and then gone. It is always the way.

"I don't recognise this work," I say finally, looking around at the walls of sameness. "I can't see anything of you in it."

"It pays the bills."

"But that was never what it was about."

"Ideals?" he said. "Ha. Naivety more like. We all sell out in the end, become part of the machine – artistic merit irrelevant, branding everything. It's an unavoidable truth."

"You can't believe that."

He's silent for a moment. The air feels solid, taut. I want to leave but I cannot go with this unanswered question. He moves behind the counter, takes a drawing pad and pencil from a shelf underneath, sketches rapidly across the page. A quick portrait of the camera, perspective exquisite, proportion perfect. The merest effort and yet an instant display of skill, wantonly tossed off, careless and so beautiful. He turns the paper towards me.

"Imagine," he says, "I was, as my last client so kindly intimated, a Hockney. This sketch, unsigned? Nothing, worthless, a frivolity. A small amount of graphite, one sheet of quality paper – no proof it was drawn by me – and neither material can be reclaimed for its individual worth. Sentimental value only. Is it art? It isn't *worthy* art."

He sounds more like himself.

He spins the paper back again, signs his name, an angry squiggle I've never forgotten, the final E curving back upon itself to encircle the rest.

"But now," he says, handing it to me, "a rare Greene. Still-life pencil sketch, a light-hearted piece from two thousand and seven, a glimpse into the private, the personal. A thing of value – a grotesque sum, in fact, far exceeding the effort that's for sure. It becomes worthy – for its rarity, its possible meaning, for its obtuseness. Signed, this will be fed into the machine without quality judgement. But is it art yet? Does it mean anything? There's no ethereality, no soul, it says absolutely nothing, it becomes what its owner wants it to be – something pretty for the wall, something to brag about at the golf club, an investment for the future. Hockney and his ilk could crap on a plate and it would sell. I paint rotting boats. It's a game. You grow up, you realise that."

We became lovers, I think, because I became his muse. There's an argument to say a person shouldn't fuck their inspiration, but it wasn't a view Spencer held. Quite the opposite – for him I was fuel, I had to be consumed, possessed, penetrated, permeated. It was not enough for me to be there, in the room, close and in reach. It was not enough to talk and touch, to kiss. He needed to devour me – we needed to devour each other. Just as I was his muse, so he was my strength, my secret source of power against life, the world, against myself. We charged each other. A sublime force. If there'd been a way for two to become one, we would have done it. No matter what the cost.

Before then, I'd only been in his studio as an eager student. He would often be focused on a detail, a minor point, a technical thing. I'd observe. Always observe. Silently in the main, though often I'd ask a question to prompt another flow. But something changed that night and I can't even remember what I'd said. His focus expanded, the small things no longer mattered, it was the vastness of thought that took him. It took me too. He paced the room explaining. So alive. When he'd finished, he came back to the sofa, sat on the floor, trailed a hand across my face. He was trembling, his eyes were wild.

"It's you," he said. "You've done this, see?"

He took the joint from my hand, placed it in the ashtray and lay beside me. We touched at every point, binding together like twisted rope and it was both unexpected and yet also known that we would make love. There were no words, only the unspoken peeling away of unwanted fabric. Only touch, flesh against flesh, eyes unblinking, fixed. Only him, me, us. Words were redundant. Every lover since has talked and it's a comparison I can't ignore. It's there, always, each time they open their mouths and suggest something or ask for something or even say *I love you* or *I want you.* Words, words, unnecessary words. Then I think of Spencer, and it ruins the moment. I always think of Spencer. It's kept him with me for three decades. When I remember it now, it can still make me cry. Him. Me. The way we knew all that could be said. The way we didn't need to say it. It has to be a truth. Because if it isn't, then I've never had anything.

"You always said people filled their lives with too much stuff," I say.

"It is fact."

I wave an arm around the gallery. He shrugs, pushes hands into pockets and walks slowly towards me. I see him assessing the years, trying to find the girl he remembers, just as I search his face, mouth, eyes, to find the man I knew.

"You said it was how they avoided the truth, by filling their lives with love and work and finance and business and politics and war..."

He laughs. Quietly, head down, one foot scuffing the floor.

"... and religion." I say.

"Yeah, sounds about right."

"*That comfortable lid*, you called it. *The place where all thinking ends.*"

"You clearly have a better memory than I."

I walk deeper into the room, towards the expensive end. I can see this is his best work, yet it is more of the same. Just bigger, more complex, well lit, expensively framed.

"*I've seen life for what it is*, you said."

I look at him. I want to see a flicker, a wince, a reaction. A sign he remembers, knows, can see what I now see.

"Do you remember what that was?" I say.

"I talked a lot of crap. Youth. It's a long time ago and no, I don't care to remember, I don't dwell on the past. Counterproductive, don't you think? We can't return whence we came. It really is so *good* to see you. Can I get you a glass of wine? I have a bottle open, wait here, don't go." He puts out a hand. I think he might touch my arm and I step back. I don't know why.

"*An ephemeral sense of urgent hope. Nothing more.* That's what you said."

He stops, hand still outstretched as though he might touch. I catch the flicker I sought. A brief shadow across his eyes, a suggestion of depth still at home.

"Yeah, yeah, sounds like the right sort of pretentious crap for my youth." He lowers his hand. "Let me get that wine."

"What's it like, in your head? What do you see?"

"I see everything." He takes her hands, pulls her slowly around the room, he walking backwards, naked, eyes shining. *"Everything. And in seeing it all I recognise much of it is nothing. The whole is too vast. Too, too vast for any of this minute stuff to matter."*

"I don't understand. What's 'the whole'?"

"It's a matter of perspective, don't you see? Viewed from down here… well of course it looks like it matters – it's all around us, it's all we see. But from up there…" He points out of the window into a sky that seems blue but which he says is not, and she follows his finger, feels herself unsteady as she focuses on the softly floating clouds.

"Up there. Think it through from up there," he says. *"Imagine you're an enormous lens zooming out from the world at a distance others can't even contemplate. A place where small measures of time do not exist. Where you can't see houses and roads and fences and cars and people and industry. Where you can't see borders, strategic alliances, or information travelling through fibre optic cables. A place where there is only emptiness. The sheer bloody expanse of nothing; human existence no more than a fleeting blip so insignificant it doesn't register. Our world is nothing, we are nothing, all the effort is nothing. For me, there's only one thing to do - pan back into this world, the grey faces of those trapped in its machinery, and capture them in the context of that truth."*

It was vast. He made it so. I believed every word. Held onto them, even when all else was forgotten. I carried his vision with me – I've always kept it – those words have sustained, defined and guided me. I wonder when he sold out. When he stopped believing it himself. When he became part of that mechanism – the grey faces, filling space, filling time.

"What happened to your Dark Works?" I say.

"A long time ago," he says. "Worthless shit. History."

He's walking away, across the room towards a door that presumably leads to the wine he has offered. I'm struck by the thought he may walk through that gap and vanish, and I will be left here, in someone else's gallery, surrounded by the sort of painting I despise, and wondering how I came to have such a vivid flashback to a time long gone, a man long dead.

"*They are in their caves looking at shadows...*" I say.

It cuts the air.

He stops. Turns. Now I see a look in his eyes I know. Now I see the man I thought dead. Now I'm sure it was true, he will not vanish, I am living this moment and all of it was real.

"*... And I am in the sky,*" he says. "Jesus, you remember that."

Time might stop, right now, right here. A dimension long gone may open again and take us

– him and me – wrap us in its dark, cold, empty mist and just take us. We stand still, facing each other. We do not speak, but we each look into eyes we now recognise, hear an echo fill the room. The threat is overwhelming. I see it. He sees it. The silence is filled with all those words we have never needed to say. I am in danger. I apologise for having taken the camera, I don't want a glass of wine, I say, but I am sorry about the camera, it's valuable, I shouldn't have stolen it. I leave. Quickly. Before I can change my mind.

Sometimes a thing is so powerful it can only be destroyed. Sometimes you just have to break a thing before it consumes you. You're not at all sure, the breaking feels wrong, yet the drive to keep hacking is there, unavoidable. Once you've started you must carry on. Do the job properly. A half-broken thing cannot be fixed and can tempt with dangerous possibility. The trick is to destroy it fully and never glance back, or wonder, or question, just move on. It is done. It is broken. It cannot now hurt you.

I see people content with their lot and wonder *could that have been me?* Was there a point, one solitary moment in time, where I too had the choice of growing into the person who is content? If there was, if at some crucial point I stepped fractionally the wrong way, then I missed it completely. I can't possibly trace it now. I will never know where and when it was.

I don't know why I left Spencer.

I don't know why I would have broken something so beautiful. I just don't know. I'd always assumed him dead, yet I must also have contemplated him alive as well because many times I've pictured a point when he and I would meet, would reconnect. But I always knew each imagined conversation could never then happen, had been cursed by that very imagining. Scenarios we dream can never materialise. There are no prophecies. I should have learned over the years to pre-empt conversations I do not want to have by way of this method. Negate them completely by the mere act of scripting them myself, alone, in my head before they can happen for real. But we don't. We daydream desires not fears.

I've done mine and Alice's grocery shopping. I'm becoming quite adept at thinking for two, splitting the basket into halves, selecting the things I think she might like – things she might eat in large enough quantity to keep the flesh on her frame. She likes fish, so I charm the fishmonger into providing well-boned slivers of nourishing smoked mackerel, small portions, individually wrapped. He now picks out only the finest scallops because, after all, if the old lady is only going to eat four then she must eat four of the best. Alice will be able to phone and place an order when I'm gone. When she must once more care for herself. Now as I put things away, I run through the suggested menu for the week. She listens, nods, makes appreciative noises at the choices I have made. She's grateful I don't insist on her eating large platefuls of stodge. I think she's also grateful someone is making the decisions for her. I suspect she finds it hard to co-ordinate these things herself. Yet she doesn't lean on me. Doesn't expect more than can be given.

But I still feel responsible.

She's baked a cake and now makes a pot of tea. I will stay for a short while, though I am struggling to keep up a dialogue today. Spencer occupies my mind, all of it, and there is barely enough room to negotiate Alice's cluttered mental storage system without trying to recall who Phyllis Evans is and where her recent fall fits into Alice's world. She asks whether Fen might run her to the hospital to visit, *do you think he'd mind, dear?* I say I don't know, we haven't spoken for a couple of days, but I'm sure he'd be happy to take her.

"Are you alright, Christine?" she says.

I carry the teapot to the table.

"Yes of course. I'm fine."

"You and Malcolm haven't had a fight?"

"No, we haven't had a fight."

We sit and drink tea, eat cake, and I ask her what she loved most about her young Dunkirk man, just one thing. She sighs, satisfied, grateful for the chance to reminisce, puts her cup carefully back onto its saucer with a shaky tinkle. Then she retreats, gazing towards a point high on the far wall as though it were a portal for recall.

"Just one thing?" she says after a long silence. "It would be his thoughtfulness. He was such a kind young man, always thinking ahead, always considerate. Courteous, dear, you know?"

"Would that have lasted, do you think? For sixty years?"

It's a cruel question. I realise this as soon as I've asked, but there's no taking words back and to apologise would merely draw attention to the hurt, so I wait and watch her face as she considers the possibility.

"Goodness, I couldn't say, my dear. I'd like to think so, really I would, but I just can't possibly say. Do you think it wouldn't? You could be right, I suppose, but maybe not. People do take others for granted, and sixty years is a long time, but a kind man would still be a kind man, all other things remaining equal, don't you think?"

I tell her about seeing Spencer, that morning, about how different he is from the man I knew, the artist, the lover. I explain how it was him and yet not him, how my memory now feels false, distorted, how I don't now know whether I was wrong or he has become wrong, or when, or how, or why.

"I wonder if he would have changed had I never left."

"Well of course he would have *changed*, dear,

people do. They grow and mature. Being together is more than the initial excitement and newness. It's about living, sharing dreams, sharing life's disappointments too. I never got the chance with my young man, my Albert, but I couldn't have expected him to remain exactly as he'd been, especially not after the war. We are moulded by life. People grow together, sometimes they grow apart, but I would have hoped the thoughtfulness would be there, would have stayed the same, even if the man did not."

She picks up her cup again, holds it in two hands, two stiff and tired hands. She doesn't look back at the portal, but stares instead at me.

"And what did you love most about your young man," she says. "Your artist?"

I try but I can't put it into words. I can't see beyond the missing years, the enormous void between going and returning, breaking and reconnecting. Thirty four years of lost time. Thirty four years of growing together, changing together, sharing dreams, sharing those disappointments. Thirty four years that can never be reclaimed. Thirty four years that might have changed everything.

flashbacks in colour

COLLECTING FACTS was Malcolm Fenchurch's stability. A person in possession of information is a person equipped. It had always been this way. As a child he'd made lists, collected cards, grouped books in logical order – not merely alphabetical, but also within the relevant classification, by genre, by subject-matter. The playground game he hated most as a child was blind man's bluff. He found it hard to hold onto relevant details in the dark. He needed visible objects onto which he could anchor fact. Darkness was a chaotic void where thoughts swirled and collided in random panic. Everything was clearer in the daylight.

The drawback to being a compulsive fact-collector came when a particular piece of information just could not be gleaned. The frustration was intolerable. To know a fact existed somewhere and yet persisted in being just out of reach provided the sort of obsessive challenge he'd never been able to ignore. Finding Pat was proving to be one of those intangible quests. He was compelled to keep searching.

"Anything?" he said to Rose.

She sighed and shook her head, pointing with irritation at her computer screen as though it was the cause of the futility.

"Not a sausage," she said. "Nothing. And that's the *local* paper. I mean surely..?"

"You're searching on the right year? Have you gone a couple in either direction? She might have got it wrong, she doesn't remember much."

"I've searched seventy to seventy five."

"Try seventy six."

He tapped his pen repeatedly on a blank notepad, creating a swirl of dots expanding ever outwards. This hunt was probably as pointless as his reasons for doing it. Chrissy wasn't going to stay. She wasn't going to be content with settling down with him, here, forever. It wasn't as if by finding Pat, putting her memory to rest, Chrissy would transform into the sort of person who craved domestic stability. She was not one who stayed. She was already preparing to go, he wasn't stupid. He'd not remained single all these years without learning to read another's subtle clues. A person needs to spot when the end is coming, be ready and equipped to cope. Chrissy, for all her mystery and vagueness, gave hints only an absolute amateur could miss.

"If we just had a surname," Rose said, "it'd make all the difference. I could check *births and deaths* and we'd definitely find her. Can't she remember? At all?"

"She says not."

"Well, the only thing I've found remotely in the vicinity is some local businessman collapsing and dying in The Smuggler. Seventy three, December, but it's a man – chap who ran the Haddock Bar by the harbour – it's not even close."

"Wait." Fenchurch moved across to her desk, stood behind and leaned over, peering at the computer screen. "Find that again. Find it. It's relevant."

But there was no mention of girls on the lifeboat house roof. No mention of anything to remotely connect with the story Chrissy remembered, other than Jim Maddern's daughter, Marion, being with him when he collapsed. It had to be the same night. He scanned the text again, scrolled down as far as the article reached, just in case there was a clue, but nothing. Not one word to say Chrissy and Pat had been there, on that roof, wild and out of control, one falling, one rescued. Nothing.

The girl with the mousy hair and her glamorous side-kick are at the harbour. Pat in dramatic stance, arms wide, on the wall's edge – one step separating solidity from a fall into the oily sludge below, singing Can the Can *progressively louder until its echo bounces back in accompaniment. Holidaymakers scowl. That sort of rebellion they can get at home thank you very much.*

The girl with the mousy hair rests on cool stone – hands in pockets, elbows tight against ribs – egging on her friend with indifference.

And Marion isn't there yet.

They're sixteen and crackling with something, *and they don't yet know Pat has nearly reached her pinnacle, is an engine revving on limited fuel, a map with colour but no text.*

They're buttons waiting to be pushed.

For Chrissy, the mousy hair is a chrysalis, her slower wit a sustainable pace, the ability to detach a skill for life. But she sits, ignorant of this, legs dangling over the harbour wall, wishing she could be like Pat, glad she isn't.

When Pat realises Chrissy is ignoring her she sits too and their boots sway together, heads close, breath mingling in a warm murmur. They talk for a bit whilst they wait for Marion. They laugh and call her a swot because she has private extra tuition on Thursdays. But then she comes and they're pleased because she's the wadding between grit and wound.

And anyway, she's brought chips from her dad's shop.

A rare coherent memory. The sort of snapshot that fades only softly, never losing its impact, never draining completely of its colour. This memory is one of strained solidarity, the last gasp of a friendship about to expire. It's the final image of innocence in my album.

Now I sit here again. On the harbour edge, legs dangling, a cooling cup of coffee on the café table behind me. I hold the poems resurrected from my bedroom floor and cannot work out why they are only mine. I thought we'd put Pat's under there too. I don't recall the past in any form more tangible than an empty grasp into mist and I feel cheated.

I watch the tourists heading home after another busy day. Another day of activity they will fail to remember in future years. Another day of activity which might beckon to them at some distant point yet which will also remain, as my memories, the merest wisp of thought, of understanding, of having once been. Logic says moments of huge impact would be retained – memories so severe they cannot, and do not, evaporate. Lesser moments are easily forgotten. Yet I can recall that night, with Pat at the harbour. Just an ordinary Thursday, one of many, with nothing more outrageous than her finally managing to climb the harbour pillar and stand arms outstretched to view, as she put it, The Whole. Why can I remember it so clearly and yet fail to piece together that other night, only weeks later, when together we jumped the icy gap and alone she flew away?

Shortly after that ordinary Thursday, Pat started to question Spencer's mores, to feed me with insecurity, with doubts, with an urge to prove things were as I believed them to be.

She was jealous. I see that now.

Spencer had come between us in a way Marion could not. Where she had been the wadding, he was the inevitable blade – impenetrable to Pat, dangerous to me. Her take on things became my truth as she slowly ground against him. She was the strong one, I'd always known that, and she persisted – refused to settle on a diagnosis, solve the problem, draw a line under the issue and move on. What had not been a cause for concern became, for me, the *only* cause for concern. She was so rarely without solution. It scared me. Where I had seen strength and Faith, I now saw vulnerability, loss of Hope, a further cut waiting to happen. She was right, I was in danger. She was right, I was raw. By the time I realised she'd been wrong, it was too late. I'd broken it. The only thing left to destroy was us.

Dawn. Naked. Alone in the canyon's early sun.
The brief suspense between ground and flight.
Unexpected recall, memories long forgotten.
Ice. Fire. Pitch. Light.
Darkness, its shadows, the unknown sound.
Simmering spices in a half-starved mind.
First breath inhaled, ultimate breath out.
Still. Deaf. Mute. Blind.
Relentless disease, no treatment or cure.
Brief recognition in the eyes of a stranger.
Denying a question to prolong the riddle.
Faith. Folly. Safety. Danger.

Love. I've read the poem several times. It's the naive outpourings of a teenaged heart, there's no literary merit. Yet it reads, to me at least, as though it might. It's as raw as I once was. I wonder whether I shouldn't just burn these memories, remove them as I removed my parents' junk. To keep them is a weakness, a failure to accept what has gone is done. But I know I will keep them. They're proof I have loved. And there are times – have been times – when such proof might have helped, might have allowed me to love again.

I watch two girls across the harbour. They are probably the same age as Pat and I were that night. They too look brash and confident, their voices carrying, deliberately, across the void. But I know they're not at all sure. They're anxious and confused, unclear as to why they are here, what purpose they might have, what future lies ahead. Despite the glossy shine of their hair, the careful artifice with which they have masked themselves, they don't understand the games they must play. They'll learn the rules by success and failure, as we all must. With an irony reserved only for mankind, it's the failure they'll remember most – they'll love and lose, and if they're lucky they will love again.

Spencer had almost finished his Dark Work series back then, in late seventy three. Beautiful, angry paintings, placed in sequence around the walls of his studio, resting on the floor, leaving lines of paint on the boards so desperate was he to remove each from the easel, align it with the rest, fill its vacant spot with a fresh blank canvas and begin again.

But the Pat stuff started to niggle. I ceased to be quiet, to inspire, and instead began to question. How did I know he loved me? How could I be sure I was not a momentary passing interest? How could I measure what we had when I had so little with which to compare? If he could just do or say *something*. If he could open a door on his past, show me a fragment of what had once been, something in which I would find resonance and yet see difference. If he could just contrast what was with what had gone before, it might be enough. For me, I had Pat. No other. But in her I had known the most ardent of Faiths; in her I had felt the meeting of souls. It had been spoken. Often. She and I were clear, vocal, expressive. That we were inextricably connected was given and yet was not an unvoiced assumption. We felt the need to *say it*, to reaffirm regularly what we collectively knew as Truth. In its simplest form I needed to know they loved me.

Pat provided the proof, willingly. But Spencer refused. He said love was not a negotiation – it existed or it did not. He said to believe its existence required a leap of Faith, not a provision of proof.

And Pat said *if he loved you he would just say it.* But he didn't. He returned to his painting and found something spoiled. The colours wouldn't come, the shading was edged where blending was desired, the light was too dark, the dark too light, the cohesion had gone. He paced and ranted, slashed at it with a scalpel, ripping away the wet canvas and covering his hands, the blade, his clothes and the floor with dirty smudges of ivory black. He told me to leave. I was hindering, not helping. I was no longer part of the creative process. This failure was all my fault. I think of him like that still, even now. Covered in ivory black, pushing away that which he loved. I did not have a canvas to tear and destroy. I did not have a room wherein I could pace and scream and break things and cry. I did not have anything other than Pat, a stolen bottle of vodka, the long night ahead and a heart filled with venom. So we went to the churchyard, we liked it there, and I transferred the blame. My loss of Spencer. His loss of creative flow.

It was all her fault.

I told her this.

I could barely form words but I told her this. The colours converged, transforming everything.

"It was you and me – you and me against the world – before *him*..."

"You're supposed to be my *friend*," I said.

"You and me, that's what we promised, you and me always. Bitch!"

Pat kicked out. At me, at the gravestones, at the sleeping foliage growing around their bases. She looked for things to throw, but there was nothing that was unfixed, nothing that wasn't firmly rooted in the damp, cold earth.

"It's always us, that's the problem. You, always there, criticising, judging. You're like my bastard of a father – always telling me how shit I am, how wrong, how useless."

"Because I love you!"

"You don't! You're jealous I have someone."

Had we been able to stop, stand back and watch, we'd have believed ourselves already dead.

"Just fucking choose," Pat said, when we began to exhaust all meaning. "Me or him."

With the creation of anything there's a point at which a person must stop. Must recognise all that can be done has been done, that it's time to end the process of one's efforts, to mark a piece as complete. Destruction is a viable creation. To remove a thing is as valid as to place it in situ. Emptying a space as much of an art as filling it. I knew my work was almost done.

"Him." I said.

Pete had never seen this photograph album before. Again, a worrying glimpse of a past to which he had not been privy. He'd never thought Marion to have secrets, though that was perhaps too loaded a term. These were inconsequential elements of her life – in as much as one half of a couple might see consequence in the past actions of another – nothing sordid or character damaging, just events and people she'd never before mentioned. Strange rather than sinister. Omission rather than lie. But indicative of an unknown strand of her character that begged the question why she'd felt it worth hiding. Now she'd finally told him about the events of the night at the lifeboat house, he was left with a sensation of it having been a false absolution. Confession under inquisition does not taste as sweet as that freely given.

"See?" she said, flicking between two clumps of pages. "All these when we were little, less and less as time moved on. She was a lousy friend. Started college, that was it. Other people, other ways to spend the time. I hardly saw her."

She turned to the back of the album, a solitary snapshot of a female silhouetted against the sunset, standing on a stone pillar at the harbour, arms outstretched, head tilted back, hair a jagged outline falling away from curved spine.

"Don't know why I cared. You never knew who you'd get anyway – Dr Jekyll or Mrs Hyde – life was easier without her. This is the last one I have of her, just weeks before she left, that night, the night dad died."

But Marion seemed calmer now, as though the telling had been enough to expunge the worst of the hate. For her this was almost over.

"She's come back," he said. "Sought you out. Surely there's meaning in that?"

"Is there? I don't think so. She hasn't exactly come back to repent. I still blame her, I can't forget or forgive, if that's what you're thinking I should do, but I suppose talking about it at last has been a blessing. But I won't forgive her, Pete. I can't forgive her. You just don't know what she was like, how hurt I was to be left, just left, as though I'd never mattered. She wasn't there when I needed someone, she was never there when I needed her. And all these years without her, well I grew used to that, it was better. I didn't need her to come back. I didn't need her in my life."

"Any one who professes to be in the light and yet hates his brother is still in darkness." He leaned over, kissed her head. "I'm going up. Night, love."

Spencer pours another whisky. It leaps up the side of the glass, pitching over the edge and trickling down his hand. His clean hand. His neat, manicured hand. There was a time its flesh was seldom seen, when he could move through days and nights without pause, his skin an extension of each worked canvas, its colour echoing progress – *Prussian Blue, Viridian, Indian Red, Mars Violet, Ivory Black.* Those colours no longer grace palette or skin. Those colours belong to another time.

He stands behind the glass shop door and watches holidaymakers weighed down with bags of beach hut aesthetics, compulsively acquired for an urban setting. The wrong shades, the wrong light. They'll never understand beauty as context, arrangement, balance, harmony. Year upon year they'll remove pretty pebbles from the beach only to later wonder how their beauty expired.

Beyond them, buildings curl around the harbour. Uneven, cluttered, almost absorbed into the landscape, ivy grasping and pulling walls and roofs into the rocky green incline behind. Context is everything. Individually, each structure is flawed – a heavily repaired cottage, modified, extended, patched up in places with modern brick; a shed with ugly corrugated roof, tainted by dull orange rust. *Yellow Ochre, Gold Ochre, Raw Sienna, Vandyke Brown.* He's painted the scene a hundred times.

He's knocked back pigments to capture the patchwork of stone marked by damp, ingrained with the dirt of centuries, bleached where the sun touches, dulled where it inhabits shade. *Raw Umber, Davy's Gray, Naples Yellow, Bronze.* He's spent hours on this intricate process. It's uninspiring, this contemplating colour with an analytical eye. He once *felt* colours, knew them instinctively, was inspired by a context uncontrived. A context he *lived*. A wholly different way of painting.

He'd been an artist, he was now merely a craftsman. An impassive judge of light, shade and form. An objective calculator of what might sell.

A man who can break down the pigment structure of everything – a walking, breathing index; a catalogue of artistic trivia. He couldn't remember the last time he dreamed freely. Woke alert, alive. Felt his mind expanded by vivid context. Rose naked to paint in darkness. Forgot to eat, forgot to sleep, was unable to name the day. When had that beauty expired?

He pours more whisky. Spills more. He doesn't care. Barely notices the cold trickle now, so numb is his flesh. He knows where he must go. Upstairs, to the store room – past the completed paintings queuing for their moment in the gallery below, past the work in progress: more of the same, well-judged images created in appropriate moments between eating and sleeping, between the washing of hands, the ironing of clothes, the weekly supermarket shop – to a door on the far wall, currently blocked by blank canvasses, beyond which lies another storage space.

A space he has only entered once.

The day he filled it with his *Dark Works* and closed the door.

Left them to age, together, alone.

He hasn't looked at them in twenty years.

He sways a little as he negotiates stairs he's climbed thousands of times, heads to the studio where sun shines in through vast skylight windows. There's nothing in this room he cannot name, locate, instantly recognise as his. The stench of rags and brushes soaked with turpentine are as familiar an olfactory presence for him as latex and cash is for the whore; the individual note of each pigment as identifiable to his nose as the chink of coin in bowl to a beggar's ear.

He moves onwards, to the end of the room, where he hauls blank canvasses to another wall, stacks them recklessly, kicks away other random debris, clears a path to that closed door.

Opens it.

Fumbles for the light-switch.

The bare bulb is of too low a wattage to provide anything but moderate assistance for the vaguest of perusals. It's a blessing. His hand touches the sheet, feels the fabric grainy against his skin, layered with two decades' worth of dust.

He should have brought the whisky bottle.

He should wait until nightfall.

He should wait.

And so he turns, walks back into the studio and the light of an ordinary day.

dream about drowning

YOU CAN'T TRUST the memory of first love. It has to be seen in context. Whatever you think it was, it wasn't. If ever a person needed proof of the distorting effect of rose-tinted spectacles they need only go back. Revisit an old lover three decades on and see how things would have panned out. See how mundane life becomes when a person gives up on every inspirational dream from their halcyon days.

Pat did the right thing by jumping.

And I did the right thing by running away.

Yet there was still something of the man Spencer had been. There, in his eyes, when I finally got through. Though the chasm between the two was immense. I can't have got the first image right. The man I knew could never have given up. And yet he had. Therefore I have to assume what I once thought was the man, was not. That it was the projection of an impressionable teenaged mind. That it was, in its entirety, no more than wishful thinking. I'd taken away a wishful thought, which in turn became a wishful memory, a stored falsehood. The touch, the passion, his physical beauty – those things had been real. But the drive, that inner core – the things that made *him* – had clearly not.

Because the man I knew would never have given up.

Alice appeared, early, at the kitchen door with a bunch of flowers wrapped in cellophane.

"Malcolm called last evening," she said. "You weren't in so he left these. I popped them in the sink overnight, dear, keep them fresh. Aren't they're lovely?"

"Oh. I was at the harbour."

She'd also brought a large plastic jug – a colourful modern item I couldn't imagine having a place in her home. She waved it at me with a smile.

"Knew you wouldn't have a vase, dear, but didn't trust myself to carry glass."

She hadn't been right since the fall. Not properly right. I wondered if she ever would return to that stoic, fit woman, or whether this was it – this was as strong as she was likely to be for however long she had left.

I don't much care for cut flowers. An illusion of life – the brightness of their colours already on the wane the moment they're snipped from their source. The gaiety they suggest is a falsehood, revealed within hours as the first petals fall. But I peeled open the cellophane, filled the plastic jug with water and placed the stems into its palliative sustenance.

"Are you avoiding him?" Alice asked.

A flower arrangement is an artistic endeavour, of course. It's important to remember that. And in the process of creating, things do sometimes get destroyed. There can be no art without pain.

"Your young man," I said, "Albert. Do you think he was really worth it? I mean, the memory? Was it worth holding on to? You know, when you think what it might have cost?"

She waved me out of the way. Adjusted the flowers, tugging them gently to fill the spaces, turning and twisting until their heads faced forwards. But they fell naturally again to the sides, leaving a gap in the centre. The jug was too big, the flowers too few, it was not going to be a perfect display.

"We do silly things when we're young," she said. "Think silly thoughts. Everything may seem important and forever but it isn't. There's a whole life to come, new people and places and experiences and all we thought was real and lasting will be gone. A brief moment, dear, so insignificant it'll be hard to recall one day. I've forgotten almost everything about him. I don't even think it's his face I see. I never had a photograph."

She rooted in a drawer, found my mother's kitchen scissors and began to remove selected stems from the jug, trim them down and place them back in the water.

Essentially she and I were the same. That she chose to hold onto a false projection all her adult life mirrors my illusion perfectly. That she chose to spend sixty years alone is no less fulfilling an option than decades of temporary lovers to whom no sense of self will be offered. We have both created a space. Have loved and lost and avoided any repeat of same. We will both die alone and with Regret.

"You can't keep avoiding him," she said. "Malcolm. You have to tell him, dear."

She pushed the last stem into the jug. The flowers now sat perfectly, faces forwards, stems straight, small at the front, tall at the rear. The end result energetic, fresh, alive and quite beautiful in its simplicity.

Already a petal had fallen.

They're near the old lifeboat house. Pat has the vodka and she's not sharing anymore. She swings the bottle towards her mouth, misjudging speed and direction, her arm numbed by drink, anger and cold. Now her cheek is doubly wet. She's ahead of them, walking backwards so she can see their faces – "I hate you" – then turning, staggering on, up a narrow road that leads nowhere. They follow because they knew this would come. It has to be seen through. Even though it's freezing and she's hogging the booze.

Marion's trailing. She just can't keep pace. But Chrissy has never felt so alive – she's sharp, edgy, and can walk all night if she has to — she's not even cold. She's just alive. Vibrant. She's waiting for Pat to really start, and she doesn't give a damn because this has been coming forever. They reach the lifeboat house. Pat stops, as though this was always the destination, leans against the wall, dangerous, reckless. She's smiling, but it's twisted and ugly. It could go either way from here. There's a part of her that wants to be stopped. Chrissy says "are you going to share that bottle, or what?" Marion gives her a look. Pat stops smiling. She says "want it, bitch?" and throws the bottle over the wall.

Pat's hands are free now, so she climbs. The wall isn't very high, but there's a hell of a drop the other side. She points to the roof of the lifeboat house, which is just about level with the top of the wall, and she's swaying a bit. Marion looks nervous. The sweat makes Chrissy shiver. Pat shouts "on there, you and me, winner calls the shots, right?" and jumps the four foot gap, over a lethal drop onto teeth of granite and the sea's raking thirst. She's clawing at the frost and scrambling up to the ridge. Marion looks at Chrissy. She's terrified, you can see it in her eyes. But it's not as if they haven't been on there before. In summer, to watch the sunset. Sober.

Pat's at the top, straddled across the ridge tiles, hair blowing. She looks elated. "Come on then, bitch, if you're brave enough." For Chrissy, it's no longer about Spencer. It's about every challenge levelled since she was six." Can you stand on one leg? I can. I bet I can do it longer than you."

Can you sit on a cold roof?

Unless she does this there'll never be an end to it. One of them has to fall. One of them has to finally get the last word. It's perishing. The wind's getting up. The tide's coming in. Pat shouts again. Marion says "don't be stupid" as Chrissy climbs onto the wall, stands with arms wide to counterbalance the drink, the wind, the adrenalin. "Oh my God, you silly cow, you stupid silly cow, oh Christ, I'm going for dad… don't move… I'm going for dad."

Marion runs round the harbour to the chip shop, while Chrissy cuts numb fingers on the edges of freezing tiles. She's glad it's dark and she can't see the fall, only a moving shine on the water, blinking and shifting; a vague sense of the drop. But at the top, astride and facing Pat, she's big again, in control, safe. Like a giant in a fairy tale.

"That's the easy bit." Pat's voice hacks across the icy gulf. Her hair's whipping around her face, going into her mouth. "Now we sit. Now we fucking wait."

Chrissy says nothing because her teeth are tight and her jaw is aching. She has nothing to say, though her head bursts with it, and she's glad she has the advantage of the oncoming wind. She leans forward slightly, lets it sweep her face clean, jutting out her chest like a figurehead. If she could open her mouth, let the air in, sweeten her insides. But it's tight. It's so very tight.

Her hands have gone dead. She can't even feel her legs or feet now. She wonders if she's still touching the tiles, or is actually lifting away from the roof. She senses this is the end, this is it, there won't be anything more and really, now, she just wishes it would happen. Close her eyes. Float away.

They sit in the wind and darkness. It feels like forever. Invisible spray hits the walls, arcs high, scatters and falls on them like dew. Pat doesn't look so confident now. She's stopped shouting. She's crumpling – she'd probably fall if her legs weren't frozen into place – and crying. She's really crying. Maybe she wants to let go but can't. Chrissy has never seen her like this – so empty of anger. But Chrissy can't open her mouth. It's all she can do to bring one frozen hand to her face, wipe the wet from her lashes. If she could unclench her jaw, her teeth would begin to chatter, her whole being to shiver and shake, and she'd lose control. If that happened, if she lost that rigidity, the momentum of hate and fear and pain would be unstoppable. So she just watches Pat, and it hurts, but she can say or do nothing.

They're no longer soft, pliable bodies but grotesques cut from Parian marble. Hard and permanent, shaped around the frozen ridge tiles, stiff hair etched across their faces. Feelings are muted beneath the chill; shrunken by the vast blackness around them. She knows she could fly, really fly – the measured dipping and rising of her dreams – higher and higher. Defeating the cold, abandoning her body to its worldly limitations, soaring warm and easy, fast and slow, zooming in, zooming out. Pat looks up. She's had the same thought. It happens. Her fingers uncurl and she forces unwilling arms to spread, to move up and down jerkily – not the smoothness of dreams – and Chrissy watches in catatonic wonder. She unhooks her own clawed hands from the ridge, wipes the hair from her face with a shaky movement, stretches out her arms. She's trying to hold her teeth together, grimacing in a way that could be pain but could be laughter and her chin bobs up and down with the effort. It's laughter. She's laughing. Pat is laughing too. Their arms stretch into the darkness – elegant, unfurled, arced – and they glance down towards the source of the spray, the jagged bed on which their nest sits. Pat shouts "come on, let's do it. Let's fly. Just once."

The answer to everything. Disappointment, Futility, Pain. To soar greatly, just once, must surely be enough. They force dead legs to life, squat like fledgling chicks, facing across the void, bonded but mistrustful. Filled with Love and Hate but no strength for either, they call to each other in voices raw and broken.

Marion's back with her dad. He's a bit thinner than he once was but he's still too fat to climb so he runs into The Smuggler and brings out a few strong men. One is Jack Crozier who used to fish but now takes tourists round the bay. It's Jack who gets onto the roof. It's solid and almost dry. It doesn't dip and twist with the wind, doesn't keel over and make a man pray. It's a pleasure trip. Jack's glancing from one girl to the other – he can't be in two places at one time – and shouting "ROPE GET ME ROPE I NEED ROPE" and somebody must already have it because it appears near his feet just seconds later.

Just as Pat takes off.

It lands in a loose coil, clunking against the slate and slithering halfway down the roof again. In the silence between flight and fall; the brief halting of wind, sea and the jangle of the harbour – in the silence of a communal held breath. But there's no splash. Chrissy looks at the sky.

Pat must have done it. She must have flown.

Between them, the men from the pub get Chrissy down. The landlady of The Smuggler brings a blanket, wraps her up and takes her inside. She sits across from Marion in front of the fire and thaws. Marion is crying. Her dad says she has her A-levels to think about, she doesn't need this, and though she doesn't say anything, you can tell Marion agrees.

When she can move again, Chrissy says thank you to Jack and the landlady and the other helpers because tomorrow this will be all round town and her parents need to salvage something. She says she needs the toilet – "it's fine, honestly, I'm okay by myself" – walks steadily down the dingy corridor keeping her back straight, her pace even. But she doesn't stop at the entrance marked ladies. She walks through a side door which leads into the delivery yard, goes to Spencer's place because she knows he isn't there, breaks a window, opens the door, lets herself in, takes one of his cameras from the flat – it's his best one – and empties the cashbox he keeps under the counter in the studio. Then she goes home, packs a few things, and just makes the last train.

Jack Crozier readied his boat at his usual easy pace, untroubled by the customers waiting above. Ten twenty was the stated departure time and ten twenty was the moment he'd pull away from the harbour wall. Changing a routine wasn't something a person should do on a whim. A decision made in haste was, in his experience, always one for later regret. A boat must be ready, no matter whether for a harsh winter night's fishing or a beautiful summer morning's leisure trip. That meant checked, properly, with safety in mind. These things were not something the experienced sailor would rush.

"Morning, Jack." The harbourmaster waved a clipboard as he approached along the walk above. "Fine day for it."

He glanced up, called over the throaty rumble of the engine. "Aye, I dare say it do be a fine day for them what's not got work an' all."

"You're not wrong there, Jack, you're not wrong there. But there'd be no wages for the rest of us if not for those who don't have to work, eh?" The harbourmaster winked at the waiting customers. "How's the missus today?"

"As fine as this sunny morn' an' just as pretty." He replaced the cap on the oil tank, wiped his hands on a dirty rag, straightened up and stepped stiffly over the gunwale and onto the stone steps.

"I hope you told her as much."

"Tells her every day, I does." He unlinked the

chain across the top of the steps and moved back down to let the customers descend. "An' every day she says *Jack, youm be a rum old dog, youm be, but I loves you all same.*"

The customers made their way cautiously down the worn steps, holding onto aged iron railings and gratefully taking his proffered hand, despite the lingering smudges of oil, as they reached the boat. When the last was on board, he climbed back up to reattach the chain.

"Does the missus know you've got an admirer?" The harbourmaster turned and nodded his head to a woman sat at a café table close by, focusing a camera in their direction.

Jack glanced at her as he untied the mooring line from its bollard. She'd been around for days now, pointing her camera at him. If he were to find himself on a set of postcards next summer he'd expect a fee. He coiled the rope, tossed it onto the deck and waved into the camera's lens.

"Be up for a *private session* if youm payin' a fair rate."

She lowered the camera and laughed. Stood up and walked across. He had to admit she was eyeable. Might be he'd waive a fee for this one.

"You don't remember me," she said.

He glanced at his watch – ten eighteen – and clicked the chain's clasp into place.

"Gets a great deal of ansum ladies on this boat," he said. "Though yours be a face I'd not expect to forget and if I has, then more pity me. A man'd be warmed in a squall with the memory o'youm 'fore his eyes. But," he tapped his watch, "I must be lovin' and leavin', it being ten twenty an' all."

He stepped lightly back down to the boat and into the cabin, took a last glance up at the woman, standing, staring, camera loose around her neck, before upping the throttle and pulling away from the harbour wall.

I hadn't imagined Jack Crozier would remember me. There was little to recognise of the mousy, wrecked girl of a long-distant night, even if he did recall the event itself. Which I imagined he would. But there had been no time to ask. Those in work do not have the luxury of idle chat. I should have come at the end of the day, when he might have a moment to remember a time he could leap across a lethal drop without worrying about aching joints.

ROPE GET ME ROPE I NEED ROPE

A waitress brought my cup of coffee. Barely into the day and she looked weary as she replaced old with new, wiped the table with a fragrant cloth and a laze of movement to defy any real purpose.

"Enjoy your drink," she said. As though without instruction I might be so forgetful as to consume it without notice. As though with platitude I might believe she cared.

She moved to the next table, gave it a token swipe with the cloth, pushed in wayward chairs and returned inside. I'd been here since eight thirty. I liked mornings at the harbour almost as much as evenings. There was something satisfying about watching a town wake up – slowly, cautiously – and later, wind down, ease into sleep. Unlike cities which never stop, and rural enclaves which barely surface, the small town has a comforting rhythm. For a short stay, for a change. It wouldn't do to get stuck in a place like this and fall under the spell of such endless repetition. Wouldn't do to become part of this machine. But it was fine for now whilst I contemplated, tried to make sense of my own rhythm, my own cycle of wakefulness and sleep.

The past had always been the dream to me. That hazy, confusing whirl of colour and disjointed events. A thing that had somehow made sense at the time but afterwards was clearly wrong, clearly unstructured, clearly impossible. The first year after I'd left was my morning, the slow awakening, the hesitancy between the unconscious and the conscious. The equivocal hour when upturned chairs on tables are righted, urns are filled and switched on, ovens are warmed, mail is delivered, curtains open and the future hangs on the continuing momentum of the present.

At least this is what I'd thought.

The years since that time had been my

working day. Hectic and packed with meaning, if a person chose to find it. Movement and purpose and no time to stop and reflect, to remember two silly girls on a frozen roof, to remember the dreams of the previous night.

Zak and Mervyn and nameless lovers beyond – all had been part of that working day. All had been part of my wakefulness; life, living, alive. Spencer and Pat were figments of the night – compositions of fragmented memory, shuffled and muddled and forced into an order quite incomprehensible to the woken mind, but perfectly rational in sleep. They had been the dream. They had been the beautiful impossibility. They had been night's imagined reality.

This is what I had thought. Until yesterday. When I faced the spectre of my dreams and did not feel an ease back into slumber, did not sense the twilight drawing in, a return to rest after a long hard day. But was, instead, stirred by morning sun, revived by an early tidal breeze, lifted into wakefulness with a sense of refreshed vigour, of having slept well and long, of having cheated death and risen, victorious, clutching onto life.

Awake. At last.

This was the new morning. The past three decades were the dream.

I focus the camera across the harbour. Over and through boats and their masts. Zooming closer to the tip of the lifeboat house, just visible beyond the harbour wall. It is only a brief glimpse. To see the whole is a five minute walk around the harbour and up the lane. Five minutes waking time, to unwind thirty years of sleep. I can see part of the roof and one stone corbel. The farthest one. Not the one to which I was strapped with Jack Crozier and his rope. The other one. The one from which Pat flew. Jumped. Whichever.

It looks empty through the lens.

Now we sit. Now we fucking wait.

As though I'd expected to see her there. Her back against its rough support, her face white and wet and exhilarated. But there's nothing. Not even an idle gull or the shadow of a passing cloud. Nothing beyond the clarity of my mind's photograph – that night, that girl, that manic end.

Come on, let's do it. Let's fly. Just once.

I don't know what happened to my real snapshots. The harbour, the cliffs, the beach. Pat and Marion. The shabby buildings littering the town. The broken windows of the old pilchard factory where Fen lives now and which, without the photographs, has had no life other than whitewashed walls and luxury living. If that is the dream, what happened to the reality? Were those pictures left behind that night, to go the way of my albums and posters? Did my father burn my wakeful hours?

I'm still focused on the small section of lifeboat house roof. Still waiting for a bird to land by the corbel. But my eye is its own lens and has self-adjusted, taken the image out of focus, blurred with an effect that does little to enhance the view but everything to negate its emptiness. I sense someone beside me, lower the camera, turn my gaze.

It's Spencer. He's unshaven, has dark paint on his hands, his clothes. He smells of whisky and turpentine but his eyes are alive, radiating an energy to surpass such weariness. The high-octane pressure of the creative phase. He's been working.

He sits. Indicates my untouched coffee. "Can I?"

"It's probably cold," I say, but he drinks it anyway. I signal to the sulky waitress, order another two coffees and then, as an afterthought, ask for a couple of pastries too.

"Any kind, it doesn't matter."

I stare across the table at him. He stares out to sea, the empty cup clasped between two stained hands and pressed against his chin. He's dirty – utterly unkempt – and behind him well-groomed tourists trawl the pavement, peering into gallery windows, admiring what they see, yet oblivious to this artwork sitting facing me now. Too raw. Too honest. Perhaps they'd see him as vagrant, perhaps they'd judge him idle, too lazy to bother, too uncaring to follow the rules. For them, the smart Spencer is the plausible choice. The schmoozing salesman they understand. This shabby artist is a pastiche. A cliché. A fragment of the past. Art, like all else, is commerce and the wise creatives do not hang on to old imagery. This man is merely grubby, does not understand the world. This man is a relic of days long gone. But, to me, *they* are the spoils, *he* the seaside find. The piece of beautiful driftwood amidst the ugly tidal clutter. I want to touch him, look at him, keep him forever.

"It's the vastness I love," he says, his eyes still on the horizon. "But you know that. The sea, the sky, the sheer bloody space."

"It's the vastness I fear."

He now looks at me. Lowers the cup. "You never feared it, you *understood.*"

"I dream about drowning," I say. "Sometimes in water, sometimes the sky."

The waitress brings our drinks, the cakes. I slide both onto one plate, push them across the table towards him.

"Eat."

"Enjoy your food," she says.

I smile and watch Spencer consume without notice.

"She wants you to taste it," I say. He looks down at the pastry in his hand as though unsure how it came to be there.

"I got them out," he says. "The Dark Works."

"And? How do they look?"

"I finished that last one, the one I was working on when you left."

He puts down the cake and reaches for my hands. I laugh at the crumb and paint combination around his mouth, the manic glow in his eyes. I laugh at the impossibility of this moment, after all this time. I laugh because I'm alive.

"Then I saw you from the window," he says. "Serendipity. You in my line of vision just as I'd laid them out. That last one, finished, and you here, out of my window."

"What, and you think the two are connected?" I laugh again but watch his face. His stare matches mine and we are drawn again into mutual consumption. Nothing has changed. We are still as we always were.

"I *know* they are," he says.

Malcolm's father had always prided himself on recognising when damage limitation was the best course of action. Charles Fenchurch did not believe getting one's fingers burned should be accepted as an inevitable part of life. A situation correctly judged was a situation under control, an ability to spot the approach of stickiness the measure of a successful man.

Work on the basis they all want to shaft you. You'll not be far wrong.

Whilst there were many aspects of his father's tutoring Malcolm suffered only because he had no alternative, damage limitation awareness was not one of them. His father had been referring to clients, other lawyers, judges, politicians, tradesmen – business affairs rather than the romantic variety – but by his mid-twenties, Malcolm had clearly seen how the principle could, and should, be applied on a wider basis. Like now. With Chrissy.

She flicked the edges of a stack of papers on his desk, the movement wafting a stray sheet he'd been reading, causing it to twist out of line. She took a pen from his pot, examined it, put it down on the desk. He picked it up, replaced it in the pot, readjusted the sheet of paper. She looked around, waved a hand in the direction of filing cabinets, more scattered papers on their surfaces.

"You have a lot of stuff," she said.

"We generate paperwork. It's the nature of the legal process, generating paperwork. Not usually this messy but Rose is having a filing session."

"Oh. Right."

Few people understood how he could break off a love affair before its natural end. His friends meekly followed the long route of disintegration, arguments and withdrawal before they conceded a relationship was over. Malcolm had taken that approach once. Never again. Yet whilst his friends could clearly see how the damage limitation concept applied to their career, or maintaining a car, or buying a house, they refused to accept it could also work for their love lives.

They thought it a cold approach – especially his female friends – as though there was somehow more warmth in prolonged delusion.

"Been busy?" he said.

She walked over to the filing cabinets. Glanced at the columns of papers, stacked, waiting for Rose to return from lunch.

"Don't move any of that," he said.

"Looking after Alice," she said. "You know, shopping and things."

All relationships end, it's only a matter of drawing the line to suit. It's like when a person falls in love with, say, a particular house and leaves themself vulnerable to a shafting because the owner can clearly see how much they want it. There's always a choice. You either stick with the dream, knowing when the novelty wears off you may find yourself wondering why you ever paid over the odds – or you walk away. Sometimes you just have to recognise when to cut your losses. The point at which disappointment now is better than the same, but worse, later. Even if it doesn't always feel that way at the time. Whilst they'd never admit it, several of his friends were in up to their necks in mortgage repayments for houses they'd forgotten they ever loved, because they'd failed to walk away. Some were slowly rotting in relationships that wouldn't survive the decade either. No. There comes a time when damage limitation is the best course of action.

"Come on," he said. "Let's go for lunch."

Marion shuddered as she watched the woman on the television game show shrieking and clapping when she realised she'd won. After jumping up and down on the spot, wiggling in ways she'd doubtless regret when she watched the recording later, the woman left her place behind the podium and threw her arms around the host, still screeching, almost knocking him over, leaving a red lipstick smudge on his cheek as he finally prised her away.

Marion would, she knew, never be chosen for such a show. She was sure they must vet contestants before letting them take part. To make sure they get the screamers. It's what the audience wants. The sight of another human freed from inhibitions somehow satisfies a primitive urge in those watching. She wasn't sure whether her horror outweighed the jealousy or vice versa. All she knew was when it happened she couldn't look away and yet she cringed through every second of watching.

The doorbell rang.

"Who the hell's that?" she said.

"What am I?" Pete said, rising from his armchair. "Psychic?"

It wasn't that she was an unemotional person. Tears could be provoked with the right film, the right documentary, the right sentimental charity appeal. She was emotional enough; she wasn't a cold fish. Yet she'd never been able to let go in situations where others so readily did. Dancing, for example. She'd never been good at it, even when she was slim and fit. And cheering. She wasn't the sort of person who whooped and hollered. She was more an enthusiastic clapper, with a broad smile and a *well done*.

The woman was crying now and thanking her fellow contestants, her family, her bosses for letting her have time off work. The game show host hugged her firmly around one shoulder, all the time manipulating her to face the appropriate camera, so it could zoom in, catch her swollen face and disastrous mascara run. It was what the audience wanted. It made them feel good about life.

Pete came back. With Chrissy.

"What do you want?" Marion said.

"I was passing," Chrissy said. "And I wondered if we could go out sometime, maybe this week, a drink or something? I want to explain, put things right. I'd really like us to talk."

"Shall I put the kettle on?" Pete said.

Marion glared at him. "No. I'm tired, want an early night."

"I won't keep you," Chrissy said. "But say yes. Please. Tomorrow? Saturday?"

She had a look on her face Marion had seen before. That night. When she'd turned up drunk at the shop, swinging a vodka bottle and not making much sense, and then had left as abruptly as she'd arrived. Marion went after her because her dad said it was the right thing to do. *Keep an eye on her, love, make sure she gets home.* But Chrissy didn't go home, she went to the harbour and Marion followed, caught up, and Chrissy asked *am I the sort of person people can't love?* What a question. What's a person supposed to say?

The right answer – the answer Marion had wanted to give – was to hug her, tightly. Tell her of course she was loveable, of course she was loved. To hold her, comfort her, take away the bottle and say all the things she needed to hear. The truthful things. Just the way it was – it was not a call to lie. But she'd hesitated. Hugging wasn't an instinctive gesture. She couldn't just *do it*. And in that moment, in that bolstering pause, she'd seen this very same look in Chrissy's eyes. A fear, a realisation – a hurt that negated anything that might now be said. Marion had rushed, said the first thing that came to mind: *don't be silly*.

Don't be silly.

Chrissy backed away a few steps.

"Okay, you don't want to. I'll go. I'll not bother you again."

Pete frowned, put out a hand to stop her. "Hang on, love."

It wasn't disapproval in his eyes, it was disappointment. Marion breathed – slowly, deeply. "Okay," she said, "okay. Yes, tomorrow then. You're right, we should talk."

The loud jangle of an advert filled the air. A woman bounced along a pavement in a way few seldom do, a ridiculous over-spring to her step, all white teeth and perfect skin. Her hair shimmied behind her, causing heads to turn as she passed. *Bring out the real you,* the voice-over said, *with Vous shampoo.*

As though it were that easy.

a matter of perspective

I ARRIVE AT the gallery. Spencer opens the door as I approach. He's been waiting. We don't speak. He waves me in with an impatient flick. The shop lights are off and the sign on the door is already turned to closed. We stand for a moment in the darkening gloom. The natural twilight drains the last of the colour from pastel canvasses. He now looks alien in this neat space. Loose, stained clothes and edgy gait. Outside, people pass without note, their voices muffled through the glass, tugging on cardigans and lightweight coats as the sky darkens. It's going to rain.

I'm looking at this ageing man but witnessing his youth.

And I wonder what he sees.

He stands and stares as though he, too, might recognise what once existed. He too might recall the younger me; the one without constraint. But I'm not sure. That person left long ago and I am well-practiced in this disguise.

"Come, come," he says, grasping the arm of my jacket, propelling me towards the rear of the shop. The touch transcends the fabric.

"You need to be ready," he says. "that feeling of *right*, remember?"

He looks at me, searching.

"You know this, you do, you know this." He's almost incoherent. "You've had this a thousand times, this moment, this point where you *know*."

We move into a room off the gallery – a bare space, a sort of kitchen area, with an old wooden table on which sits a bottle of whisky and two glasses. He pours me a glass, refills his own, his hand shaking, driven by sleepless energy.

"Drink, drink," he says. "You need to be ready before you see them."

"Ready?" I laugh, raise my glass, tap it against his. "I *am* ready. Thirty four years in the making and you want me to wait even longer?"

"You're actually here." He touches my face, just to be sure. Leaves his hand there, against my skin.

"And you're alive." I cover his hand with my own, feel the roughness of dried paint, let my fingers slot into the contours of his with a familiarity that aches. I have touched them a thousand times.

I wonder whether I'd have stayed away had I known for sure he was here. I wonder why I ever left. The weight of years lost presses against my skull and I want to rewind time like a faulty roll of film, back to the point at which it failed, and start again.

"Everything I aimed for," he says, "before,

back then, that last painting in the series. Something always missing, always something not quite there. I couldn't understand what it was, what was refusing to come. And I thought it was you, the demands, you know? But you left. You just went and I saw I was never going to find it then. You had not been the reason for the failure. Do you hear that? It wasn't your fault. And I needed you."

He indicates my glass, drinks down the contents of his own. Refills both.

"Close your eyes," he says. "You know this. You know this moment. When you look through the lens and realise you've caught it, when you think you won't work your finger fast enough to press, click, grab it while it's there, exactly the right shot. *You know that feeling.* I want you to remember. Can you? Can you feel it? Can you conjure it again?"

How could I not know? He'd been there when I felt it the first time. Sketching in his studio – the small rickety one now occupied by holidaymakers and wet swimwear – me, picking up the camera, the Hasselblad, and trapping him in the lens. Perfection. Sheer bloody perfection. Insanely photogenic. And it had all been there, in that lens, in that moment – all I wanted to capture of him. The loose black curls, uncombed and matted in places, fighting to obscure his face. Fingers, stained and neglected. The paper, the pencil, the way they relaxed in his hands, comfortable, at home, in exactly the right place. The filth on his rough jeans. Shabby. Almost a vagrant. A beautiful dark cherub fallen on hard times. A stunning homeless angel. He'd been oblivious to my approach and my shaky finger pressed the button, got the shot, and at that moment I knew – I had it. What I wanted. I'd caught the essence of him.

"Yes. I know it, of course I know it. You taught me to use the camera, remember? To recognise the moment when it came."

He takes my glass, places it and his own on the table.

"Good. We'll go up."

He's laid out the ten large canvasses in a wide semi-circle in the studio, propped against chairs, a table, and easels. Nine of them are exposed – dark, shadowy paintings that seem to swirl, as though the viewer is being sucked in and spun. They are beautiful. And, of course, I recognise them. But to see them again, together, like this, after all these years is chilling. The subtle swirls of colour at the edges of each joining with the swirls of the next, like a mist floating around the room, vanishing in the gaps between each canvas, reappearing against the dark paint of its neighbour. I'd forgotten how beautiful they were.

"Christ," I say, "we're up there, just as you wanted, up there and looking down."

"It's a story," he says. "But not just one story, every story, this is only one sequence, one perception, one interpretation."

The tenth canvas is under a sheet. This is the painting I haven't seen – the one he was working on that night, when the colours were wrong. That night, when my two big passions collided and fragmented. I breathe slowly as he pulls the cover away.

"Here it is," he says. "Finished at last."

I start to move closer but he stops me and I let myself be guided to the centre of the room to face the semi-circle, to stand before the paintings like performer and expectant audience. Scattered equipment lies around the room, carelessly pushed against walls to make space for the show.

"That is us," he says, turning me and pointing to the new painting. It's similar but different, dark yet light. He has tamed the colours into amazing duplicity.

"You and I," he says. "Us. The ill-fated lovers. The eternal lovers. It is now, it is the future, it is what will come as envisaged from the past, it is a false clarity, it is the knowledge we think we possess. It is all of these things, depending where it sits in the sequence."

He's close behind me, taking hold of my shoulders, his breath against my ear. He's removing gravity with his presence and I am lighter. We turn slowly as one to stare at each canvas in turn.

"Can't you see?" he says, "What's happened? You, coming back, and this?"

"It works," I say. "It all works so beautifully. You're right, it's that moment, the moment viewed through the lens. It's everything, as you said, *an ephemeral sense of urgent hope*, just as you said it would be. Jesus, why did you keep these hidden?"

I say these words and hear the pitch of my voice rise and think it might be someone else. For so long I've listened to my own harsh tones, my cynical drawl, my dispassion, my refusal to relent expressed in rhythmic sneer. But now I hear the me of long gone. The one who was unafraid to voice delight. The one who let passion bubble, erupt and transmit no matter how much of herself was exposed. I want to laugh, to scream, to sob. I want to dredge up every word I can find to describe the beauty of these paintings and shout them out, hear them echo and bounce around the walls. I want to ask Spencer how he *feels*. I want to listen and nod and not wince at the raw emotion I know would come.

I want to love.

I want to *bend*.

But I stand. Still, but alive. Feel him warm against my back, hear his words as though they were inside my own head already.

"It wasn't enough," he says in dry whisper, "to finish that piece. It needed more. The *whole* needed to *breathe*."

He spins me round, eyes fiery, manic.

"Light!" he says, "I needed light! Lots of light!"

He points to a large metal box on the floor behind us, bulbs projecting on jointed arms and thick wires tangling and crawling towards a shadowy corner. He moves to turn off the studio lighting and returns, flicks a switch on the box, turns to face me again, persuading me further into the semi-circle.

"It's timed," he says, "to perfection. I spent most of today getting it right."

As we stand, facing, eyes locked, the machine hums and the lights begin to warm, to glow softly – red and orange and yellow and green and blue and purple – slowly becoming brighter, the arms quietly rotating, the growing beams floating and crossing in the air, soaking us in colour. I cannot take my eyes off him.

"And now," he says, touching stained fingertips to my mouth, "silence."

The lights fade and we stand once more in the evening's dusk. I hear him count, a whisper, *one, two, three*. One solitary beam of orange light now begins to rise, its depth intensifying before it pauses and fades and the next colour takes its turn. And I move too, turning slowly to follow the display as it bleeds between our bodies and hits the painted canvasses. There is a rhythm, the colours lighting each individual canvas left to right – the designated story – and I anticipate and shift my view in readiness. They go through the cycle repeatedly, the paintings shining and seeming to move under roaming beam, changing hues, the shadows where they pass, the transfer of my vision.

With each cycle the pace gathers, the lights no longer taking patient turns but competing – lighting up opposing canvasses simultaneously, ever faster, ever more colours joining the fray. I am caught up in the speed, the unpredictability as this new story is told, unable to turn quickly enough to face two directions, unable to second guess the order. I'm missing and catching the colours as randomly as they are revealing themselves. I'm missing and catching the story in fragments.

And I think of that night.

The frenzy. The wind.

The spray bouncing off the rocks.

The lights pick up a new rhythm, becoming faster, multiple beams coming to life with increasing vitriol, like lightning. Sparking and flashing around the semi-circle, hitting our bodies, the paintings, the walls, the clutter behind. Random – totally random – some fast, some simultaneous, some slow, and some for such a fragmented moment I can hardly tell it happened. I can barely name the colour.

I watch the artwork in fascination.

See the story angry and raw.

See again the fury of that night. The raucous

voices, the love, the hate, the fear and exhilaration. The sense of being utterly alive and yet so close to death. A knowledge once learned never forgotten – how death lights up life.

But Spencer watches only me.

He reaches out, to undo my clothes, his clothes, hands and face coming and going in the light and shadow. I view his touch in the colours, feel it in the dark moments, see my own hands in unfamiliar tones on his shirt, caught in stroboscopic pause, the dull edge of buttons against fingertips the only proof of movement.

We are now the artwork. As perhaps we always were. Pressed together in a kiss so familiar I may only have dreamed the years in between. Colours covering our revealed skin. Playing tricks with our nakedness to kindly remove, to wickedly enhance, the imperfections of age.

Our clothing drops to the floor. Its own hues hidden in the momentary flashes of other shades, dulled by shadows once colour has passed. There's an inevitability to all this – that I should stand, naked, disorientated, in light and shadow. That I should remember another night, another long-gone time when I was also without the protection of facade, when I was also wholly exposed.

The years in between are the lie.

I have never been other than this.

I want to talk to him but the silence is exquisite and I cannot break it. I want to touch him but do not want to cut through the tension between us, do not want to destroy what is momentarily delicious. The trickster lights causing moving limbs to appear still, still limbs to seemingly move, slow to a less frantic pace. Individual colours glow in patient sequence once more, slowly reaching strength, slowly ebbing away. And the canvasses cease to move and now stand still, their story a calm one, their narrative controlled and linear again.

    Beams of light arc gently, caressing our bodies. Where a shade lingers, he touches. I watch colour cross his chest, catch the pause with my own hand – flat, fingers spread – two surfaces becoming one, bathed in the same alien tone.

    The light curve lowers, sweeping downwards across the floor, leaving our upper halves in shadow, dark and dull, almost colourless. But below we are coated in orange and purple, spanning back and forth yet never leaving our flesh.

    I sense his smile in the dim light. He almost speaks too as he brushes my mouth with his and I taste whisky, feel the hint of a word, soft and raw and speaking of everything. Then he kneels and traces the colour where it fades to a shady edge across my waist, follows it down, his hands moving into the light, his head haloed with its shine, features raised and sunken erroneously – a statue, battered by the elements into barely recognisable form.

Detached from the world like this, I have no regrets.

I stare down at him, bowed, his arms wrapping around my thighs, merging into me, two partial bodies becoming one – distorted, incomplete, a broken sculpture.

The warm colours ebb.

The cool colours flow.

I reach out to touch his hair, expecting it to feel hard as the blue light sharpens its edges. But it is soft against my fingers, seeping through the gaps like spring water warmed by the sun. The cold shade bathes me, him, us, but his mouth is hot and the thrill of the contrast infuses me.

I could die right now.

But what story is this?

The canvasses now ignored, he pulls me to the floor as the lights pick up on their earlier beat, multiple colours in competitive dance. We lie on the abandoned clothes. I feel something harsh against my shoulder but don't care. It is not important. The flashes are predictable again, their sequence lulling and luring us into its pulse only to then intensify, become increasingly tempestuous as we twist and turn on the floor like mirrored fragments in a kaleidoscope.

Maybe we are already dead. Maybe this is a continuation of that other night. Maybe all I think has existed since has not. I know only one thing. At this moment, as we fuse together in the light of another story, another perspective, another known and unknown narrative, we are repeating and creating, reliving and continuing. I have been this story before. And yet I know nothing – I wish to know nothing – beyond the swirling of colours on flesh, the devilish shadows on my lover's face, the deep intake of our breath and its involuntary release; resigned, finite, like the last gasp of life.

I am home at last.

an old adversary

Fenchurch leaned over his balustrade, watching the harbour wake. There was a time when it would have come to life by dawn. But now nothing much happened before eight and there was little to watch other than a few enthusiastic canoeists taking advantage of the calm water, and Jack Crozier, the guy who saved Chrissy, preparing his boat for the day's work.

Malcolm mused on life's serendipity as he watched Crozier go through ritualistic checks and preparations. Had Jack failed to bring down at least one girl safely from the lifeboat house roof that night, then he, Fenchurch, would never have known her. Would never have known this summer's passion, its intrigue, its fun. He'd have done something else for a few weeks – something more mundane – or perhaps have met another stranger, known other passion, other intrigue, other fun.

Life was like the tide. A person never knew what it might bring in, or what it might wash away and when. But to regret a loss was to undermine what had been. He'd prefer to think of this summer as having been good. At least he knew where he was now. If there was one thing he couldn't stomach it was uncertainty. Far better to have a made a decision he could live with than drift in a mire of questions. But there was still a loose strand. He needed to find out what happened to Chrissy's friend, Pat. Tidy up the summer's events. Complete the story so it could be filed away.

The harbourmaster came out of his office carrying two drinks in polystyrene cups and walked over to Crozier's boat. The old man came up the steps to greet him and take his drink. It was a routine Fenchurch regularly watched. They'd chat now for fifteen minutes or so. It would be a good chance to catch them together – to ask what Chrissy had failed to ask them.

"Here be Trouble," Jack said as Fenchurch approached, his smart suit out of place against the backdrop of worn rope, old boats and hard labour.

"Now Jack," the harbourmaster said, "don't be getting on the wrong side of the only legal eagle in town. Those lady passengers with their doe-eyes and all. Only a matter of time till you've got an angry husband on your hands and be needing the help of this feller."

Crozier laughed. "Not been rumbled in forty years."

"What can we do for you, Malcolm?" the harbourmaster said.

Fenchurch explained about Chrissy, the night on the lifeboat house in nineteen seventy three when she had to be rescued. Did Jack remember?

"Aye," he said. "I remembers well enough. Crazy kid, stormy squall. Night and a half it was."

"A rum do," the harbourmaster said. "Wasn't Jim Maddern's daughter involved?"

"Marion, aye, it be Jim that called for help. Poor kid lost friend and father in one night. Rum do indeed."

"The girl who fell?" Fenchurch said.

"Fine bloke, Jim Maddern," the harbourmaster said. "Terrible shame that, terrible. Big loss. Good community man."

"Just as Marion be," Jack said. "A rare old chip off the block."

"But what happened to the girl?" Fenchurch said. "What actually happened?"

Jack drained the last of his tea and the harbourmaster took his cup. Placed it into his own and checked his watch.

"I's havin' a pint in the Smuggler with Bert Wilson and Joe Scott," Jack said. He looked at the harbourmaster. "Remember Bert, Rob?"

The harbourmaster laughed and nodded.

"Jim see, he comes running in," Jack said, "terrible state, says there be someone on boathouse roof. We all goes out, everyone, and she's there teeterin', standin' up, arms out, flappin' like a stranded gull."

"Which one?"

"Crazy drunk, she was, fearless." Jack shook his head, turned and stared across the harbour, towards the lifeboat house now bathed in early sunshine, innocuous against the perfect blue of sky and sea.

"Bert goes fetch his jeep, I gets onto the roof. Bloody cold, bloody wet, but I'd only had a couple of pints – late getting finished, see? Knew it be squally later, so I mends a cabin leak, made me late for the pub, good job as it turns out."

"The other girl?" Fenchurch asked again. "What about her?"

"Bert Wilson and that damn jeep." The harbourmaster laughed. "Those bloody lights. But useful that night, for sure. How many years has he been gone now?"

"Must be a good fifteen," Jack said. "Wasn't it ninety two? Ninety three?"

"The girl?" Fen said, louder. "On the roof?"

"Oh, she be fair hysterical," Jack said. "Couldn't make head nor sense, but she were weakenin', see? She's squattin' by this point, legs givin' up. She'd have fallen afore long."

He shook his head again.

"So I grabs 'er, see? No, no." He frowned for a moment. "I shouts for rope, Bert chucks a length and then I grabs 'er, tied pair'n us to a corbel. Bloody pulls it tight, I does, sits on her and holds her still. Crazy kid."

"And after all that," the harbourmaster said, "She buggered off. Ran away."

"Aye, young Marion were heartbroken. An' losin' her dad an' all."

"But what about the other one?" Fen said. "The girl who fell?"

"Other?" Jack said. "No, weren't no other, jus' the one. She were shoutin' mind, shoutin' into the wind like a mad thing, but weren't no other. Jus' the one crazy thing."

Marion watched a father and two young children squatting beside the railings with buckets and crab-fishing lines. He was unwrapping something he'd bought to use for bait and the children fidgeted, peering over his shoulder impatiently.

"Wait, wait, wait." He said, laughing as the younger child jumped up and down.

"Come *on*, daddy."

On the table beside Marion and Chrissy's sat a woman, presumably the mother, guarding the family clutter and reading a book. Marion tried to make out the title but the woman's hand obscured the second word. *Invisible* something. Whatever it was, she was clearly engrossed, detached completely from the rest of the family, her feet up on another chair, cardigan loose around her shoulders, focused on the page and oblivious to the older child now trying to attract her attention.

"Mum, look." He waved a strip of meat his

father had torn from a piece of bacon but, when he saw she wasn't listening, crouched down and began to tie it onto the line.

Chrissy returned with wine, a couple of glasses and a menu, followed by an apologetic waitress who cleared away the remains of someone else's meal and said she'd return shortly to take their order.

They sat, sipping their drinks, Marion still watching the two young boys with their father, dropping their lines into the water, unravelling the string with intense concentration. Waiting. The younger of the two asked when he could pull it up again. The father explained how they must be patient, give the crabs time to find the food.

"I'm sorry I just left," Chrissy said. "Without saying anything"

Marion picked up the menu, cast an unfocused eye down the list.

"Nothing made much sense that night," Chrissy said. "I can't really remember, but I know everything was chaotic. I'd gone before I sobered up, you know? And then there just didn't seem any point getting in touch, months went by, life changed. There was never a point where it would have seemed right, and the more time passed the less likely I was to ever get in touch. But I'm sorry, and about your dad. I didn't know."

Marion put the menu back on the table. She wasn't hungry anyway. She took another mouthful of wine and stared into the horizon.

"Did you ever think what it was like for us? Me? Your parents? Did you never think we'd be worried?"

"No, I didn't. Life sort of just moved on. It wasn't a conscious thing."

There was a sudden excited squeal from the younger boy over by the railings and the father bent down to help him wind up his catch. The older child peered over the edge, tugged on his own line with a frown, glanced at his younger brother and said it was probably just seaweed. But it wasn't. It was a small crab and the younger child flashed a satisfied look at his brother. He removed the creature carefully under his father's instruction, holding it with finger and thumb, his other digits stretched out of the way of tiny claws that could probably do little harm. He dropped it into the bucket of water. His brother tugged again at his own line, kicked the railings grumpily.

"Come on, Michael," the man said, ruffling the older boy's hair. "You'll hook one soon."

The mother turned another page in her book.

The man reminded Marion of her dad. Patient. Kind. Always time to explain things, no matter how busy he might be. She'd give anything to talk to him again. To talk to either of them again. This was all life was about – these moments this family were now experiencing. Small fragments of pleasure which, added together, can make a person look back and smile.

"I couldn't understand why you didn't contact your mum," Marions said. "Thought it heartless. Still do, if I'm honest." The wine was certainly encouraging her. She picked up the menu again, scanned the list and settled on a crab sandwich.

The waitress returned and they each ordered the same. Chrissy asked for another bottle. The small child wandered across to his mother, carrying the bucket of water and crab carefully. She put down her book, leaned over and looked.

"Wow, you caught one," she said. Marion caught her eye and smiled. The woman winked. "What are you going to call it?"

"Michael," the boy said. His mother laughed.

Moments. Life consists of moments. Some happy, some nondescript, some tragic. A person learns to appreciate the good ones, deal with the bad, get on with the mundane. But Pete was right, life's too short for grudges.

"Look," she said to Chrissy, "Let's not labour it, eh? You went, you had your reasons, it was a long time ago. I know you weren't well, and all that stuff with your parents, you were never happy. Have you been happy? I mean since?"

"Don't know. Maybe. Sometimes. Would I know it if I saw it?"

"It's this," Marion pointed towards the family, waved an arm to the sky, still blue, still sunny. "It's all this. Things that make us smile, laugh, a good wine, the chance to sit and relax.

Aren't you happy now? Right now? At this moment?"

Inside the house her father is frightening her mother again. This is something he does now. The girl with the mousy hair stays in the garden when her father is like this. She digs holes in the soil and lets her tears drip into them. One day she might cry enough to make a small puddle and conjure up a fairy.

Today her father is making her mother sing to his toy soldiers. He finished painting them yesterday and now they are in the house. After he'd done that, he smacked the little girl because he said she went too close to the shed. She's not allowed in there. Ever.

But today he's ignored her in favour of frightening her mother. The girl dressed herself – she's good at that, even though she's only six – and poured herself some cereal. She had to ask mummy to get the milk from the fridge because she can't reach, and her mother did this in a hurry and dropped a bottle. That made her father angry. He doesn't like mess.

Now the girl sits in the garden, with her stick, and pokes small holes in the soil. The window is open. It's July. It's hot. The soil is dry and tumbles back into the holes. It needs wetting but she can't cry today. She used up all her tears yesterday.

When I look at the man and his kids dangling their lines over the edge of the harbour wall, I see people engaged in pointless activity. I wish I could see it as Marion clearly does, but I can't. They start with no crab and when they've tipped them back into the water before they leave for the day, they'll be left with no crab. All that effort has been pointless. I envy their ability not to see this.

The woman with her book. Marion said it's another moment, a time of peace and carefree self-indulgence for someone who perhaps ordinarily spends her days running around after those children, after that husband. But to me it's a sadness – watching a person enjoy a book, losing themselves in someone else's world, thrilling at events they're unlikely to ever experience for themselves. It's a painful thing. The best I can think for this particular stranger is perhaps she's not escaping *into* happiness but is maybe *extracting* it. Perhaps, when she finishes that last page, closes the book for the final time, she will feel better about the world, will carry some of that pleasure into her own reality. But I doubt it. I think she'll rush to the bookshop to buy herself another piece of someone else's life – another world into which she can escape. I wish I had Marion's faith.

"What about the dreams?" I say. "The happy moments a person expected but didn't materialise?"

I perhaps shouldn't have touched this nerve. Her face shadows over. The waitress arrives with our sandwiches and wine. I pour us both a glass.

"Did *your* dream turn out to be everything you wanted?" she says. "Maybe sometimes the dreaming itself is the moment. I don't know. Yes, I wanted university but there's no saying it would have made me happier than I am, is there?"

"It wasn't good with Zak," I say, "not for long anyway. Yeah, the dream was better than the reality. A person just can't conceive, can they? When you're that teenager, thinking all things are possible? Can't conceive how wrong you might be."

"I think if we knew how things might be, we'd give up before we'd even started."

We're talking. More than that we're talking like friends. Though we have still not yet broached the subject of that night. Have not mentioned Pat. We drink more wine and I tell her instead about Spencer – she never knew who the mystery man was then, back in nineteen seventy three. She's surprised a tutor would fall in love with a student. *Didn't he worry he'd lose his job?* I tell her she's clearly led a sheltered life, tutors often fuck their college pupils, it's a perk. She says I've clearly led a wild one. And we actually laugh. Like friends.

I'm not sure mentioning Pat is a good idea.

But I must.

"I need to stop moving on," I say.

She starts to pour us another glass, but only a trickle comes out. The bottle is empty, the sandwiches only half-eaten. We look at each other and laugh.

"Are you going to stay?" she says.

"Maybe. But I need to know what happened. I need to know about Pat."

She gives me a strange look. "Oh, Chrissy, not that."

Through the window comes the sound of mummy singing. Her voice warbles to match the song, which is about a bird. She sings "bye, bye, blackbird" and something in the words and the way her mummy's voice sounds now does make the little girl cry. She bows her head so the tears run down her nose and drop into the dry soil. She's nothing if not resourceful. That's what her teacher says. It's something to do with using things she's found to make pictures. She's good at that.

No one here can love or understand me. The girl understands that. It's her favourite bit of the song too because whoever made it up must have known what it's like to be sad and on your own.

Her father stops her mother singing and makes her start at the beginning again. He keeps doing this. The girl covers her ears. Mummy's singing is going all wrong and it's making the sad song just too sad.

It's July. It's hot. The holiday children will be at the beach, playing in the sand with their buckets and spades. The little girl sometimes goes there with Alice but she's not here today. She's visiting her sister.

She could go to the beach herself. She knows the way and how to be careful crossing the road. She won't get lost. What she likes to do most is climb the steps to the top of the cliff and watch the holiday children. From up there they're pretty coloured dots and squeals and she can look at them for ages without getting bored.

Without taking her hands from her ears, the girl with the mousy hair gets up and walks around the side of the house to the gate.

I'd like to think Marion means it's too painful a topic but there's a tone in her voice that negates this. I can't quite put my finger on it but can clearly see she isn't traumatised for herself – Pat's name has not drawn a shadow across her face – and I'm struck by the strangest sense. A discombobulation of self. I feel Pat's presence. All those glimpses I'd once expected – the catch of her laugh, the flick of her hair – are colliding here, now. Arriving and consuming me. I am not alone. She is here. I can feel her. If I stayed quiet long enough I would hear her voice.

"Have you been up there," Marion nods in the direction of the lifeboat house.

I shake my head.

"Shall we go?" she says.

We walk up the lane, the evening sun still warm, the harbour breathing with the labours of a day's end. A local drunk approaches, mumbling, weaving and tripping but never letting go of the bottle in his hand, never actually falling. He never does. His steps are only unsteady to those who watch. He glances up as we pass, waves the bottle.

"Venge ma mort!" He hacks out a laugh. "Venge ma mort!"

We walk in silence for the last fifty yards.

No trace remains of that wild winter's night. No clue as to the truth of it. No blood smears on jagged tiles, no broken vodka bottle on the rocks below, no lingering scent of fear. It might never have happened. It might have been a dream.

Standing at the top of the cliff it's breezy but still warm. The grass tickles her bare legs and the sound of sea and people's voices is far enough away to be soothing, like cricket on the radio. She can still hear her mother's voice. As though it could reach all this way – but it's there, in her head, warbling like a blackbird and she wishes the sea was angrier to take the singing away.

Blackbirds aren't the best birds. They hop around on the ground too much. Birds should fly, high, swooping up and down. Seagulls are better. She sometimes dreams about flying – up into the clouds, zooming back down again, gliding over people's heads and making that loud caw, caw, caw song. It always sounds like seagulls are laughing at people and she thinks if you could fly then you probably would laugh at all the people stuck on the ground, having to walk everywhere.

She stands close to the edge. Closer than Alice would allow. There's a fence but it's old and bendy. The cliff juts out in places and gulls sit on clumps of grass. Occasionally one stands, opens its wings and takes off. The girl with the mousy hair watches, amazed at how brave they are – how they don't look down and worry, they just fly.

Perhaps it's like fairies. If you believe, you will see them. Those who don't believe – like adults – won't. It doesn't mean the fairies aren't there, laughing at them, like the gulls watching humans walk everywhere. What would happen if she tried? If she really, really believed she could?

"I can fly. Can you? Can you fly like a bird?"

The girl with the mousy hair looks up to see another girl, about her age and pretty, with shiny black hair and exciting eyes. She's leaning against the dangerous fence.

"I don't know."

"It's easy. You just close your eyes and jump."

"But what if I fall?"

"You won't fall if you fly! But if you can't then I suppose you'd die, all bloody and broken."

There are small moments of clarity in every dream. The difficult rescue, Jack Crozier tying us to the corbel, freeing up his arms to get a determined grip. He'd perhaps pictured himself pulled through the spray onto rocks that had long wanted to claim him. He must have seen that desperate blackness, Death's advance, and recognised his old adversary. And perhaps that's why he'd called for rope – *not yet yer old bastard, not my time* – and so was here still, now, defeating Death, claiming even more years as his due.

Today the lifeboat house is calm. Grey slate and orange lichen against shades of blue that stretch forever. Water quiet, gulls content on warmed granite beds, children in the distance squealing in fun. A pastiche of summer delight. But the rocky base descends into a murkier place – beneath the blue and green, beneath the lapping, beneath the sun's affectionate touch. Down there is the truth. Down there the storm waits.

The sea is evil.

It's only a hundred and thirty million years old, Spencer had once said, *what do you expect? It's a petulant child, wants to devour the land in one greedy mouthful.*

"Do you remember?" Marion says, putting a hand on my arm.

Come on, let's do it. Let's fly. Just once.

I nod my head. Then shake it. I don't trust myself to speak.

"Did you think you were shouting at her?" she asks. "That she was actually there?"

I am the polar image of the drunk. My gait stable, poised, controlled and yet with each disjointed step there is a danger I will fall. I am unstable, despite appearances. I have always been such. But the drunk's steadiness exists. That we cannot see it does not render it impossible. He does not fall and for as long as he does not fall he is steady, despite the perception of those watching.

"I can fly. Can you? Can you fly like a bird?"

Pat didn't fall. She flew.

a moment of madness

december 1973

THEY'RE NEAR the old lifeboat house. Chrissy swigs vodka from the bottle, jerking it towards her face, spilling more than she manages to pour into her mouth. She doesn't break momentum, doesn't slow that pace. She staggers, pushing on and on, swearing and screaming at the darkness. Her voice is breaking and still she shouts. It's freezing. Marion's tired, she can't move fast enough to keep up. She wants to go home, back to the warm, the calm, but she can't leave her friend like this – incoherent, crazy. She yells against the wind – *slow down, wait, stop* – but Chrissy doesn't hear, doesn't want to hear, isn't sound enough to hear. It's often been this way, but never quite like this. Never as frightening as this. If Marion could catch up, if she could put out her arms, stop the impetus – just for a second – but she's not fit enough. Not strong enough. Not driven enough.

If she had half of Chrissy's passion.

But she's never had that.

Not even close.

They reach the lifeboat house. Chrissy stops and faces the wall, shoulders rising and falling, coughing as the icy wind fills her throat. And Marion catches up.

There's the low wall, rough and worn, and beyond it the roof of the lifeboat house. Beneath, a sharp fall onto peaks of granite and a tide engaged forever in futile attack. It's a long way to fall. Marion's almost close enough to touch, to take her friend by the shoulders and still her rage. Chrissy stares only towards the wall and shouts *are you going to share that bottle or what?* Marion moves to see Chrissy's face, looks into eyes that seem incapable of sight. And the words are aimed at the wall but can surely only be intended for herself. It is Chrissy who has the bottle.

The temperature drops another few degrees.

Chrissy throws the bottle over the wall and Marion can't even hear it hit the granite because the tide is angry and the wind is ripping at boat masts, penetrating the hill's crags and lashing its trees, peeling in frenzy across rooftops searching for something to take, to break, to carry away in the spin of its fury.

She doesn't know if Chrissy is talking to her.

Or the wall.

Or herself.

Or the person only she can see.

But Marion has to do something because now Chrissy's climbing onto the wall and she's trying to balance and is looking towards the lifeboat house roof which is just about level with where her feet are placed, and she's swaying. Oh God she's swaying.

Marion shouts *no, don't be stupid* as Chrissy jumps the four foot gap, over the lethal drop, and claws and scrambles her way to the ridge.

Oh my God, you silly cow, you stupid silly cow.

Marion can't think of anything else to do other than fetch her dad. She runs back, round the harbour to the chip shop. Her face is wet and she can barely breathe and by the time tears reach her open mouth they're chilled and slide across her burning lips, falling into the corners where she catches their cold saltiness with her tongue.

Chrissy is going to fall.

She's going to die.

Marion stumbles through the shop door and somebody catches her, steadies her, says words which don't register but whose meaning is clear. But she can't be calm, she can't succumb to those comforting sounds.

Her dad lifts the counter hatch and he's coming towards her, his greasy white coat pushing through the queue. The customers move back, towards the wall, watching her, watching her dad as he takes her from the stranger, wipes her face, holds her by the shoulders and says *what's happened, what is it* and she can't speak. She can open her mouth but only animal sounds come out. She tries again and again until she eventually hears herself; *Chrissy, fall, boathouse.*

Her dad rips off his white coat but there's no time to grab anything warm and they leave the shop. Somehow she has energy enough to run again back round the harbour, up the cobbled lane towards the lifeboat house roof. She can't believe her dad is running too. She can't remember the last time she saw him move this fast. These are the thoughts in her head as they keep going, keep on towards the lifeboat house – she's barely able to breathe, barely able to see, but still she runs. It's dark, the only light a yellow glow from the windows of The Smuggler and the wind is fierce, bringing in the icy tide that will surely end her friend's life.

Jesus Christ the stupid little bitch.

Her dad's cursing, blaspheming, panicking. He runs into The Smuggler – there's no way he can climb up there himself – and brings out some men. Thank God one of them is Jack Crozier. If anyone can climb a roof in a storm it's a man who's been out at sea in worse.

There's a lot of noise now. People have come out of the pub. Someone drives a Landrover out of the car park, points the roof spotlights towards Jack, Marion's caught in their glow, mesmerised as Jack inches closer to Chrissy on the roof. She hasn't noticed the crowd, hasn't noticed Jack. She stares out across the roof, standing on the ridge, arms out to the sides and *flapping*, up and down as though she's pretending to fly. She's laughing, in a sickening way, her hair stuck across her face, her clothes twisted against her body. She's soaked. Marion can barely watch but she can't look away either. Her jaw is in spasm, every muscle in her body tight and her legs feel as though they are melting. She thinks she might sink.

Jack is almost upon Chrissy and she still hasn't seen him. He's glancing from her to the space across – maybe he's trying to see what she sees – and he shouts *ROPE GET ME ROPE I NEED ROPE* and somebody must already have it because it appears near his feet just seconds later. It lands in a loose coil, clunking against the slate and slithering halfway down the roof again.

And Jack grabs.

He has her. He's wrapped an arm around her body and she crumples to the tiles and he just keeps on holding her, his other hand patting around for the rope. He circles them both in its coil, straddling the ridge tiles, his legs over hers – he's almost sitting on her – and his hands are looping the rope around a corbel, swiftly tying a knot with a skill that does not need to be supervised. And he pulls tight, checks its grip, and then wraps both arms around Chrissy, holds her to his chest.

They sit for a couple of minutes. Chrissy shaking. Jack still.

Now there's a ladder leaning across the wall, resting on the edge of the roof, and two men hold it steady whilst a third climbs. Together he and

Jack untie Chrissy – she's limp now, she's quiet, she's calm – and they gently ease her down the roof, never letting go, and others reach up as she descends. There's always someone touching, they all want to save her, nobody wants her to fall.

Now Marion's muscles relax.

Completely.

She stumbles to her knees and her stomach heaves. There's nothing left to come but still her body rises and falls as she retches air. She sounds like a hurt dog – she can hear it, she knows it comes from within, but she can't control it.

Her dad is there. He leans forward, pulls her up, holds her tightly and strokes her hair and talks to her as he did when she was a baby, *it's okay, there, there, it's okay*.

He's still out of breath and isn't a good colour but he urges her up, coaxing in simple words, as though she were a small child. Together they walk into the pub, to get warm, to sit for a while. Behind them the waves continue to pound the granite, pushed on by the wind.

Their fury is endless.

About the author

Born in Lancashire, a stone's throw from the infamous witches' cairn on Pendle Hill, Sandie Zand was educated at the local grammar school where she excelled in English, Art, History and Detention.

She has lived in various parts of the UK, but now resides, works and writes in Shropshire.

The Sky is not Blue is her début novel. Details of current works in progress and other random scribblings can be found at:

www.sandiezand.com

MAD BEAR BOOKS

Mad Bear Books is an independent publishing imprint — owner-run, free from big-business corporate pressures. We publish books too edgy, controversial and non-compartmentalized for old-guard publishers to touch.

Other recommended titles:

Honour by Freddie Omm: A chilling, spellbinding thriller about sex, love, faith and greed—and a toxic evil at the heart of modern society.

www.madbearbooks.com

Lightning Source UK Ltd.
Milton Keynes UK
UKOW03f1246100913

216908UK00004B/19/P